Portals
Book One of the Into The Galaxy Duology

Ann Christy

All rights reserved. No part of this work may be reproduced, distributed, or transmitted in any form or by any means, electronic or mechanical, including photocopying, recording, or otherwise, nor may it be stored in a database or private retrieval system, without the prior written permission of the author, with the exception of brief quotations included in critical reviews and certain other noncommercial uses as permitted by copyright law.

This is a work of fiction. Names, characters, organizations, places, and events appearing or described in this work are either the product of the author's imagination or used in a fictitious manner. Any resemblance to actual persons, living or dead, or to actual events, is purely coincidental and the product of a fevered imagination.

ALL RIGHTS RESERVED

Copyright © 2018 by Ann Christy

www.AnnChristy.com

Original Cover Art by Tom Edwards
Illustration © Tom Edwards
TomEdwardsDesign.com

Also by Ann Christy

The Silo 49 Series
Silo 49: Going Dark
Silo 49: Deep Dark
Silo 49: Dark Till Dawn
Silo 49: Flying Season for the Mis-Recorded

Strikers Trilogy
Strikers
Strikers: Eastlands

Between Life and Death Series
The In-Betweener
Forever Between
Between Life and Death
The Book of Sam (prequel)
Christmas Between Life and Death

Perfect Partners, Incorporated Series
Robot Evolution (Volumes 1-5)
Hope/Less

Dark Collections
The Ways We End
And Then Begin Again

Anthologies
Wool Gathering (A Charity Anthology)
Synchronic: 13 Tales of Time Travel
The Robot Chronicles
The Powers That Be (A Charity Anthology)
The Z Chronicles
Alt.History 101
Dark Beyond the Stars
Future Chronicles: Special Edition
The Time Travel Chronicles
The Doomsday Chronicles
Dark Beyond the Stars: A Planet Too Far
Dark Beyond the Stars: New Worlds, New Suns
Chronicle Worlds: Tails of Dystopia
Bridge Across The Stars
Best of Beyond the Stars

For Those Who Dare

One

My brain cells are dying of frustration. I can hear tiny screams as they try to comprehend the gibberish falling out of my AP Calculus teacher's mouth. How I qualified for this class, I'll never know, but I'd happily trot myself over to Geometry if I thought I could get away with it.

What's worse, my phone is blowing up in my back pocket, making it hard to concentrate. Notification vibrations are coming fast and furious. I have zero idea why, but it worries me.

I haven't done anything lately that would get me into trouble and I'm not involved in any sordid high school scandals, so it must be some sort of emergency. Did my mom get into an accident? Is the house on fire? It's only after calculating the odds that I might peek without getting caught that I realize I'm not the only one with this problem.

The guy in front of me is lifting one side of his butt as his phone vibrates against the plastic seat. The girl next to me—who is ridiculously good at this calculus thing—has her hand pressed to the front of her backpack to muffle her phone noises as well. When the alert tone sounds out from a slew of phones, including one inside the teacher's desk, I decide I simply must look. Something is definitely wrong. Slipping it out of my pocket, I hold it below the edge of my desk and hope for the best.

"Lysa! No phones," Ms. Blanchette calls. As usual, she pronounces my name wrong, making the *y* long so that it sounds like *Lice-ah* instead of like a regular old Lisa. Why did my mom choose to spell it so uniquely?

Before I can correct her, or hide my phone, all the phones in the room send out a tone simultaneously. It's the one used for Amber Alerts or Emergency Broadcasts. Her eyes flick toward her desk, then she waves her hand and reaches for her drawer.

"Let me look first," Ms. Blanchette says, but her expression says she's worried. I don't blame her. She probably thinks it's a school shooting or something equally horrible. Like everyone else, I watch her. Her face crinkles a little, like she can't believe what she's seeing, then she mutters, "What the heck?"

Apparently, the class is done waiting for her signal, because I'm not the only one to put my face to my screen. My notifications are crazy. The last text from my mom is the one I hit first.

Are you alright? Text me right now!

Since I have basically no idea what's going on, I text back a nice and generic: *Fine. At school.*

It doesn't take long to see what's up, but even so, I'm not the first one to see it. Voices start rising. Combined with the sound of videos playing on different phones, a confusing mish-mash of noise makes focusing difficult. Glancing up at the teacher, I make sure she's not looking before I click. If phones are a no-no in school, then using them to watch videos is beyond a no-no. My school has a really strict policy on that.

I'm confused by the alerts because they're clearly building on some earlier story. It looks like something weird has come to earth, which can't possibly be accurate. I click back to the video referenced in the story and wind up at one of those stalker-azzi sites, the kind that make their money by spying on celebs and getting bad pictures of them with hamburgers shoved into their mouths.

The video is a few hours old, and in it a reporter is standing on a New York City sidewalk doing a live report about a nasty traffic accident involving someone famous for being famous. While going over the gory details of the accident—probably hoping to get a good shot of the ambulance and lots of blood—a window opens on the street behind him. It isn't really a window, not the kind with a sash and some glass, but it's a window all the same. The oval glows in shades of iridescent purple, with beautiful threads of deep blue swirling around inside, the two colors broken by swoops of white that make the edges of the purple seem almost pink. It really is stunning to behold, the light of a nebula brought onto a dirty, litter-strewn sidewalk.

The reporter shuffles back a step or two, his face suddenly nervous, the hungry glee at potentially seeing a smashed up semi-celebrity vanishing from his heavily-powdered face. After a beat, he grins and remarks that it looks like they're going to get a visit from a street magician, or maybe an illusionist that freaks out crowds for fun.

The crumpled vehicle now forgotten by whoever is manning the camera, the image shifts until the oval of light nearly fills the frame, the laughing people nearby on the sidewalk crowding the edges. I pause the video to look at the spectral window more closely. It's almost mesmerizing, the kind of thing you can look at all day and see new patterns emerge, each more stunning than the last. I wonder how a street magician could even dream up something so beautiful, let alone project it into the air like that. It looks real.

Hitting play again, the video catches one of the bystanders leaning toward the newsman. He grins and says, "Hey, that's more creative than yet another accidentally-on-purpose leaked sex tape."

That comment garners a few giggles from the crowd, and even I smile a little. The laughter hitches and a few gasps sound out when a man hops out of the glowing oval of light. He looks just like any other man. Actually, he looks exactly like one of the men on the sidewalk watching the show. He's wearing a tan overcoat buttoned over a suit and a pair of nice shoes. His sandy hair is far too perfectly tousled to be the product of the wind alone. He's like a twin taking the concept of dressing like their sibling a little too far.

And what that man does when he pops out of the window of swirling color is kind of surprising. He grabs the man who looks exactly like him, his hands firmly around the man's upper arms. For his part, the man being grabbed does nothing. He seemed to freeze when the new man hopped out, like a switch had been flipped on his motor reflexes, though I'd guess it's shock at seeing his twin.

The duplicate says something too low for the microphone to catch, all the while considering the face of the original man with a vague intensity. And then he tosses the original man straight into the oval of light. As if to finish the performance, the window winks out of existence without a sound or any other disturbance. The man who came from the window tugs down his coat sleeves and proceeds to walk down the sidewalk as if nothing happened, his hand absently smoothing that perfectly tousled hair as he steps past the crowd.

The camera jerks back to the reporter, who is standing there gaping at the retreating man just like everyone else. He puts his hand to his ear and startles a little, as if someone just told him to wake up and smell the coffee because he's on live TV. He gives a small, nervous laugh, reorienting himself and plastering that newscaster look back onto his face.

Everyone else on the sidewalk looks a little unsettled too. I mean, they seem entertained, but also confused.

Where were the flourishes? Where was the illusionist, who should now come out and take a bow, then make a grab for some bonus media coverage? A few people shake their heads or purse their lips, as if they find something so frivolous distasteful while the sound of ambulances fills the air with warbling urgency.

I'm still not sure how this video relates to an emergency big enough to disturb class. I mean, it's a magic trick. I click off the video and return to the news site. Almost immediately, I understand. A different newscaster is showing a snippet from a security camera overlooking a large kitchen loaded with industrial stainless steel. People are busily working, then the edge of a window just like the one on the street pops into existence. A man wearing a chef's cap and holding a clipboard stands with a woman in an apron near a counter. Both jump back in alarm when the window opens just feet from them. Then, like the man on the street, the woman freezes with her hands raised to her chest and a look of fear on her face. Again, like the street scene, someone exactly like her steps from the light.

Unlike the street scene, the duplicate woman doesn't shove her counterpart through without opposition. Instead, the chef whacks the new woman with his clipboard and starts pushing her away, using his clipboard like a weapon. It's raging up to become a brawl as he shouts, people running from off camera to join the fray.

None of it works though. The new woman straight-arms the chef backward with barely any effort, then grabs the still-frozen original and tosses her into the light. Just like on the street, the oval winks out immediately, but the scene doesn't end with laughter. This time, the chef gets up, crouching a little and wary of the woman. Suddenly, this new woman puts her hands to her temples, as if struck by a sudden migraine. I see her mouth opening in a pained shout, or maybe even a scream. Then she shakes her head and looks around like she doesn't know what's going on. The chef lets her know by grabbing one of the big knives from the counter and plunging it into her chest, while everyone else stares at the pair in shock.

The video flies up into the corner of the screen and the newscaster resumes talking, telling eager viewers that the same sort of scene is being reported in many locations, both in the U.S. and abroad. No one knows the precise nature of the phenomenon, or why it's happening, only that it's not right. A word normally avoided by reporters of any repute is relayed in a near hushed tone: *aliens*.

When I look up from my screen, my teacher's face has gone pale and her fingers are tapping away at her phone like a pro. I can't even text that fast. She drops it when the school speaker comes on and a voice tight with nerves announces that school is cancelled.

It looks like I won't have to finish today's AP Calculus class after all.

Two

When I get home, my mom is sitting on the coffee table, which is as close to the TV as possible without standing in front of it. She looks sweaty and nervous, biting at one of her fingernails. A few wisps of her almost-black hair have begun to frizz out of her up-do. There's even a run in one of her stockings, which is weird. My mom is one of those women who believe bare legs in a business skirt over the age of forty is gauche, and she always carries a spare pair in her purse. To say she's normally the buttoned-up type would be an understatement.

She hops up from the table as soon as I walk in and wraps me in a hug. A relieved breath whooshes out of her, as if she'd been holding her breath until I got home. It's one of those hugs so tight it almost hurts, like the one she gave me when I went to summer camp for the first time, convinced I'd catch a tropical disease or get bitten by a rattlesnake.

"Mom! You can let go. I'm right here. Everything is fine," I say, my voice constricted.

She gives a soft, nervous laugh and releases the hug, but only so she can grip me by my upper arms and stare at me. "You're really okay? None of those things came to your school or anything, did they?"

Judging by the way she's staring at me, I wonder if she thinks I'm one of the duplicates. I grin and point to the scar on my chin where I took a header skating. "Nope, still me."

She rolls her eyes a little, but lets me go, so I'm betting she was wondering exactly that, even if only a little. Flapping her hand toward the TV screen, she says, "They're talking about aliens."

Tossing my backpack onto the seat nearest the door, I answer, "That's stupid. What would be the point?"

"The point?"

"They're taking people to put another person right back in their place. Why would any alien do that?"

She's already standing in front of the screen—apparently the coffee table isn't close enough after all—but she shoots me a look. "Clearly, it's something. Who knows what an alien might consider reasonable? I'm pretty sure no one on this planet can do that. Bring those light windows and create duplicates, I mean."

Joining her in front of the TV where two guys are almost shouting each other down instead of talking, I shrug. "You're the one that works at the Pentagon. You tell me if anyone can do it. You'd know, right?"

She snorts and says, "I'm an office manager."

"Still."

"Still, nothing. It's a big place with a lot going on, but if anyone in the world could do something like teleportation then it would have leaked out. No, this isn't us." Before I can respond, she puts up her hand, a cue to pay attention to the TV. The two men have calmed down a bit, but only a bit.

The one with the slightly reddened cheeks of the very irritated purses his lips like it's taking real effort not to start yelling again. He motions for the other guy to talk and says, "Go ahead. Your turn."

The little banner on the screen indicates he's from NASA, which is sort of funny since there are no spaceships involved. He's also got a little gleam in his eye, like he's pretty sure their funding won't be cut for the umpteenth year in a row.

He takes a deep breath and says, "What I'm saying is that panic isn't called for. We need calm heads and thoughtful reasoning. Until we know what this is, we can't react appropriately. For all we know, this is a natural event…or even something being done by humans right here on earth. We just don't know."

The red-faced guy looks a little less red, but he's still irritated. The banner below him says he's a national security consultant. He doesn't interrupt, but there's not a microsecond between the end of the NASA guy's sentence before he starts in.

"We don't have time for that. Less than five minutes ago, another report came from inside a movie theater. One of those things popped up during the movie! And there are more, we're getting calls and video from everywhere. It looks like these things…these *portals* as the government calls them…are showing up every fifteen minutes or so, and no one knows how many are showing up each time. It could be dozens. Or hundreds! People need to act fast and decisively. If they see one, they should use any and all means to avoid being taken. Any force necessary—"

"Do you hear yourself? I mean, are you actually listening to the words that you're saying?" the other guy interrupts, his expression incredulous. "What if this is being sent by our future selves? That makes more sense than aliens. I mean, if any alien species can go to the trouble to create these portals, then they can probably do a lot more. Why bother with this if they mean harm? And why replacements? You saw the report on the man taken while waiting in line at a bank. The duplicate had no idea he was a duplicate. He didn't even appear to remember tossing himself through a portal! I ask you again; What would be the point? It would be the stupidest invasion ever!"

"Stupidest invasion ever," my mom whispers, then shakes her head and looks at me. "What's going on?"

I can tell she wants to hug me again. She's got that mom-needs-a-hug look on her face. I lean in and let her squeeze my shoulders until my collar bones hurt. The things I do for my mom. When she's done squeezing, I say, "Don't worry, Mom. We'll just wait and see what happens. It will all work out."

*****

Have things worked out? Not so much. It's been two weeks and our world has changed drastically. We live in the world of the Portal Invasion, though there's still no way to prove anything as far as I know. Even school is sketchy now, with more of my classmates not showing up and the halls less deafening between classes every day. The whole thing is too weird to be believable. Is it aliens? Is it the future? Is it bad…or is it good?

Is there a way to be sure?

We've thought up lots of different kinds of aliens. We've thought up even more ways those aliens might invade us. You've got your parasites, your insects, your robots. We've even dreamt up aliens so ill-suited to our environment that they really should have preferred Mars and skipped harassing Earth altogether. If it's scary, improbable, weird, or even remotely interesting, then we've probably thought of it and told the story to each other in some form or another.

The one thing we haven't thought of is the thing that's happening. What's more, we can't even be sure that what we're seeing and experiencing is really what's going on. The Portal Invasion is a total head-trip. If this were a movie, I'd love the originality. It would be a hit, an honest-to-dollars hit. Unfortunately, it's not a story and I'm living it. We're all living it. Originality is not good when the real thing comes to your planet in a blaze of beautiful light.

We've learned a lot since that first newscast at the traffic accident. We now know the portals appear in hundreds of locations at the exact same moment. We're still not sure how many come each time. The world is a very big place, and no one is watching most of it. We here in the surveillance society of the first world are learning just how much of the planet is unmonitored.

Even calling those things portals is a stretch, because there's no way to know their exact nature with any certainty. Most people think they're portals to another world, another universe maybe. Lots of people believe the portals are cosmic incinerators, or maybe just a way to blink that original person out of existence. If the government knows which of those possibilities is true, they aren't sharing. What we do know is that they come every thirteen minutes. As in, exactly thirteen minutes. It's so precisely timed, we could use those appearances as a time standard instead of the atomic clock if we wanted to.

I think it was a simple mistake that they created a portal in the middle of a busy intersection during that first round of abductions. Then again, no one is sure that *was* their first round. The uncertainty makes trust difficult, because no one can ever be sure another person is still who they seem to be.

I used to think we modern humans had major trust issues, but our simple suspicions of before pale in comparison to the level of mistrust we carry for each other now. They could have gone on taking us for an incredibly long time had they sent portals to bedrooms or bathrooms or couches where people spent their evenings in superficial online communication. Those public displays let us in on the game they were playing.

They learned from that mistake though. They—whoever they are—learn from all their mistakes. Portals don't show up on streets anymore, or inside movie theaters, or busy conference rooms. It must be difficult to snatch humans simply because we're so darn social. Our herd mentality is a stumbling block.

Panic has been replaced by a constant state of mistrust and fear. It's not fun. It's also confusing, because there's no logic to any of it. Why take a dentist? A factory worker? A sous chef?

Even more baffling is the question of why the snatchers are sending back exact duplicates to keep living the life of the original. If they want our planet, why put the humans back? I keep hearing the same phrase I heard on that first day; *stupidest invasion ever.*

It's as if we've been invaded so often, we've become good judges of what a decent invasion looks like. Who knows, maybe we have. I think it's much more than an invasion, and I'm not convinced we're capable of understanding the motives of whoever is doing this. I also don't think we can stop it.

And that's what makes it the best invasion ever.

Three

The dead sous chef, the guy in line at the bank, and the man in the tan coat provided three of the early subjects our government used to figure out exactly what the replacements are. I'm sure other countries had their own versions of those same people. And that's what we're calling them now; replacements. It's taken four months, but the various governments of the world have at least gotten the terminology agreed upon. They've not managed much more than that.

The people who pop out of the portals are, without a doubt, people. Just standard humans. With so many people in the DNA databanks, or having paternity tests, or tracing their genetic ancestry, it wasn't hard to get comparison DNA for reported replacements.

Even if DNA matched, something would have to be different, right? How could a replacement remember a life they didn't live? Memory testing became a huge thing. People started using code words and memories that only they would share as ways to ensure their friends and family were still their friends and family.

Of course, that didn't work.

The memories are the same. The brain scans are identical. Their DNA has no variation from the original. They don't remember coming out of the portal and many simply don't believe they're portal people at all. Those portal people are unequivocally *us*. To my mind, that's another reason to look at this with some fresh perspective. It's the most unlikely of invasions. If the whole point is to take over the planet, why take it over with more of us? I'm not even going to think about some of the crazy conspiracy theories out there. More of those show up online every day.

So, where exactly does that leave me four months after the first portal opened on Earth? After four months of portals opening every thirteen minutes to extract another thousand or so humans?

If I'm precise—and precision seems called for—then I'm currently handcuffed to my mother, making a tight fist while she chops vegetables for dinner. She's fast, ridiculously so, and her knife moves up and down on the carrots like she's a machine. She jerks my arm as she reaches for another carrot every few seconds.

The only positive is that I no longer worry about AP Calculus. I should be starting my senior year in about two months, but school is not a priority anymore. I'm not the only one who gets their education sporadically from a computer with my parent attached to my wrist, or not at all. The general philosophy seems to be that we'll catch up once we figure out how to stop the portals.

"Mom, that's enough carrots!" I exclaim as she reaches for the ninth one.

She pauses, knife in the air, then looks at the bowl of sliced carrots. "Oh, yeah, I suppose it is." She smiles brightly. "You like carrots, Lysa, so that's good."

"I do, but if you're making stew, it should have more than carrots in it."

She nods, then jerks me along as she heads for the fridge. She pushes a bag of potatoes and a huge onion at me, then rummages for whatever else she needs in the deep recesses where we have a dozen half-empty obscure condiments. I'm generally scared of all those sauces and pastes. Most of them are hot enough to make snot run out of my nose.

"We're almost out of chicken *demi-glace*. Make sure we order some."

"Sure thing," I respond, but I know I'll forget by the time she brings me anywhere near the shopping list.

I turn away while she chops the onion—another downside to being attached at the wrist—and watch the TV on the wall by the table. We have it almost always set to news. One channel that used to be general news is now entirely devoted to the Portal Invasion.

Today, the big news is that the first member of Congress has been confirmed replaced. He seems as surprised as everyone else. At the press conference, he looks like he's still waiting for someone to tell him it's a big joke. Like every other replacement, he has no memory of tossing the original version of himself into the portal, but the screaming assistant and the neatly cut handcuff chain gave him away.

"Do you think it really matters that's he's a replacement?" I ask.

My mom wipes onion tears from her eyes and tugs my handcuff in the process. "Of course, it matters! They aren't us, even if they think they are. I mean, what happens to us, the real us?"

I shrug, because I'm in the dark like everyone else. Some people have tried to toss cameras through portals—after killing their doppelgangers, of course—but nothing sticks. The cameras pop back out. So do chairs, punching bags, and random dead bodies. Everything that isn't a living person pops back out. I've even heard of dogs getting tossed in, but they always come back out too, a little dazed, but none the worse for wear. The portal only accepts a living human. Period.

Believe it or not, we've had several murder investigations after people tossed a spouse into the portal when their own replacement came through. You have to wonder what they were thinking to plan to get rid of their one-time soulmate in such a bizarre way.

Even weirder, sometimes the authorities don't press charges. No evidence and no body. Go figure.

There's the opposite camp too. It's not all bullets and bayonets. There have been some replacements who found themselves alone when they woke up from whatever fugue they're in when they first come through to our world. Whole families link up and jump through if a portal comes. And it works. As long as they're touching and close together, they go through. But where?

As to what happens beyond the portals, we've got nothing. No camera images, no returnees, no nothing. There are rumors that the government has sent soldiers through, but I'm not sure I believe that. No one knows where the next round of portals will appear, and no one would miss it if there were soldiers stationed every twenty feet around a city to catch one opening. If we have sent a soldier over, then it's by luck or chance.

Or because they were replaced.

So, my mom's question about what happens to the original version is completely unanswerable. Still, we ask each other all the time. Everyone does. I know I wonder about it almost constantly.

I'm not sure it's anything bad at all. It could be something amazing. I keep those thoughts to myself. My mom would flip out, and everyone I know would immediately view me with suspicion. More than likely, I'd be reported as a possible replacement and hauled away to wherever they take known or suspected replacements. And just like all the people who went through portals, suspected replacements taken by the government never return either.

"It can't be an invasion," I say. This situation has been going on for months, which means millions of those replacements are wandering around our world. Some have been caught, yes, but that's really a drop in the bucket. Everyone replaced while out of sight of another person is still out there.

Mostly, anyway. There are a growing number of people like my mom, and they're cutting down on the number of replacements that survive. They take readiness to a whole new level.

Even the government encourages this kind of readiness. *Treat the replacements as an imminent threat.* That's the guidance from the government and people are following it, a first when it comes to governmental edicts regarding what we citizens should and shouldn't do.

There are signs, brochures, and web pages devoted to the best way to dispatch your replacement if your time comes. Gun sales are brisk…to say the least. At first, people wondered why those being replaced didn't fight to the death, even with their fists. It turns out we don't have that option. Once a replacement gets close, the original freezes, unable to do more than lift a finger in their own defense. If you're going to fight, you have to do it within a few seconds of the portal opening.

That's a very short window for defense, so people take it seriously. Including my mom.

My mom starts in on the potatoes like they're portal potatoes that simply must die. She hates it when I say this stuff. Between chops, she says, "It is an invasion. It has to be. There's no excuse or explanation for it other than an invasion."

"It will take almost two hundred years to replace us at this rate! It's stupid! There must be another reason. And they're just people. Why invade us to replace exact duplicates?"

My mom's hand pauses and she gives me a sharp look. "You sound like those religious people. Is there something we should discuss?"

I'm almost tempted to say I've had some form of religious revelation. She'd be more likely to understand that. As it stands now, she can't find any logical reason for my views. It's not like such a belief would be unique. Big parts of the population—whether members of established religion or not—have decided that the portals are being sent by their deity of choice. Some think it's the rapture, with the portals coming for those who will ascend to heaven.

Technically, we're Hindu, though my mom isn't big on formal observances. She's left me to figure out what I believe without pressure. She says faith is very personal and all people will find their way to their own hearts if given the space to do so. So, she's given me space. She might be regretting that now, given my views on portals.

While I don't want to make any blanket statements, I've searched online and it turns out that many Hindus are in the camp of the non-fighters when it comes to portals. They aren't the rapture people, but they don't fight being replaced either. I think my mom is worried I'm letting that influence me, but my views are based purely on logic.

"Don't worry, Mom. I'm not about to take holy orders on you. I just don't want to assume this is a bad thing. We have no way of knowing, so why assume it's bad?"

The knife in my mom's hand slams down and she rounds on me, her face red. "No more! No more talk of that—"

The strident beeping from my mom's phone makes both of us freeze in place. One minute till the next portal. We do this every thirteen minutes. At night, we take shifts. One of us wears earbuds with the alarm on high volume, while the other sleeps. It's been hard on both of us, but harder on her. She doesn't truly trust me not to fall asleep, so she takes more shifts. With a jerk that makes the cloth around the handcuff chafe at my wrist, she grabs one of the two guns off the table and shoves it into my free hand. Then she grabs the other.

"Safety," she says.

"Check. Safety is off."

She nods and presses me against the wall, squeezing next to me as tightly as she can. No matter how many times I run the numbers for her—yeah, yeah, go ahead and tell me that my AP Calculus was good for me—she acts like she received a telegram saying I'm next with every thirteen-minute window.

"You remember, Lysa, you shoot the moment a portal opens and anyone walks out. You got it? You shoot. I don't care what they look like." Her hand is tight on the fully-loaded semi-automatic weapon in her hands.

She gets the big gun that needs two hands, while I get the pistol. We have to make concessions, what with the handcuffs and all. It helps that my mom used to be in the military, so unlike most Americans who've bought guns recently, she actually knows what she's doing.

She gave up the excitement of her beloved Navy career when I was little and starting school. With a brand-new divorce decree and her parents too far away to help provide stability when she deployed, she chose the life of a Pentagon paper-shuffler over the career she loved. Even so, she's still military at heart. The way she readies her weapon gives that away.

Even if she's serious and ready, I'm very tired of this. The odds are so slim. We're wasting our lives defending against something that will probably never happen. I roll my eyes, because what else can I do? "I know, Mom. If I see any purple glow, I'll murder it in a hail of bullets."

Her fingers dig into my dangling hand and she hisses, "It's not murder. I don't care if it looks just like you or me, it's not us, and it's not here for any nice reason. You eliminate it. That's all. Don't pay attention to anything it says or does."

I've pushed her buttons too far. Her face is sweaty and red, her breathing too shallow and fast. She dreads this as much as I do. We've learned from the experiences of others that it's incredibly hard to shoot yourself, which is essentially what we'll be forced to do.

It's even harder to kill someone you love, like a daughter. The person that comes through will be one of us, no differences at all. I think that's why my mom sweats and shakes like this. She fears it will be me. And to stay here on Earth, we will have to shoot it. She would have to shoot her daughter and I would have to shoot my mom. That's a tough situation to contemplate.

The alarm sounds on the phone. Thirteen minutes. Both of us suck in a deep breath and hold it, searching the open floor plan of our house for any hint of a white or purple glow. After a few seconds, there's no sound of footsteps or anything else.

The aliens—or whatever they are—are always on time. We're safe. For this thirteen minutes, we're safe.

My mom wipes her forehead and upper lip, her pent-up breath coming out in a rush. With a shaky hand she lowers her gun, then tugs me along to put it on the table.

"Another one down," she says, patting the gun I place next to hers. Our nice table is now covered in scratches from putting our guns down like this every thirteen minutes over the course of so many months. Given how often my mom scolded me for leaving sweating glasses that might create rings on the polished surface, it surprises me to see how battered it is at least a few times a day.

Yeah, another one down. The rest of my life means a whole lot more of these events. What's going to happen when I finally meet someone I want to date? That's assuming she ever lets me go anywhere to meet someone. Will she tag along with a rifle and stand us back to back every thirteen minutes?

"Mom, I need to go to the bathroom."

She glances at the clock and slips the key from her neck. "Okay, but you've got ten minutes and no more. Hurry."

"Jeez," I answer, embarrassed. She knows way too much about my private stuff now that we're locked together.

It feels good to have my hand free, even if only temporarily. My wrist is chafed and sore, the skin red and thin for a good three inches centered on my wrist bones. Even with the cloth padding, it's tearing me away layer by layer, leaving a delicately painful ring of nearly transparent skin where my wrist used to be. I know it's doing the same to her, but she never complains, so I try not to either. I don't see the point of the handcuffs anyway.

Of course, this is better than going to work with her. That's another whole ball game and involves me breathing other people's rebreathed air for twelve hours in a tiny, underground room packed with spouses and kids. Four marines stand outside the entrance with automatic weapons.

No room for the portal means no portal will come…which means the marines have a good chance to kill anything that comes out before it can get through the door to us. There are squares marked on the floor of the room just big enough for a single, straight-backed chair. Every person gets a chair and a square, no more. We fill the room entirely. It's so comforting and so very creepy.

Yeah, even the handcuffs are better than that.

When I shuffle back into the kitchen, stretching my arms and shaking out the stiffness, she's cutting chicken for the stew as if nothing happened. The potatoes are already in the slow cooker. I might have already mentioned that she's really fast with a knife.

There are clocks all over the house now, at least one always an easy glance away. She looks up, then says, "Six minutes."

I sigh, and her shoulders bow a little over the chicken. She feels guilty about the life I live now. I see it in those hunched shoulders, as if it were written across her back.

"I'm sorry," I say.

"So am I."

With a final plop, the last of tonight's dinner is tucked into the cooker. The little red light tells me I'm going to be eating well tonight. This is one of my favorites. A little chicken, a little spice, and a lot of vegetables, all swimming in a thick gravy that begs for a biscuit. My mouth waters even though breakfast is only an hour gone.

As she wipes the counter, she says, "Go on. You've got a few minutes. Go crazy." She grins over her shoulder at me and I want to hug her for it. Her expression might convey this is no big deal, but letting me more than arm's reach away is torture and I know it. This bit of freedom must hurt her like a case of full-body shingles.

I'm out the back door and into the yard in two shakes, running like my hair is on fire and my arms pumping with the freedom to move. I can't go far, so I run around the house. We don't have a fenced yard, so I only have to jump the little line of rosemary plants that borders our walkway. I let my shoes brush against them and the burst of sharp sweetness envelops me along with the sunshine of a perfect summer day. It feels so good that I push myself faster, going at a reckless speed that makes me feel like I'll trip with every footfall, a dizzying pace that brings me back to life in the best way.

"Time!" my mom shouts from the window.

My brief taste of freedom is over and my spirits plummet once again. Time to be a prisoner. Time to be afraid. Time to wait for it to be my turn.

Four

The whole house smells of stew and my stomach growls loudly as I sit next to my mom on the couch. She's working while I play a mindless game on my tablet. Since she needs both hands for her keyboard, I don't have a lot of choices. I'm bored with all the books I've got right now, so it's bursting little colored dots on the tablet screen for me. It only takes one hand.

The alarm goes off and I ask, "Only three more alarms till we eat?"

She smiles tiredly as she helps me up from the couch. "Maybe four."

"Close enough," I say, giving her a nudge with my shoulder. She may be doing a lot of this to herself by worrying, but she's exhausted and growing more fragile by the day. Affection is sometimes called for. It adds a little gas to her rapidly-draining tank. Plus, I love her and all that.

We're up against the wall with a few seconds to spare. Instead of that paranoid jerking around that she usually does, she leans her head back and looks at me. "I'll rethink this. I promise. I'm just not ready yet."

"That's—"

I don't get a chance to finish, because at the exact moment the alarm goes off, the portal opens not ten feet from us. Half the couch disappears and all I can see are the beautiful purple and white swirls of light. The glow of it tingles against my skin. My initial response is to tilt my face toward it and soak up infinity. It looks unfathomably deep and as shallow as a mirror's surface at the same time. The blue tendrils swirling inside seem almost alive, moving with sinuous grace through the swirls.

"Shit," my mom says, her mouth hanging open.

Out of the portal steps my mother, her face blank of any real expression and her eyes traveling briefly around the room. When she sees my real mother, she steps forward without hesitation, as if she doesn't see the guns in our hands pointed vaguely in her direction.

My mom is already frozen, her mouth still forming the end of her last word. No one knows why that happens, but the freeze is part of the process. She can't do a thing to protect herself. That means I have to do something fast.

I raise the pistol and point it at the replacement. My finger is ready to pull the trigger, but my brain is screaming at me, *That's your mother. Don't shoot your parent.* I swear I'm trying to shoot, but I just can't. That's definitely my mom. With a grunt I try again, my finger tightening the tiniest bit before I push out a frustrated breath.

I can't do it. I can't shoot her. She's my mom. My finger loosens on the trigger and the barrel moves away from her face.

She has no bolt-cutters with her, so I'm not sure how she thinks she can get my mother through the portal. Her hands rise, reaching for her neck where my mom wears a key. I guess this replacement has her own key, which means we're screwed. The replacements won't toss in someone other than their original, but if she can unlock our cuffs with my mom frozen…well…it's all up to me to stop her. Still, my finger won't squeeze that trigger. My beautiful, kind, loving, and fun mother is not someone I can shoot.

"Mom!" I scream.

She can't do it, because she's frozen. Her face is almost as blank as her replacement's, their expressions a near mirror image. Her gun barrel bumps into the other's chest as the replacement pulls the key over her head, her dark, wavy hair flopping down no differently from the way my mom's did earlier when she unlocked me so that I could pee. The freeze may have happened already, but I don't think it's a total freeze. I've never seen a portal up close before, so this is all new to me. My mom's eyes blink and water. Her nostrils flare. Her chest moves with her panicked breaths.

That means it's not complete, but enough so that she can't punch the replacement in her mouth.

"You must go. It's for your own safety," my replacement mother says, her fingers closing around the little key and reaching past the gun for the handcuff.

My mother's breath comes out in a whisper. "No."

It seems to take incredible effort for her to shape her lips into that one simple word. Sweat dots her forehead and a vein on her eyelid swells under the pressure. I don't need to hear more to know what that tiny, strained word means. She wants me to shoot and I can't do that. I see sorrow replace the terror in her eyes for a moment. It's so brief that I might have imagined it.

Then her gun goes off.

The replacement flies backward like a superhero power-punched her in the chest, an explosion of blood and other unsavory bits showering us with an unpleasant warmth that I'll probably freak out about later. But not now. For one eternal moment I stare while yuck drips off my face, then I'm running through all the things we have to do as fast as we can.

"Quick! Get her through!" I shout, yanking at my mother. She's standing there with her mouth opening and closing like a fish, covered in her own blood—except that it came from another body. She looks like a horror movie. She unfreezes, almost like a switch clicked.

I totally get that she's in shock, but really, we've got a portal issue here. If she's unfrozen, then we need to move. Unless the replacement is dead, she shouldn't unfreeze.

"Come on!" I shout, this time yanking the gun away and dropping it next to mine. "We've got to get her through before she dies."

My mom comes along, but she's more like a zombie than the energetic and slightly nervous person of five minutes ago. The truth is, I don't think the replacement is alive. I think she died the instant that gun went off against her floral-patterned shirt. If the explosion that it made of her chest is any indicator, she has to be dead.

Even so, I yank the key on my mom's neck and lift our joined hands, so I can maneuver the key into the lock. She doesn't so much as blink. I leave the handcuffs dangling from her wrist when I free myself. There's no time for quibbling over details.

I pick up the replacement's shoulders and bite the inside of my mouth hard enough to taste blood at the sight of her face. Even her hair is curled at the temples like my mother's.

"Mom, pick her up," I urge her, my voice going all funny with the tears that I'm doing my best to hold back.

She snaps out of it, or she mostly does anyway, her head shaking and her fists clenched. "She's not me. She's not human." With the portal gleaming at us in the place where we were sitting a few minutes ago, it's pretty hard to ignore that we've got a big problem.

One of the replacement's shoes has come off and I see her toes. The sight almost makes me drop her. There's a bandage between her toes with a cartoon character on it. It's exactly where my mom's is after trying to break in a new pair of sandals and earning a blister for her efforts. I don't mean similar. I don't mean the same brand or stuck to the same general area. I mean *exactly* where my mom's is, right down to the crooked end where she pulled it to stick it to her foot.

"Oh my gosh," I say, staring at the foot in my mom's hand. The whole thing is too surreal. No wonder people have a hard time doing the deed when it comes their turn.

My mom looks, then drops one foot to rip off the bandage. Sure enough, there's a blister there.

"Talk about attention to detail," she whispers.

We toss the replacement into the portal and she's swallowed like she never was. I'm pretty sure she was dead, but exactly how dead is an issue. Maybe the deciding factor is brain activity or electrical impulses or something else, but not having a heartbeat isn't a complete deal-breaker when it comes to the portals accepting what we throw back.

Why we don't just leave the portal alone and let it shimmer there for the entire cycle is also a question I've entertained. Why are people so adamant about tossing something in and letting it close? Now I understand. I absolutely and completely understand that urge. The portal is disturbing at the deepest level. All I want is for it to disappear, but at the same time, I feel compelled to look…to stare into whatever might be beyond. The portal is off-putting and compelling in equal measure. I can almost feel the atoms of my body vibrating as they bathe in that mysterious light.

I shake my head and back up a step, forcing my eyes away from it.

Plus, well, if the government finds out we got a portal, both of us will be hauled away to wherever they're taking replacements. We've got to get rid of this body or we're toast. And if anyone sees this portal through the window, we're equally toasted. They'll call the hotline and that will be that. No one can ever find out this house was visited by a portal. Also, if the portal doesn't keep the body, what will we do with it? Bury it in the backyard in the middle of the night?

Silently and slowly, I start counting. I make it all the way to five before the corpse bounces out like a bizarre pinwheel of limp arms and legs, then slides to a disorderly halt at my feet.

My mom falls back against the front window, the glass making an ominous cracking sound when she does. "No," she croaks out, eyes riveted to the crumpled form once again leaking fluids all over our living room floor. Her dead face is turned in my mom's direction, the two identical people now staring at each other, except that one of them is sightless, her face already pale with death and blood loss.

No one can handle seeing that. No one.

Her handcuff rattles when I grab her by the shoulders and pull her away from the window. There's a spider web of cracks where her head impacted the glass. It skews the view outside, turning it into a frightening scene rather than the suburban Arlington street it was only moments ago.

"Mom, it's not an invasion and if it is, she's dead. You're safe," I say, cupping her face in my hands so that she has to look at me. I wish I hadn't done that, because it smears the blood on her face, spots and streaks turning into large, red swaths shaped like my hand. She doesn't look at me, her eyes pulling so far to the side that it must hurt. I shuffle over a step to get between her and any view of the body.

Finally, she looks at me, but she's so shell-shocked I don't know if she understands what's going on. "They'll come for you next," she whispers, specks of blood on her lips smearing as she shapes the words.

I shake my head. "You know it doesn't work like that. It's random or something. And you know they only send a replacement once. No one has gotten one twice. It's over for you. You're safe. I'm safe."

Am I safe? The truth is, I've never thought I was in danger. Not really. For whatever reason, I'm with that much-maligned minority that thinks there's something other than an invasion going on. I don't think it's religious either. There must be a logical reason, a purpose. There must be a sensible explanation.

My mom *really* hates it when I say things like that.

She slides to the floor, her eyes wide and frightened as they shift from the dead replacement to the portal, then back again. She's completely overwhelmed, and understandably so. I feel the portal behind me like a physical thing instead of a hole in our reality. If I were to close my eyes, I think I would feel it like a hand on my back, urging me onward, while comforting me at the same time. I swear I can feel it right this second, whispering for me to come through and enjoy the sights. I turn and look at it closely for the first time.

It's comfortably sized for a person to get through, taller than it is wide. Edging around the glowing oval to get a more complete look, it's the same from the back as the front. The portal is so thin it almost disappears when I look at it from the side.

The longer I look at it, the more beautiful it gets. There's something attractive in it, something that draws me closer.

"Get away from it!" my mother shouts suddenly, breaking the trance I'd begun to fall into.

I look back at her and say, "It won't hurt me. This isn't meant to hurt us."

She moans a little and whispers, "Can you feel that? It's horrible…"

I have no idea what I'm thinking or what other influence is pressing me forward, but I know what I'm going to do. This might be my only shot to find out the answers I'm desperate to know. I could go the rest of my life and not see another portal based purely on the odds. And I can feel it urging me in some way, a feeling of deep longing that works on me right down to the roots of my hair. It won't hurt me. I just know.

So, I obey that urge. To the sound of my mother's screams, I race forward two steps and fling myself through the portal.

Five

There's the briefest moment of complete disorientation. I don't mean feeling a little wobbly or dizzy, I mean utter and complete loss of balance. I don't know which way is up or down, if I'm two dimensional or three. Even the concept of up and down is suddenly foreign. Am I a being of physical proportions or only the idea of one? Thank goodness it doesn't last long.

Even as I pop out of the portal, I see another one right in front of me, this one a deeper purple with streaks of richer, darker blue inside. I'm aimed right for it and I put up my arms—or at least I think I do, considering that I'm not sure if I have arms—but it winks out as I fly toward it.

I fall onto soft mats, all my sensory abilities slamming into my head at once. Gravity, inertia, the force of muscles and bone, the lightness of air in sunlight…all of it returns to me at the same time. Of course, that's not good for a body, so I immediately puke. I don't mean your standard puke, either. I mean projectile vomiting like I've only ever seen in horror movies or comedies about college misadventures. Behind me, I feel it when the portal goes away, like a bit of the air is sucked out of the room.

"Oh dear," someone says faintly, but I'm still puking.

As the last of my innards are wrung out of me and deposited onto the puffy mat in a splattery puddle, I feel better. That's also nearly instantaneous, and I wheeze in a frantic breath or five. I'm kneeling on some sort of plastic-like mat. It's very soft and bouncy. I have the odd thought that I landed in the gym where I used to practice gymnastics as a little kid. Almost without my wanting to, my fingers press into the mat, sinking in to confirm by touch that it's real.

"We've got another one," that same someone says.

I look up to see a grey-haired older woman, the kind that should be wearing an apron and perpetually smell of freshly baked cookies. Her chubby hands are pressed together at her waist and her expression is exactly what I'd expect from a grandma whose grandchild just got a boo-boo in need of kissing all better.

"What the heck?" I ask, wiping runners of bile off my chin. My hand comes away with a load of blood as well as bile, which alarms me until I remember what happened to my replacement mom.

"Are you hurt?" she asks, concern evident in her tone.

She must mean the blood. I shake my head and she looks away, her face rather sad. The expression is replaced by something more neutral almost immediately, like she doesn't want me to see her sadness. Then she plucks a little towel from a stack and steps forward cautiously, as if waiting to see if I'll attack her. She holds it out, while keeping her body just beyond the reach of my arms.

"You've got a little something," she says, motioning with one dimpled hand in the general area of my face.

I'm utterly and completely confused. This is what's beyond the portal? Grandmas in romper rooms for kindergarteners, all laid out with nap mats and childproofed against falls? I feel my eyes darting everywhere, trying to catalog what I'm seeing, but everything seems remarkably mundane. The light is normal and coming from round patches on the ceiling, though I can't see actual fixtures, only light. The mats look new, but they're fairly standard mats. It's all very, very average.

What's left for me to do except accept the towel? It feels like any other towel to me, not in the least bit alien. Actually, it's sort of nice, the thick kind you get in good hotels.

"Thank you."

She smiles and nods, clearly relieved I'm not going to do anything to her. I wonder how often they're attacked. Probably a lot. I sniff at the towel to be sure it's not coated in ether or any other serial-killer type thing, but I try to do it discreetly. All I get from it is the scent of clean cotton toweling. As I wipe my face, she opens a little box on a counter that runs along the opposite wall and withdraws another towel. This one is tightly rolled and sending tendrils of lazy steam into the air.

"Here, this will help," she says and hands it to me, still keeping her distance.

It's exactly like the ones my mom and I get at the Japanese restaurant she loves so much. I liked the warm, wet towel more than the sushi when we first started going there. My confusion grows.

I wipe my face and arms down, staining the towel bright red. She's right, it does help. It helps a lot. I sigh and sit back on the mat, putting a little distance between me and the mess I made. It smells bitter and unclean. With one last swipe on my forehead, I point with my eyes at the puke and say, "I'm sorry about that."

Her smile is genuine, truly. Her expression is real in a way that we rarely see smiles in adults. Unguarded is what I would call it. "Oh, never mind that. It happens. That's why everything is washable and—"

A voice seems to come from everywhere inside this room, cutting her off. It's officious, not nearly as warm as hers, but also not hostile. Mostly, it sounds like a man having a busy shift that isn't exactly going well. "Let's confirm her identification. Standing down 8-8-9 for the next cycle."

The old woman looks toward the ceiling, then shrugs at me a little guiltily. "He means you, dear."

"Who are you? Is this an invasion? Is this like an alien ship or something?" I ask, standing up and holding out the towel the same way she did, at full arm's length.

She laughs and waves her hand as if that's the funniest thing she's heard all day, then drops my towel into a hole in the wall above the counter. "Not at all, sweetie. I promise."

"Who are you?"

"Oh, that would help, wouldn't it?" she says, her eyes twinkling and her cheeks dimpling with her smile. "My name is Rosa and I was supposed to be here for the transfer of Barbara Choudra. You're not Barbara Choudra. What can I call you?"

I'm not sure why I do it, but I step forward and hold out my hand for her to shake. Now that I'm here, I might as well make the most of it. And like my mom always tells me; I can get more bees with honey. So, I'll be polite and not a scared ninny. Rosa seems surprised by my extended hand, which somewhat confirms the notion of them not having great initial meetings with people who get tossed through the portals. Still, she takes my hand. Hers is warm and dry, soft just like a grandma's hand should be.

"I'm Lysa Choudra. Barbara is my mom."

She frowns at that, squeezing my hand a little. "Oh, my goodness! That's terrible! Did she...I mean...oh, dear."

It takes a half-second, but I realize what she's thinking. Given all the husbands and wives who have tossed in a spouse, the sheer number of people who have tossed in a stranger that happened to be nearby, or damaged their replacement and tossed them through, she must think my mom pushed me in to save herself.

"No," I say, laughing. "She didn't push me in. I'm not sure why, but I went in myself. I have absolutely no clue why I did it. But, *uh*, we did...*uh*...well, the replacement didn't make it."

The reality of what I've done doesn't click until I say that, but it does once I say the words. The sensation is like a full-force body slam of reality in my face. My heart jumps painfully in my chest and my innards seize up. *I can't go back*. No one has gone back that anyone knows of. I've just walked out of my world with no clue what might happen to me. And I helped commit a murder on my way here to top it off.

My chin starts to shake, this hit of reality too much for my system. I put my hands to my head and squat back down on the mats, overwhelmed by the incredibly stupid impulse that just ended my previous life.

"Oh my gosh. I *walked* through."

Rosa hurries over and rubs my back with a firm hand while I squat there, my face in my hands and my whole body tucked tightly into a ball. I can't help but notice she's wearing white sneakers with hose. How odd.

"*Shh*, it's okay. I'm right here. You're fine. We'll get this sorted," she murmurs as she rubs my back.

As strange as it is to say this, given that she's probably an alien that snatches a thousand humans every thirteen minutes for unknown, and possibly very bad reasons, her touch is super comforting. I really want to hug her. Is that weird?

After a few minutes, I wind down, my body done with processing the reaction and the initial shock. My brain isn't done by a long shot, but my body is for the moment. And now my knees hurt from squatting like this. When I hold out a hand, Rosa helps me up and then surprises me again by pushing the hair away from my face, then gripping both my hands in hers.

"Okay?"

I nod, but I'm really not okay at all.

Six

Once she's sure I've got myself under control, she leads me over to the counter gently and says, "Since you didn't go through, I'll need to confirm your identity. It's simple and won't hurt, but it is important. With so many incorrect transfers, things are getting to be a bit of a muddle."

Transfer? That's an interesting word. It tells me we probably aren't dinner for aliens at any rate. But transfer to where?

Along the counter is an array of things I don't understand. I know the box the towel came from and the hole where it went after I used it, but all the rest are absolute unknowns. Nothing looks overtly aggressive or dangerous though, so that's something.

Rosa takes the hand she still has clasped in hers and tentatively pulls it over a shiny oval set into the counter. "I'm just going to lay your hand right here. You'll see a light, but it won't hurt. Is that okay?"

I nod, watching the oval intently. Anything could happen, but I believe Rosa. She seems so sincere and so much like a grandma. I don't have a grandma anymore, but if I imagined the perfect replacement for the one I had, she would look a lot like Rosa. I wonder if that's on purpose.

"Is this what you really look like?" I ask suddenly.

Rosa's eyes crinkle when she smiles. "Go on, pinch me if you like. I'm just as I am."

I nod, feeling a little embarrassed for being suspicious. Then again, they did just send a portal with a replacement for my mother. But Rosa seems so *nice*.

As soon as my hand touches the cool surface, an extremely bright light pinpointed around the center of my palm makes the flesh of my hand glow. It's just like when you press a bright flashlight into your hand and the edges glow like you might be able to see through it if the light were only a little brighter. Except this one is brighter, and I can see right through my hand in shades of pink. The bones are visible as darker lines and patches.

"Whoa!" I exclaim, ready to snatch my hand back.

Rosa's touch on my forearm grows firmer. "It's okay."

The light goes out before I can even decide if I want to pull harder or not. A small, musical *ping* sounds out in the room. As Rosa and I look up, another voice that I think might be a computer says, "Lysa Ann Choudra, Arlington, Virginia, North America. Non-transfer."

Rosa's cheeks dimple again, but this time from pursing her lips instead of smiling. All she says is, "Ah."

"What does that mean? Non-transfer?" I ask, alarm ringing through me.

If the people who get replaced are transfers and I'm a non-transfer, does that mean a portal wouldn't have come for me? Wherever it is that we're transferred to, what happens to those who aren't supposed to transfer? Am I headed for the dinner table after all?

Rosa once again rubs my back, up near the shoulders just like my mom does when she's trying to soothe me. "It's okay, Lysa. We'll get this sorted, like I said. It just takes a bit of doing. You're quite safe."

Again, I believe her. She's so stinking earnest. Rosa comes across as someone who has never so much as uttered a white lie in her life. Of course, sincerity is the hallmark of the best liars, so there's that.

"I'm really scared."

"I understand. I really, truly do."

She gives me some space, a minute or two to calm myself and catch my breath. When I'm a bit more under control, she presses a silver patch inset into the counter surface and another box opens. From within she withdraws something that looks like folded pajamas, deep grey with a lovely purple piping along the edges.

When she hands them to me, they feel like a soft cloud. They may look like flannel, but they feel so much softer. Next, she pulls out a pair of socks with a soft sole along the bottom.

"Your clothes are...*umm*...a bit soiled. Perhaps you'd like to change?"

I look down to see my t-shirt is liberally splattered with blood, as are my jeans. Even my favorite pair of Converse sneaks have big smears of red all over them. I'm horrified. "*Ugh*."

"I'll just step out while you change, but if you need me, you only need to say so. I'll come right back in. There are more hot washcloths in that box, so you can clean up a bit more. Just leave your clothes on the floor and I'll take care of them."

She waits for me to nod, gives me another smile, then steps over to a place in the white wall that looks no different from any other. It slides open at her approach and I crane my neck to try and see out, but all I see is the other side of a corridor, another featureless white wall. I wonder if there's another person like me, or maybe the correctly replaced person, on the other side of that wall.

The door *snicks* shut and I'm left alone with the counter and the puffy gym mats. I guess the mats are here because of the fall we take coming through. How considerate they are, particularly for alien invaders.

It takes a half dozen or more of those hot, wet cloths before I feel clean, though in truth, I really want a long shower. I still feel like there's blood all over me in a sticky, gross residue, even though I can't see it. And I can feel it in my hair, wet clumps drying into sticky, stiff clumps. The washcloths don't do much for that. It's strange to stand in this room without my clothes on, but I don't see mirrors or glass that would indicate anyone is watching me, or camera lenses on the walls. Given their tech, I doubt I would see anything as obvious as that, but I still feel better for not seeing any.

The pajamas fit perfectly, as do the socks, which is a little weird. There are even pockets perfectly placed for cramming my hands into. I'm rather tall and a bit curvier than average, so it can't be coincidence that the pajamas fit me so well. I'm not fat, just cushiony as my mom calls it. When she really wants to embarrass me, she says I'm voluptuous. It always gets a rise out of me when she says that, and she laughs that wicked laugh of hers, her shoulders hunching up a little and her eyes wild with humor.

My mom. I left her with a corpse of herself.

I'm the worst person in the world.

"I'm done," I call out, but my voice sounds shaky. It feels weird to be loud in this room.

The door opens immediately and Rosa strolls back in, waving to someone as they walk out of sight. I barely get a glimpse, but it looks like a kid, no more than ten years old if I go by height. So, they have ten-year olds wandering around. That's interesting.

"Oh, you look so much more comfortable!" Rosa says, smiling. She plucks at the end of my sleeve and adds, "It's very becoming. Grey is a good color for you."

I don't wear a lot of grey, but now that she's mentioned it, the skin on my hand isn't quite so green looking. It's more creamy than pasty. I wonder if they did that on purpose and if so, how could they know what would look good on me? And why would they be so considerate as to think of how I would look in a specific color? Once again, I'm left with that feeling that whoever these people are—still assuming they're people—they aren't interested in hurting us.

She glances up at my hair and says, "You'll need a more substantial washing. You'll be able to get a shower or bath soon. Don't worry."

"Is it bad?" I ask. When I shake my head a little at the question, a clump of something falls from my hair to splat onto the mat.

Rosa makes a little face and says, "Well, it's not so bad. Would you like me to help?"

I nod and she whips more of those hot towels out of the box. A little recess fills with water when she passes her hand across it and she dunks the little towel in. Stepping closer to her, I let her drape a dry towel around my shoulders, then bend so she can wash out my hair with the wet cloths. They come away red, then pink.

This is the most bizarre thing that has ever happened in my life. An alien invader is towel-washing my replacement mother's innards out of my hair. Honestly, I can't even process this.

When she's done, she smiles at the bird's nest that is my hair. I may be only one quarter Indian, but I got the hair from that side of the family. My hair is so dark brown it's almost black and that makes the wildness seem even wilder. There's not much that can be done about it, so I finger comb it as much as I can, then shrug.

"Ready?" Rosa asks.

"For what?"

"Well, there's a sort of waiting station I'll take you to. With all the mix-ups and wrong people coming through, we're playing a bit of catch up here. What a muddle!"

She seems genuinely confused by this, as if she has no idea how upsetting and frightening it is for us on Earth. Could it be that they don't get it? That seems incredibly unlikely. Haven't the other thirteen million plus people that came through let them know?

I hold up a hand and say, "Sure, but can I ask you a couple of questions first? While it's still just us?"

"Of course."

She seems sincere enough, her hands clasping together at her waist in precisely the same way they were when I first popped through. "I have to know. Why are you doing this?"

Rosa sighs, then says, "That's complicated and because you're a non-transfer, I shouldn't be the one to talk to you about it. You'll get that information from someone far more qualified than I."

That answer could be ominous, but it only sounds regretful coming from her. So, moving on. "Okay. If you're not intending to hurt us, then why don't you just tell people what you're doing? On the other side, I mean. Do you understand what's happening when people see a portal open and a doppelganger step out?"

She wrinkles her face and shakes her head in disapproval. "Well, I know that we're getting far too many incorrect transfers, and the violence is quite shocking." Again, she shakes her head, as if trying to rid herself of a disturbing memory. "But we simply can't say too much, dear. We've changed things as much as we can. The stand-ins tell them they have to go, don't they?"

"Yeah, a creepy zombie-like duplicate says that in a dead voice and that's supposed to be comforting?"

"It isn't?"

"Uh, no. It isn't. Not at all."

"Oh dear." I swear it looks like she's about to cry. Yep, she's going to cry.

"I'm sorry. Please don't cry," I say. I feel like I have to hug her, which is so weird. What is it with these alien grandmas?

She dabs at her eyes with her fingers and tries to smile at me, waving me back. "It's alright. I just want things to go smoothly. I've never seen anything like this before. It's just so…so…*wrong*."

"That's humans for you. No one can say evolution didn't prepare us for responding to threats."

"But we're not a threat," Rosa says, looking into my eyes as if pleading for understanding. "We're truly not. We're here to help."

The voice from somewhere else comes back as soon as those final words leave Rosa's lips. "Please take the non-transfer to the waiting station. Welcome to our humble hub, Lysa."

There's a reprimand for Rosa and a warm welcome for me in those words, even though the tone doesn't significantly change. I just feel it. Rosa holds out her hand like I'm a little kid who needs to be held close when crossing a street. If my mom did that, I'd laugh at her, but I don't feel like that at all with Rosa. I take her hand without hesitation.

The truth is, I feel like stepping beyond this door would be the equivalent of crossing all six lanes of the freeway while wearing a blindfold. I'm awfully close to peeing myself. Wrapping my cold fingers around her warm ones, I follow along like a duckling.

Seven

The hallway is long, very white, and utterly featureless. "Wow," I say, wondering how they find their way around as we approach an intersection that looks exactly like the one behind us.

Rosa waves her free hand and says, "There are twelve-hundred rooms like the one you arrived in. Other transfer rooms are configured differently. In total, there are thirty-thousand in this module. We have six modules, and the whole place is called the hub."

With that, she motions me toward the opening at the end of the hallway, which curves around in a graceful arc. There are other hallways branching off before the curve hides the rest from view. Everything is white, very white, but there's a discreet dot of color inset into the wall just below the ceiling. I turn around and see my hallway is marked by a pure yellow dot. The next one is yellow with the faintest of green tints.

"You send a thousand portals at a time, right?" I ask, finally noticing the difference between the number of rooms and the number of portals estimated by officials on Earth.

Rosa tugs me along by my hand, a little smile on her face as she speaks. "As you already noticed, not all of the transfers go as planned. Lately, we get as many as half that are incorrect. Either no transferee, the wrong one, a non-transfer, or something else altogether. Some of the rooms aren't ready by the next round. There *should* be a thousand human transfers each time, but there are usually far fewer. We're getting another section going so we can keep up the pace. It won't do to fall behind. Won't do at all."

I'll just bet they have rooms not available. I can imagine some of what comes through. The image of that second, slightly darker portal comes to mind. In particular, the way it winked out as I approached it. Or rather, how it winked out as I hurtled toward it through a portal out of my world. *Transfer*. If my mom would have been tossed through as planned, would she have gone through that second portal and landed somewhere besides here?

I could be mistaken. It's possible that the second portal was some artifact created by the mere act of going through, a sort of mirror image or something. But the word transfer keeps ringing in my head.

We round the curve, which just keeps right on curving, and more hallways branch off from this central area at precise intervals. This place must be monstrously huge given how long this curve is taking to get around. The colors graduate from greenish-yellow to green to a sort of blue that I remember from a trip to the Caribbean; not quite blue, not quite green. It's one of my favorites. It doesn't take a genius to understand their labeling system. This is the human color spectrum, a march across the rainbow.

As we get to a pure blue, Rosa stops and faces the interior. It looks no different from any other spot on the wall, but she holds up her hand and a fairly standard looking elevator control glows from a spot in the white. I bend to peer at it, wondering if I can see through whatever it is, but it really does appear to come from within the wall itself. Rosa waves, and the down arrow glows brighter, a countdown evident in the blinking of the arrow.

Rosa sighs while we wait, and I suppress a laugh. It's so normal. Sighing while waiting at the elevator is a totally human thing to do. She clears her throat as the countdown continues and asks, "You don't have motion sickness or agoraphobia or anything like that, do you?"

I have no clue what agoraphobia is, but I do have a tendency for nausea when I sit in the back seat during road trips. I like to read, but it's a sure recipe for a queasy stomach on a train or bus. "I do get a little car sick sometimes."

Rosa looks around, like maybe she's trying to think of where to get another towel, so I say, "It's not bad. Mostly it happens if I sit in the back seat or don't keep my eyes on the distance."

She smiles rather mysteriously at that. "Well, then. You should be fine. Everything is distant from here."

With that enigmatic statement, the wall dings and a door slides open. It's just an elevator, but the walls are glass. Through the glass there's only the pale grey of the elevator shaft at the moment. We step in and Rosa waves, scrolling the lighted numbers that pop up until they reach H4. I notice we're on 4-MA19.

"Get ready," she says, squeezing my hand. "I'm right here."

What are we going to see? An alien planet or a ship or something even more bizarre? Clearly, it's something that will be new to me, or else I wouldn't need to prepare myself to see it. The elevator starts smoothly, none of the jerking most elevators have when they start and stop. I'm looking, but so far, there's only the grey walls. That's it. Rosa is looking at me expectantly, and I know it's about to happen when she squeezes my fingers again.

And then it does. The gray walls rise and in their place is the universe. A vast blackness filled with stars so bright and numerous that the sight is dizzying. The blackness is clear, and so very, very dark. It's like I could reach out and touch the stars.

I stumble against Rosa for support. All I can manage is a weak, "Oh!"

"Does that answer your question about where we are?" she asks, her voice amused.

"Yeah. Well not all of it, but yeah."

"Look over here." She tugs my hand, so I'll face the opposite side of the elevator. Her free hand waves like someone displaying the view from their living room.

A pair of braces the elevator is riding on bisect the view, but opposite the vast black of the universe is the overwhelming sight of what must be a space station. To say it's huge is entirely inadequate. The place we were is a blob above me, but if that module is like the other five spaced around the perimeter of this circular structure, then it's surprisingly beautiful from the outside.

The modules, or whatever they are, look a bit like stylized beehives attached to a circular ring. The ring surrounds yet another structure in the center. The one in the middle is a substantially larger version of those on the periphery. The central structure isn't just bigger, but longer, like a beehive stretched out by trick photography or something. And that one isn't featureless on the outside.

Bands of what look like windows stripe the central structure. They look like very thin lines from my perspective, almost too small to distinguish. Lights dot the stripes at different points, which serves to reinforce the notion of its massive size. Based solely on the tiny strips of windows, the structure is too enormous to exist. If I estimate the height of each level the same way they are in houses, let's say ten feet, then it must be at least two miles tall. At *least* that high. I'm probably vastly underestimating given how long it's taking to get to the ring connecting the modules.

A flash of movement to the side draws my eye. A ship—an honest-to-goodness spaceship—zips away from the ring in the distance. It looks tiny from here, but it must be gigantic if I can see it all the way from here.

Lights flash on the ring, then go out as the ship moves away. A portal just like the one that appeared in my living room opens in the blackness and the ship disappears through it.

"Holy macaroni," I whisper, letting go of Rosa's hand to press my fingers against the glass. I do feel dizzy now, but not in a sick way. I feel dizzy in an OMG-I-can't-believe-this-is-happening way.

Rosa chuckles and says, "I wouldn't call it macaroni or holy, but it's home."

"Home," I wonder aloud. How cool is it that she can look at this and call it home, like this amazing place in space is just another house in the suburbs?

I like science fiction in books, movies, and on TV. I'm that sort of girl, and I have a pretty good visual imagination from all the reading I've done. No one has ever imagined it like this, including me. No movie, no matter how elaborate the special effects, has ever captured space like this or made me feel this overwhelming sense of wonder before.

This is real.

Eight

The view disappears suddenly, hidden once again by the walls of the elevator shaft.

"Here we are," Rosa says brightly, once again taking my hand as the elevator stops and the door slides open.

"Where are we? Are we in that big circular part? Is that the hub or is where we were before the hub?" I stop there, because I have a bazillion questions.

She laughs, but answers freely enough. "The whole station is called the hub. Where we were before is called a module, like I said. It's really a diminutive name for something so large, don't you think? And yes, you're in the ring right now."

"What about that big thing in the middle?"

"That's called the central station."

A thought occurs to me and I could slap myself for not thinking of it when we could see the stars. "Where's Earth? I mean, we can't be too close, or someone would have seen something as big as the hub, right?"

She nods as I ask, still smiling her little smile as we walk down another hallway, this one a very pale beige color. She waits a tick before answering me. I wonder if she's waiting for that voice to break in, or maybe for permission. I don't see anything like an earpiece—and I did look while we were in the transfer room—so I don't know how she's getting the information if she is.

After a brief pause, she says, "Earth is very far away from here, but that's about as much as I can say. I'm no good with the stars. It's not my thing."

Her response is so normal that I believe her. That does lead to some interesting questions though, like how they send portals at long distances and why they would do so. What possible interest could they have in us if we're so far away? We're nowhere near having the capability to travel beyond our solar system with anything other than an unmanned probe.

Basically, we're no threat to others out here among the stars, so why bother with us?

If we're in the ring part of the huge station, I can't tell. There's no detectable curve to it, though it isn't a simple hallway. There's plenty of stuff to look at. It reminds me of an empty airport, maybe a terminal not in use or something of that nature. There's even a darker stripe along the floor some distance from us that I'd swear was one of those moving walkways found in long terminals. The place is quite brightly lit, but it has that distinctly creepy vibe of a big, uninhabited space.

We turn off the main hallway into yet another corridor and things start to look ordinary, even familiar. There are borders around the doors, so that I can see them and latches right where they should be. There's even a push bar on one and a lighted sign with the pictogram for exiting to stairs and the little flame I've seen on a thousand emergency exits. It's a relief to see something so normal.

"This can't be an accident," I say, waving toward one of the latched doors.

"Well, perhaps not, but it's more comfortable for you, isn't it?"

I nod, because it is. It's amazing how much little things like that matter. The ordinary is comforting.

Ahead is a relatively short hallway. There's a small panel set at a tilt next to a nice, normal door that would be right at home in my high school. It even has scuff marks on the brass kick-plate across the bottom from shoes bumping into it. Rosa steps up to the panel—it looks like one of those information signs at museums, except mostly blank—and presses her hand on one of the two silvery ovals. It looks the same as the one that I put my hand on to get my identity.

There's no bright light for her, just a dim blue glow and a ping. She nods for me to put my hand on it and the same thing happens for me.

"What's that? A lock?" I ask, peering into the oval to see if there's anything behind it.

"Exactly. You've got an ID now, so it's making sure who we are before letting us in." At my confused look, she takes my hand and turns it palm up. She traces her finger on a spot in the center and says, "Right here.

When it read your identity, it also imprinted it here. This is your identification."

"Cool," I say, lifting my hand and turning it this way and that against the light to see if I can see anything. I don't.

Rosa *oomphs* as she pushes open the door and waves me through. The notion that the door reminded me of a school was a better comparison than I thought, because I'm pretty sure I've just entered a place meant to look like a college. A big reception desk awaits, with a woman in slacks and a sharp, sapphire-blue button-down shirt standing behind it. There are several short hallways in a semi-circle branching off, each one with a half-dozen doors.

The woman behind the counter smiles in welcome and waves us over, as if inviting us to cut to the front of a non-existent line. Rosa walks me up like she's done this many times. She might have for all I know.

"This is Lysa. You should already have her file."

"Hello, Lysa!" the woman says, far too excited for the situation. "I certainly do have you in our system already. All I need is your hand and we can head on back."

Another of those silvery ovals awaits me on the counter, but I hesitate before letting my palm touch the surface. Turning to Rosa, I ask, "Does this mean you're leaving me?"

Like the grandma she appears to be, she brushes the backs of her fingers across my cheek, then squeezes my shoulder ever so gently. "I must. I've got transfers to facilitate. It's my job."

"Does that mean I won't see you again?" I ask, feeling a bit like that first day of school when my mother dropped me off and I realized she wasn't staying with me.

There's a hint of mystery in her smile when she says, "Oh, I wouldn't go that far, dear."

That's better. For whatever reason, I'm okay with that answer. I lower my hand and the blue glow shines.

Nine

The woman at the counter—her name is Esme—checks me in and sets me on the path of the non-transfer, whatever that may be. While the reception area reminds me of an older school or college, beyond that it's more like a dorm combined with an office building.

There aren't any people about, which makes me wonder how many of those who've been shoved through—or perhaps gone through on a whim like I did—share my designation as non-transfer.

That's still a puzzle to me. On the one hand, it could be a good thing. Maybe that means I'm unsuited for whatever nefarious activity is planned. On the other hand, maybe that means I'm unsuited for whatever awesome thing they have in mind. It could go either way at this point, and I'm not the kind of person who worries about things I can't control.

I'm more inclined toward positive thinking. While it may seem like my impulsive act puts the lie to any claim I might have on the status of thinker, I've been thinking of little else since the portal invasion began. I've been thinking about what happens beyond the portals with a burning curiosity I didn't often share with others. My mom flipped her lid when I told her that if it came for me, I'd hop right through.

Shortly after that conversation the handcuffs appeared, so I've been keeping mostly mum since.

Yes, I've listened to the so-called smart people who yack incessantly on TV, but aside from a few reasonable people who are invariably made fun of by everyone else, none of the smart people are very smart.

Fear defines everything they say. Fear has defined everything since that first portal came. No one wants to push aside that fear and ask themselves why the portals are coming without limiting all the responses to bad ones. Everyone starts with the premise, it's happening *to* us. No one starts with, it's happening *for* us.

The exceptions are the various old and new religions that believe the portals are a supernatural thing. Well, there's also a segment of people who believe the portals are sent from our future selves, meant to help us skip past some terrible thing that will happen to the earth. That notion has a little merit, which means the fear-mongers on TV never mention that possibility.

To me, all options are equally likely. Hopefully, I'll find out that it's a positive thing, because there's no correcting what I've done if it turns out to be negative.

"Lysa, sorry to interrupt, but your catalog is coming, along with your dinner. Is this a good time?"

The voice coming from the ceiling belongs to Esme, who calls herself a general factotum and lost person wrangler. It's very cute the way she says it, clearly meant to make others feel at ease. I'm not saying I trust everything at this point, but I will say that whoever is doing this is very good at making sure everyone involved is easy to like.

"Perfect timing," I answer back, though it does feel strange to talk to the ceiling. And it *is* perfect timing. I just got out of the shower—they have incredible water pressure here—and put on a new pair of pajamas waiting for me on the bed. I don't think they're truly pajamas, or maybe humans that come here wear pajamas all the time. Either way, I'm good for the moment.

And I'm starving. I missed dinner.

"You remember about the bot?" Esme asks.

"Sure do. Bring it on."

She laughs from the ceiling of my room like I'm a hoot, then says, "When you're done, just use the panel like I showed you. You're on your own for the rest of the evening, but we'll get started fresh in the morning. If you need me, just call."

"Gotcha."

That pleasant ping sounds out once more, but this time the small sound is accompanied by a pink light above my door. I open my very normal looking door to find the bot. It looks like a rolling cabinet about the height of my belly button. So, no aggressive robot overlords after all. That was one of the many possibilities floated about since this began.

"Hello," I say. It has no head or anything even remotely head-like, but it does have one of those silvery patches on the side. A smiley face glows on it at the moment.

One of the doors pops open and a tray rolls out. "Your meal." Even the robot voice is pleasant.

"Should I just grab it?" I ask, not entirely sure what manners are called for when dealing with a robotic cabinet.

"Yes," it says, then a second tray rolls out under my meal. I can't see what's on it, so I grab the tray and hurry to set it on the little table in my room. By the time I get back, the first metal rack has retracted, and I see a good, old-fashioned catalog sitting on the second tray.

"Ah!" I say, hefting the heavy block of colorful paper. "Thank you."

"You're welcome," it says, then the smiley face changes to a winky face as it trundles off. It's sort of cute for a cabinet, a little squat and almost chubby looking, which is very weird to think, but also happens to be true.

Like I did when I first got to the room, I look down the hallway to see what I can see. There's no one around, just more doors. Nice normal doors in a nice normal hallway. It really is like a dorm at college, only without litter on the floor or posters or graffiti. Sighing, I close the door, but I can't resist making the *shh-snick* noise that doors make in almost all science fiction movies. I grin and hope no one that might judge me immature is watching.

My dinner is good, if a little odd. The texture of the meat is all wrong and I don't think it's meat at all. It reminds me of those vegetarian patties that are supposed to be like chicken. It's good; a bit spicy, but tasty. There are roasted potatoes and Brussel sprouts, which are both favorites of mine, along with a salad and cookies that taste of lemon and almonds. Hot tea and sparkling water round it out.

Whatever else these aliens might be, no one can say they aren't good cooks and excellent hosts.

I flip through the catalog as I eat. This big book is a real, honest to goodness catalog. It's also very fat, the last page numbered *1643,* and divided into sections for clothing, personal items, entertainment options, furnishings, games, and everything else you could imagine. They even have a section for bedding that includes sheets with popular cartoon characters, if that's your thing.

I'm supposed to furnish my room and pick my clothes if I'm not keen on the pajamas. My mom told me that catalogs were a big deal when she was small, and she used to love to mark all the pages with the things she wanted. I've not seen them much, except for small ones that come in the junk mail, but now I understand that wistful look when she spoke of them. Perusing for goods online is one thing, but there's a certain allure to this crinkly and colorful paper.

My room isn't empty, but it looks fairly bare without any personalization, so I take stock before I go crazy and wind up with a mountain of stuff. My room is divided into two main sections and quite large, almost like an efficiency apartment. On one side, there's a tall dresser with drawers that slide out when I pass a hand over a tiny, silver oval inset into each one, a desk with a chair, a bigger easy chair next to a side table, and then my bed.

The bed is a double, which is what I have at home. The frame is something like a box, with more drawers underneath. On the other side of the big room is a small dinner table, two chairs, and a short line of counters where the room is bisected by the bathroom door.

There's an entire corner empty of furnishings, but the catalog has a section for exercise equipment and other large items, so I'm guessing that corner is mine to do with as I like. The bathroom is small, but equipped with the basics: toilet, sink, and a shower/bathtub combo.

When Esme brought me here and told me about the catalog, I did wonder at it. How long am I staying if they're going to let me furnish an entire room? That indicates ownership or a long period in residence. I was sort of hoping this was a stopover and they were going to send me back, maybe with some information that might help.

When I asked, Esme only shook her head and said, "Even if you're only here for a few days, it should be comfortable. Don't you think so?"

It didn't escape my notice that she didn't answer the question.

There's nothing for it, so I might as well be comfortable and enjoy this no-credit-limit catalog. There are no prices. How often am I going to see that in my life? There's a pad of notepaper on my desk and a pen—both also normal looking—so I note down all my possibilities and then narrow those down to my choices. When I look up at the silver spot next to my door, I'm surprised to find that a great deal of time has passed.

That's another cool thing. The silver rectangle is blank until I look at it, then it shows the time and what's next on my schedule. I've been trying to catch it out and surprise it. If I look straight ahead and take a moment to really focus on my peripheral vision, it remains blank. The moment I lose concentration and let my eyes move, it lights up. Whatever tech they have here, it's way better than ours.

According to the calendar on my screen, my next appointment is at 0800 with a "Facilitator." I'm not sure what's being facilitated, but I'm hoping it's my return to Earth.

Esme told me that I'm an hour behind my regular time-zone in this wing, which is set to the North American average. That means I'm an hour more tired than the clock says I should be. I'm not in the mood for sleep yet, so maybe this is a good thing. When I do go to bed, hopefully I'll really sleep.

Of course, I'm in space on a giant space station where every thirteen minutes, up to a thousand people are switched out from my planet. And I'm wearing pajamas. Looking at a catalog. I'm not sure having a good night's sleep is on the docket with that much weirdness to contend with in my brain.

When I'm done, I use the silver spot—which Esme says is my interface—to punch in all my choices by their identifying numbers. I could use my voice to do it, but it feels more natural to poke at a display not much different than the one on my phone. I wish I would have had my phone in my pocket when I came over. The pictures I might get!

The interface displays my order summary and gives various delivery times, which makes me giggle because it reminds me of home. I wonder if a big brown truck is going to pull up to give me my packages. Then I'm on my own. According to the clock, it's still not quite my normal bedtime, but I'm yawning and tired already.

Rather than fight it—because who knows if it will pass and then I won't be able to sleep—I climb into the bed and face the other silver spot in the room. This one is on the wall near my bed and much bigger than the other spot. I have a good view of it from the easy chair or the bed or the dining table. The time and such come up, but I say, "TV programs, please."

Esme gave me the quick and dirty on this. She told me that I can watch pretty much anything I could get on TV at home, sort of like an all-encompassing on-demand station. When I call out my favorite show, it shows a listing for every episode from every season. Nice! I go for the most recent episode—the hot vampire finally told my favorite character that he loved her—and scrunch up my pillow to settle in. I don't even get to the all-important kissing scene before I'm out like a light.

Ten

The pinging wakes me gently, the sound at first so soft that it barely intrudes. Gradually, it grows louder until I say, "I'm awake." Where I am slams into my brain as I become fully conscious, and my stomach does a flip in response.

My mom, the replacement mom, the portal—all of it pops into my brain in a sudden rush.

Holy crap! I'm not on Earth. My Mom is probably so pissed off right now. I hope she's okay.

All of that banging into my head makes my face hot and gives me an instant headache, the kind you get from not drinking enough water on a summer day. I groan and climb out of bed, going for the metal cup in the bathroom to take a long drink.

I put my dishes outside my door last night like I was supposed to, but I should have kept the water bottle. I ordered the *Glassware for Two* set, but who knows when those will get here.

I swish out my mouth and spit down the sink. My mouth tastes like someone died in there. There's a little toiletry kit in the bathroom exactly like the ones in hotels, so I brush my teeth until the feeling of old socks finally goes away. I know it's just stress, but dang, that was bad. Then I gulp down two cups of water and feel the tiniest bit better.

Leaning back, I look at the interface. The time shows 0705. I've got less than an hour before I'm supposed to meet with my facilitator, whatever that is.

Pressing the silver spot, I ask, "Can I get breakfast?" I should have asked about that before. Esme arranged dinner, so I didn't think of it.

Esme doesn't answer me, which makes sense unless they work ridiculously long shifts here in space. Instead, there's a male voice, but he sounds young. "You can use the refreshments tab on your interface or I can take your order. Which would you like to do?"

I'm embarrassed, but I'm more hungry and thirsty, so I say, "Can you do it? How quickly will it get here?"

"Very quickly. Go ahead when ready," he answers. I can almost hear him smiling.

"Orange juice, a big one if I can get it. Coffee with lots of cream and sugar. Water. And, *umm*, do you have cereal? Never mind. Oatmeal, maybe?"

There's a very slight pause, then he says, "Got it. It will be there in a few minutes. Anything else?"

My head is pounding, so I ask, "Do you have anything for a headache? Some aspirin or something? Ibuprofen would be even better."

"Are you alright?"

"Yeah. It's just from the excitement. Maybe dehydration."

"Sure thing. It will be on your tray."

I sigh, my head giving a painful one-two punch when I do. "Thanks."

Though I would love another shower, I want breakfast more, so I settle for taming my bed-head. It's not pretty. My hair is very dark brown and wavy. If it were shorter, it would be curly. That's nice when it comes to styling, because it loves to take a curl, but a nightmare when it comes to sleeping. I generally look like I've just rolled out of a cave, Neanderthal style, when I wake in the mornings.

There's only a comb in the toiletry kit, but I had a hair tie around my wrist when I came over, so I pull it back into a ponytail and hope for the best. It looks like a worn-out broom in the back, my tail a big puff ball of crazy that stretches halfway down my back.

"Really?" I ask my reflection. "Is this the look we're going for?"

After taming my tail with water, the door *pings* and I race to answer it. My headache has settled into my face, right behind my cheeks and forehead. I can't wait to swallow a few headache pills. I snag my tray from the bot, thank it, and then hurry back to my table. The pills are in a little packet and they look like they came from Earth. They even have the little logo for the same brand we have at home.

Downing them with a full glass of orange juice—which I might add tastes freshly squeezed—I know I've still got twenty minutes or more of pain to deal with. The oatmeal is a bit mushy, but otherwise good. Even the coffee is amazing. I pull on a fresh set of pajamas since mine are all wrinkled from sleep, and I'm ready two minutes before eight.

The ping comes exactly on time. While I'm hoping for Rosa, or maybe even Esme, I know it's unlikely either of them will be my facilitator. It might not even be a human. My stomach coils up in tight knots as I reach for the doorknob.

It isn't Esme or Rosa outside my door. It isn't some officious person I'd mentally assigned to fit the title facilitator, perhaps someone like the pinch-faced assistant principal at my school. I'm surprised to find it isn't even an adult. The guy standing outside my door is probably my age, wearing jeans with just the right amount of wear and a black t-shirt with this year's ComicCon logo on it.

He raises a hand in a casual wave and says, "Hey. You Lysa?"

I nod, because really, I don't know what else to do. He's taken me by surprise. Shouldn't this guy be in school or something? And I'm standing here in pajamas, so it's super awkward. Crossing my arms over my chest, I say, "I'm Lysa. Are you my facilitator?"

He nods right back at me, a sideways grin coming up on his face that makes me cross my arms a little tighter across my chest. Whatever confidence I had in the idea of running around in comfy pajamas is entirely gone.

With brown hair mussed just so and blue eyes that tilt down a little at the ends, he's pretty much beautiful. If he went to my school, I'd be crushing on him from the first day. And yet, here he is on an alien spaceship, wearing jeans and a ComicCon t-shirt, while I'm standing here in pajamas with bad hair.

He sticks his hands in the back pockets of his jeans as he stands there, all good-looking and perfect, waiting for me to do whatever I'm going to do next.

"You okay?" he asks, his grin growing a little wider, perilously close to becoming a knowing grin.

Okay, yep, there it is, a full-on knowing grin.

"*Uh*, fine." Then it strikes me that he's simply too perfect. There's absolutely no reason for these aliens to look like us. None whatsoever. And a hot guy who's far too close to my ideal? There's definitely no reason for that.

On second thought, I'd say this guy is probably the ideal for a whole lot of people. He's got that sort of universal appeal. He's the kind of guy that winds up starring in teen movies where the plots are stupid when you think about them later, but are too ga-ga while the movie is rolling to realize it.

"Is this what you really look like?" I ask.

His grin falters a little at my question, his eyes uncertain for a flash. Then the smile comes back, but less brash the second time. "This is me."

Again, a non-answer and I've had just about my fill of those. I step into the doorway, entirely blocking his path by leaning against the doorjamb. Two can play at this.

And my headache isn't completely gone yet, so I'm getting testy.

I nod just once, keeping my arms crossed up high. "That's an interesting way to answer that question. It reeks of bullcrap. How about you take another run at an answer. And how about a name while you're at it."

That perfect grin falls away, his hands leaving his pockets to drop to his sides, and his brows drawing together in confusion. Clearly, this is not the reception he expected.

He clears his throat nervously and says, "This isn't going well. Can we start over? My name is Jack."

Still not an answer. When he sticks out his hand to shake, I glance down at it, but make no move to take it. I'm generally not a rude person, and I'm usually embarrassed to see others act that way, but I'll make an exception right now.

"I'm not biting, Jack. How about you answer my question and then maybe we can start over."

He sighs and tugs at his t-shirt collar with a finger, like he's loosening a tie or something. His head tilts ever so slightly, just as Rosa's did when I thought she might be listening to someone for instructions.

It's brief, whatever it is, because he clears his throat again and says, "This isn't quite how this is supposed to go, but I'll do as you like. Yes, this is what I look like. This is my body and I'm stuck in it. My name is Jack and I'm going to be your facilitator."

With that, he sticks out his hand again and says, "It's nice to meet you, Lysa."

I noticed that he said he was stuck in his body, as if it's a bad neighborhood he's just got to deal with, but he answered my question. I uncross my arms and shake his hand firmly. "Nice to meet you too," I say, though it didn't exactly start out so nice. That's probably my fault, but I'm not good with weasel talk. Answering questions without actually answering them is a particular peeve of mine.

Jack peers around me at my bare room, then nods toward the table and my breakfast tray. "Are you still eating?"

I think he's trying to hint for me to invite him in, so I turn sideways and wave him inside. When he passes, I get hints of shampoo and freshly laundered clothes. Even his hair looks freshly cut.

"I'm still working on my coffee, but mostly I'm done."

He nods and looks around the room like I would look around someone's house the first time I went inside. Touching the back of one of the dining chairs, he asks, "May I?"

"Sure, make yourself at home," I say, sitting back down in front of my nearly empty tray.

Jack doesn't seem at all nervous, but he has that same hesitation to his actions that Rosa had when I first came through, like he's worried I might attack him or something. While I *am* irritated, and certainly nervous about what's going to happen to me, I'm not going to stab him with my spoon or anything else heinous. I'd rather we get past this awkward part quickly. Maybe we can be as normal as possible with each other afterwards. Normal may not be the exact word, but closer to normal would be better.

I take a sip of this most wonderful space coffee and say, "I'm not going to freak out on you or jump on you or anything. I went through on my own."

I'm trying not to stare at him, but I want to see his reactions to my words. Everything he does will provide me information, even if not immediately or in a way I can put together until later. Every single bit of data I can wring from him and everyone else inside this station might be important, possibly even vitally so. That's especially true if any of those nuggets of truth can help me figure out a way back home with something I can tell people. Caveat that with tell people something they can believe, because that's pretty important too. Maybe I can get enough information that humans can either go along with what's happening, or fight harder knowing what we're fighting against.

That's the plan anyway.

His shoulders lose a little tightness, but not much more than that. He lays a hand flat on the table's surface and looks at the back as if it's super interesting. His fingers lift and tap at the wood-like surface so that the tendons flex. Maybe if he's really an alien then his hand is as interesting as he thinks it is.

When I set down my cup, thinking I'll have to say more to get this ball rolling, he says, "I suppose you have a lot of questions. I'm the one that's supposed to answer them and give you an idea of what your options are for the future."

Uh oh. That doesn't sound good.

I touch my cup again, suddenly anxious, and as soon as I do, he looks down at his hand. It's almost like he disengages from our conversation entirely. As a test, I pull back my hand and sure enough, he looks back up.

"Why do you do that?" I ask, coiling my hands together in my lap.

"Do what?"

"Look away when I touch my cup."

He glances at my tray and then asks, "Isn't it rude to talk to people while they're eating?"

"And this is how I know you can't be human."

"So, it's not rude where you're from?" he asks.

"Oh, yeah, it's rude, but not rude enough not to do it. People talk while they eat all the time, or else eating would get super boring. It's only rude when you ask a question while they've got food in their mouth. And even then, it depends on who's doing the asking. Eating is a social thing."

Shaking his head and rolling his eyes a little, I'd swear he was as human as I am, but he can't be if he doesn't know the basics of eating with others. I suppose he could be from some obscure place where those rules are true, but then why is he wearing a t-shirt from America and sporting a trendy haircut? No, he's done his homework, but there's no way he's human.

"Listen," I say, reaching for my cup, then pulling back before I send him back into snail-mode again, "I've got more questions than I've got the ability to ask. I can't even sort out my questions, I have so many. Mostly, I can't think too much beyond the fact that this is a giant spaceship, that I'm gone from my planet, that no one else has ever come back, and that I don't want to die as an appetizer at an alien dinner party. Maybe if you just got the quick and dirty version out of the way and told me I'm not going to die as a meal for squid-people, I might be able to think."

As I speak, Jack nods a few times at my concerns as if they make total sense, then grins when I mention the squid-people. All in all, they don't seem like the reactions he would give if the news was bad.

I pick up my cup and he narrows his eyes at me, so I add, "And we can talk while I drink this. It's fine. Getting answers from alien invaders trumps manners any day of the week."

Eleven

Jack shakes his head at me and says, "We're not alien invaders."

That's not a good way to start this out as far as I'm concerned. No lying and no prevaricating can be allowed at this point. "First, you *are* clearly alien even if you put yourselves into the bodies of grandmas and hot guys. Second, you *are* snatching humans right off Earth and replacing them with something else that is clearly not the original. So, yes, you're alien invaders by default."

He tilts his head a little and he asks, "Hot? I don't understand that one exactly. Do you mean American English slang for handsome or having the characteristic of higher relative temperature?"

My cup hits my tray harder than I intended and my jaw drops a little. I'm not sure which is worse, that I'm going to have to admit what hot means or that he's really an alien in a hot guy's body.

"*Uh*, slang and see, you didn't know what it meant. You would have if you were human."

He gives me another of those little grins and says, "Thank you. You're hot too."

I'm so glad my cup was already on the tray, because I would have dropped it and wasted this coffee that tastes exactly like the stuff I get from my favorite, over-priced coffee boutique. "I don't even know what to say to that," I reply.

"That wasn't the right thing to say?"

"No. No, it wasn't. You're totally not human."

He shrugs a little and says, "It seemed the polite thing to say. Also, I am human. I wasn't, but I am now. And I know lots of stuff about humans—ones from where you're from—but this age group has the most confusing social rules I've ever encountered. Normally, I would have been able to spend time on the planet and get accustomed to things more naturally. There wasn't time unfortunately, and I'm sorry if I said the wrong thing."

I can tell he wants me to answer him, but I need a minute. Maybe I need a year, but at the very least, I need a minute to process his words. So, he's human now and he knows enough about us to pass—well, mostly pass—for a teen guy. He would have spent time on Earth as a human to learn about us, which is weird, because it makes me wonder how many aliens are already running around down there. Probably my AP Calculus teacher…no, maybe not, but for sure the soccer coach has got to be an alien. At least one thing he said makes sense. I think I understand where some of the confusion is coming from if he's having problems with teen social rules and norms.

They clearly know almost everything about us, but if he's trying to be a regular teen and using our social activity as a guide, he's going to say inappropriate things much worse than he already has. I'd bet he's using social media, probably also movies and the internet in general. I don't even want to consider what he must think of teen socializing if he's using WinkChat. The things we post on there would curl my mom's hair if she saw it.

"Are you alright?" he asks, when I sit there staring at him for too long.

"Yeah, I'm fine." That's a lie, but it's time to move on. "So, am I dinner for squid-people? Or any other kind of meal for any other kind of people or whatever you have here."

He grins again and says, "Nope. You are not to be eaten, drunk, or ingested in any form. There's nothing like that going on."

"Is anyone that leaves Earth getting eaten?"

"Nope," he answers.

"Are you lying?"

That seems to take him aback and he looks confused. "I'm not lying, but why would you ask that? If the purpose was to deceive you, then would asking me if I was deceiving you make me tell you the truth?"

"No, but sometimes you can catch liars off guard."

"I see. Well, I'm not lying." He widens his eyes at me for a quick second in an excellent imitation of someone trying to be earnest, while also holding in a laugh or smile. It's cute.

"I suppose I wouldn't know if you were anyway. So, good enough. Next questions. Why are you taking people from Earth? Where are they going? What are you doing with them? Why are you sending replacements? And why are you doing it so badly if you don't mean harm?"

Jack leans back in his chair at my rapid-fire barrage of questions, that same little smile on his face. "You have a lot of questions."

"You've taken a lot of humans."

"True. You win. First question is why? The why is very simple. There is an event coming that will destroy at least ninety percent of advanced life on Earth within the next twenty-seven years, four months, and six days. The event will have only temporary impacts, but it will still eliminate almost all humans and other animals on Earth. Plants too. The probabilities have recently shifted, so there's a significant chance now that all life on Earth could perish. That's why."

That pretty much takes all the wind out of my sails. "What?"

"Too much honesty?"

"What?" I ask again. I mean, I know what he said, but I can't accept what he said.

The smile falls away and he leans forward again, his hand sliding across the table toward mine. "That was too much. You seemed very eager for the truth, but I think you probably aren't ready for it."

It takes me a second to parse the words, but then I get a flash of alarm. If they think I'm too fragile to take the truth, then they'll start lying. "No, I'm fine. I just…well, I just didn't expect that. All life on Earth?"

He nods, but hedges his bets with his next words. "Almost all life. To the best of our ability to predict it anyway. It will be a temporary event, but the immediate impact will be lethal to most forms of life, including plants, which will further hinder chances of survival. The planet will recover given enough time, if I can use such a generality."

"That seems a long time from now. Why take us so soon?"

His eyes widen and he asks, "Do you know how many of you there are? How many animals? Species?"

That information surprises me. I had no idea they were taking animals too. As a matter of fact, I don't think I've ever even heard that mentioned as a possibility. Then again, that might be something our government would want to keep secret, since that would impact everything from our food supply to people's pets. I doubt many people would be willing to keep eating beef if they thought the cows were alien replacements.

"You're taking animals too?"

"Some now, some later. But yes, animals and plants. Bugs, fish, bears…all of it."

"Wow."

"That sums it up fairly well."

"But again, why now and why send replacements? Why not just come down and say, 'Hey, you're all going to die, so we're going to take you so that you won't.' I mean, that would be easier."

"And you think that would work?" he asks, as if that were a serious question.

Now that I think about it, it probably wouldn't work. Some would believe him, most would freak, others would destroy the world just because they're angry or confused. Humans do not, as a rule, react well to bad news. I shrug.

"No matter. We've determined that it wouldn't work, though this way doesn't seem to work very well either. And talking to humans on Earth would be against the rules anyway."

"*Duh*, definitely not working as it is." I didn't mean that to come out like it did, but it *is* sort of appropriate.

He purses his lips at me for a second, then says, "Anyway, the replacements are so that your world will keep operating as normal. That's the intention anyway. A smooth transition with no hardships on those not yet transferred. And no changes in available biological organisms for the future. That's a rule too."

There are some logical flaws inside his explanation, but I'm guessing the entire process is probably super-complex and can't be relayed by a simple yes or no answer. "Okay, but aren't the replacements going to die too? What about having kids? What about all the stuff the people who are taken might have done?"

One of Jack's eyebrows rises quickly, like he's either impressed with my questions or has just realized I really will keep asking endlessly and always find more questions to ask.

"Lysa, here's the thing. There are almost eight billion of you. That only counting the humans and that's a whole lot of moving parts and decisions. Not everyone will get transferred, only a small portion really. It's very complex, very carefully timed, and very well thought out. Yes, the replacements will live out their lives and die like regular humans. There are many calculations considered when deciding who gets transferred and when. The process is exceptionally complicated."

I sit back in my chair and try to parse things out for myself. I can't imagine all the things they consider, but I also can't put an order to it in my mind. I don't understand the reasoning behind the calculations, so there's no way I can truly absorb it. I'm going to have to settle for pushing the "I believe" button. That isn't something I'm generally comfortable doing.

"Okay, I get that it's complicated and some will be chosen before others for whatever reasons. What about telling me why people don't get transferred then?"

He inclines his head for a second and I know we're getting to the meat of it. Oh, I probably shouldn't think of meat and non-transfer in the same thought train. The way his eyes soften when he looks at me also warns me that I'm probably not going to like his answer. I take a deep breath and twist my fingers together.

"There are many reasons a person wouldn't be a transfer, but only one applies to you. Well, it's the primary reason and all else follows from that. Are you sure you want to know?"

Is he serious?

"You can't set up a mystery like that and then ask that question. Do I want to hear it? Probably not. Do I need to hear it? Yes."

He nods after considering me for a moment, probably deciding if he really should tell me whatever it is he's going to say. "You wouldn't have continued your genetic line." At my slightly confused expression, he adds, "What I mean to say is that you wouldn't have had children. In addition, the profile indicates you had a high probability of death before the event, and were almost certain to have no dependents prior to that time. There are other factors, including available genetic variations, predispositions, transfer dynamics, and the like. There were other, more efficient combinations available, so you weren't on the transfer list."

I've never considered myself particularly maternal. When I imagine my future, I see working in a lab, doing cool science-y stuff, or maybe being an artist. I see myself in the field, digging up ancient civilizations or discovering something new. I can maybe imagine finding a guy that looks as hot as Jack to marry. I don't generally imagine pregnancy and diapers. It would be weird to think of me having kids.

But to have it said with such certainty. I wouldn't have kids and I, essentially, wouldn't have anyone that depended on me before I died. Alone.

And how do they even know that?

"I'm useless? Eating food and using air for no reason, so I don't get a ticket on the rescue boat. Is that about the sum of it?" I ask. I hate that I sound bitter. I hate it even more that I can feel the sting of tears filling up my eyes.

I guess it's a good thing I jumped through when I did. Otherwise, I would have just had to die on Earth all alone with no one to love me and then the world would end.

This freaking sucks.

Twelve

Jack doesn't answer me for a long moment and when I look back at him, he looks distinctly uncomfortable. There's a rosy flush near his neck and his eyes flick away when I meet his gaze. He's sorry he had to break this news to me. That's as clear as if he'd written a sign and hung it around his neck.

Still, the whole thing is supposed to happen in twenty-seven years. Of course, I would be over forty, but maybe I was divorced or had a long-term boyfriend. Maybe we were adopting and waiting for a baby.

It could be worse. Right?

Well, the whole being dead by then thing bothers me, but I'd rather not think of that. That said, if I do find a way back, I will be careful crossing the street and never get on an airplane.

"I'm not going to have kids. So what! And that can't be the only reason. You guys take old people and I know they aren't having any more kids. Or are they? Do you make them young again or grow babies in pods for them?

Are you guys going to do something bad to me because I'm a non-transfer? Tell me straight."

I really need some reassurance on that last point. Worrying about others is hard to do when I'm worried about my own imminent death.

I expect him to give me another of those sideways smiles and tell me no. My heart plummets to my feet when I don't get that. Instead, the smile fades, and he says, "Not because of us."

My immediate thought is that I'm going to die because I went through the portal. Maybe from radiation or something. All I can say is, "I'm going to die?"

Jack takes a deep breath and then leans forward, folding his hands on the table and looking directly into my eyes. "I'm sorry. That came out wrong. No, you're not about to die. Not from us or from anything else."

"I'm definitely going to die," I whisper. He was way too quick to come out with that answer.

He tilts his head again for a second, then says, "I should clarify, because this isn't coming across accurately. You're a non-transfer because of your physical condition, the assessment of your future, and because the genetic variability required could be filled more efficiently with other humans. That said, you're here now. We can correct your condition."

I'm completely confused. My physical condition is just fine. I have nothing wrong with me that I know of. "What are you talking about? I'm not going to have kids because there's something wrong with me?" I ask. "If you fix me, does that mean I transfer?"

Now it's Jack's turn to look confused. "You don't know?"

"Know what?"

This time the head tilt is accompanied by closed eyes and a long silence. Jack is clearly listening to someone. While I want to shake him and maybe slap him around a little to get answers, I know that the answers are probably what he's listening to, so I wait.

When he opens his eyes, Jack says, "This didn't go right. Let's get this part over and then I'll begin with the rest of it." At my nod, he continues. "You have a problem with your reproductive organs caused by a genetic defect. It causes them to experience early failure. There are other effects, though most people aren't bothered by those. In your case, it will cause premature failure to parts of your circulatory system. Your assessment indicates you will likely expire between the ages of thirty-five and forty-five due to cardiac insufficiency. That's only if your problem isn't corrected."

My mouth drops open and my hands go to my belly. If I weren't so horrified by what Jack said, I'd be more embarrassed that he was talking about my internal lady-parts.

"How can you possibly know that?"

"Because you were assessed. Everyone on Earth was assessed. As you already surmised, this isn't my original form, but I've got the basics of human biology down, and we've got your terminology well in hand."

Oh gosh, that's even worse. He understands human biology…including my internal lady parts. My *flawed* internal lady parts.

"And I'm going to die from it? It's messing with my arteries or my heart or something?"

Again, he inclines his head, but this time he's not listening to anyone. This time it's body language and I know he's trying to be upbeat. "Not exactly. It would contribute to an earlier death, but only if it wasn't discovered and corrected. I'd assumed you knew something was wrong, even if not the precise details." He pauses, tilts his head to listen, then adds, "*Ah*, I understand that particular genetic flaw has not yet been discovered on Earth. It doesn't matter now. You don't have to keep that flaw. Since you're here, we can fix it. It would take only a couple of minutes."

Yeah, I'm not going to let this go on for one second longer. I can feel my arteries hardening and I swear by all the ice cream yet uneaten that my heart is thumping erratically in my chest. The sensation is probably being generated in my mind, but what if it isn't?

With that, I lurch up from the table so quickly that I rattle the tray and dishes. "Let's fix this right now. Make all that artery business good to go. You can fix the other stuff too, but I feel like I'm going to have a heart attack."

Jack gets up more slowly, looking at me cautiously, as if I'm suddenly dangerous again. "I'm so sorry this upset you. We can do that now, but it's not going to matter if we talk first. You're in no danger at this moment. And treatment might be...surprising. I think it would better if we got some orientation done first."

At this moment, I realize exactly how alien these aliens are. He doesn't understand the impact of what he just told me. He sincerely thinks I can put this aside and have a chat. Not human at all.

"Yeah, not going to happen. You can't slip news like that into a conversation and then let it ride. Let's just say that I'll be able to listen better if I know I don't have a ticker running down my life. Understand?"

He does that thing like he's listening again, but this time I'm not waiting. I snap my fingers in front of his face and say, "No, none of that. If you want to talk about me, then I want to be in on the conversation. You make it so I can hear what's going on."

Jack blinks and takes a step back, clearly unsure about me. Then he nods and says, "Please speak openly."

"I'm speaking as openly as I can—"

I'm interrupted by a voice coming from the room. "Lysa, can you do me a favor and try to calm down?"

The voice is even, pleasant, and not quite male or female, but rather some neutral point between the two.

"Are you the person that's been talking to Jack?" I ask the ceiling.

"Yes, but I'm not a person. I'm Hub."

"The space station? You're the space station?"

"Yes, that's essentially correct. I'm the central mind of the station. The entire station is the hub, while I'm Hub. One is an object. The other is a name."

"Oh." I really can't say more, because that's some weird information right there. The space station is alive? Or sentient?

"I'm terribly sorry you've been upset by this information. While I've made every effort to assess all life on Earth and created extensive databanks, the details of individual lives are not as complete as I might like. Please do try to understand that Jack is doing the best he can to give you information and work with you."

Now I feel bad. Of course, I've also got a physical problem and that's screaming in my head like a thousand televisions at high volume, but I also feel bad for freaking out on Jack. He's looking at me with that patient gaze of his.

"I didn't mean to frighten you," I say.

He shrugs and says, "No problem."

To the ceiling—because I have nowhere else to direct my words—I say, "I didn't mean to be rude, but you just gave me some really craptastic news here. I feel like I've got bugs crawling under my skin and my heart might explode."

That mellow voice answers in precisely the same tone as before, as if I'm not freaking out on it. "I can assure you that you don't have any insects under your skin. I can also accurately report that your heart is fine. The time it will take to orient you to your situation is minimal and will not interfere with my ability to repair your condition. You can put that worry aside."

Put the worry aside? The hub says that like I have a choice in the matter. That creepy bug feeling is still there just under my skin, and I have the strangest sensation that I can feel my ovaries shrinking. Considering the fact that I had no clue anything was wrong with me until Jack told me there was, I realize that's just my emotions projecting sensations. That doesn't mean it isn't terribly uncomfortable all the same.

I take a deep breath and try to convince myself I don't feel the heebie jeebies, shutting my eyes and really focusing on calming myself. It doesn't work. When I open my eyes again, the heebie jeebies are still in full force.

"Can't do it," I say. "Still freaked out."

Jack gives a little head-shake, like I'm just such a delightful mess. "I suggest we go ahead."

The hub answers quickly. "Explain on the way, Jack. Lysa, I can't always speak with you this way in other sections of the station. Jack will speak with me as needed and relay my answers or comments. Do you agree with this?"

"Yes. Absolutely and positively agree." Stepping over to the door, I open it and wave Jack out with an impatient sweep of my hand. "Let's roll."

He gives me an odd look and says, "No, we'll walk."

All I can do is roll my eyes and follow him into the hallway.

Thirteen

Jack leads me out of the dormitory hall and then out of the college looking lobby, tossing a wave at the man behind the desk as he does. Once we're out of the main door and back into the super-futuristic looking station areas, he starts talking.

"I'll give you a quick explanation of what's going on. You're a non-transfer and there are quite a few of you coming through. Right now, we're running about ten percent, which is extremely difficult to deal with. There are so many that we're coming close to our redline…which is our maximum allowable change to your planet. Luckily, Hub keeps re-stacking the transfers, which means it recalculates who's going, so that more who *were* non-transfers become transfers even while they're transiting the portal. So, even when the intended transferee sends someone else back through the portal, most of the time Hub can recalculate and shift the transfer lists to include the non-transfer. Then someone else on Earth goes onto the non-transfer list.

Unfortunately, Hub couldn't reshuffle you, so you're one of the true non-transfers. There aren't that many of those, which is lucky. Got all that?"

"So, the non-transfers are people like me? Defectives? Too defective to even shuffle the lists?"

He shakes his head and then weaves around a big unmanned cart making its way down the hallway. I look as it passes, noting many boxes with labels neatly printed with my name.

"Hey, that's my stuff!" I say, turning to watch it go and walking backwards.

I back right into Jack, who must have stopped and looked too. He grabs my arms to keep me from falling and stands me upright again. His face is only inches from mine and I get a nice long look at that heart-stoppingly handsome face. Good heavens, but these aliens know how to build a human body!

"You okay?" he asks, smiling at me. His eyes are more gray than blue now that I see them up close. And boy, oh boy, they sure are pretty eyes.

"Yeah, fine," I say, tugging my pajama top down and trying not to act ridiculous. "You know, except for the bleeping arteries and all."

He chuckles and says, "Yeah, except for that. Anyway, the bot will put your stuff in your quarters." He points to his head and says, "I just relayed the message."

"That's handy," I reply, then we're off again.

We turn away from this long hall, which is really a thoroughfare off the ring based on my best guestimate. The interesting thing is we turn the opposite direction than when I walked here from the module, which means we're turning inward, toward the station.

The space station that talks, mind you.

"So, you were saying?"

Jack points down a little side corridor for me to follow. "Ah, yes. To answer your question: sort of. Non-transfer can mean many things. A good many will die within a short period and won't significantly contribute in terms of discovery or species knowledge before that time. Others might be incompatible with life in a long terms sense. Some have personalities that would decrease stability in the transfer society. Not necessarily in a bad way, either. There are a lot of reasons, but usually there's not just one reason. A combination of things usually causes a person to be a non-transfer. Most humans won't transfer when you get right down to it, but as you pointed out, we also take older humans who probably wouldn't be alive by then either. The matrix that racks and stacks them is based on moving a sufficient variety, but not everyone. Most who will have completed their primary contributions to society won't transfer, unless they rank much higher in several other factors."

My steps slow as he speaks and then I stop short. It takes him a few steps to realize I'm not behind him, then he comes back and asks, "Are you okay?"

I shake my head. "You mean that basically anyone who's useless is a non-transfer." I can't believe how much it hurts to say that.

"No, there are a lot of people you might call useless who are transfers. No one is useless really. Only less utilized."

"Oh, so only the especially useless then?"

He's confused. I can tell by the expression on his face. He has no idea how hurtful this news is. "Did I say something wrong?" he asks.

Sighing, I look at the floor and say, "No, not if that's the truth. I'm useless, so I don't get the transfer ticket. I get it."

He bends a little, so he can look me in the eye. "That's not what I meant."

"Sounds like it."

We're in a little side corridor. The area is bare of furnishings or anything else, but Jack takes my hand and leads me to the side. He sits with his back against the wall and pats the floor. "Sit with me."

I'm reluctant to let him distract me from getting whatever is wrong with me fixed, but I'm starting to understand why he wanted to give me some orientation first. Everything he says is either a shock or a huge disappointment.

I'm useless. Great.

Jack surprises me by taking my hand in his, then folding his other hand over it so mine is sandwiched between both of his. His smile is very sympathetic. "You're not useless. It's all a matter of getting the job done. Creating the ones you call replacements isn't as easy as you think, and this is a very big puzzle with a lot of moving pieces in a constant state of change. The energy cost of each transfer is probably more than you can imagine too. Hub is shuffling the lists of transfers and non-transfers at all times. We're very good at what we do, but no system for projecting the future is always correct. There is always change. As I said, it's very complicated."

The wall is cool against my back and Jack's voice is very soothing. That itchy feeling is still there, but his words are kind and have the ring of truth in them. Before I can ask yet more questions, he squeezes my hand a little and keeps talking.

"There's also the matter of disturbing things as little as possible. We cause enough change by simply doing the transfers. In the case of your planet, too much change. You're a very odd species, you know. Highly volatile. Really, your whole planet is filled with volatile life-forms."

"You have no idea," I mutter.

He smiles at my tone and says, "I'm getting the idea quickly enough." Letting go of my hand, he says, "If anything would have changed with your condition, then you might have been shuffled to the transfer list and no one would have known the difference. Or maybe something else on the list would have changed to make you transfer. There's no way to know. You just came too quickly and on your own…which means you're stuck as a non-transfer. You're not useless and no one ever thought you were. Your life was—would have been—too short."

I take a deep breath and look around. This little hallway is very white, the hiss of ventilation the only real sound. Even so, it all looks very real to me all the sudden. Everything is vivid and somehow more tangible. Is that what happens when someone realizes there's an actual end date to life? Does everything grow more real and more important, more alive?

There's a question in Jack's eyes. Will I be okay, and do I accept?

I nod and smile. "I've got it. Now can we just get me fixed?"

He hops up and holds out a hand to help me up. "It's just through here."

He stops at a spot on the wall that looks no different to any other place except that a discreet silver square gleams in the white. A string of characters I don't recognize flits across when we approach. Immediately after that, a nice bit of English lets me know that the atmosphere is suitable for humans and I should exercise caution.

Interesting. Very interesting. How many other types of atmospheres do they have in here?

The door slides open and I'm pretty sure this is a medical facility of some kind. It isn't that far off from the ones I've seen in video games or movies about the future. There's a short row of human-sized tables with big transparent bubble-like things suspended above them. There are cabinets and shiny things—but nothing that looks like a probe—and a couple of larger silver areas that I know will be screens if they do what all the other silver spots do.

Now that I'm here, I'm hesitant. What exactly are they going to do to me and will it hurt? I mean, I tend to get some vicious cramps during my period, so won't fixing broken ovaries hurt even worse? Maybe that should have been a clue that something was wrong with me, but my doctor said it was normal for some people to have more pain during the first few years.

Well, that doctor was wrong in a big way. And now I have the opportunity to fix my body, to extend my life, to create an entirely new future that I wouldn't have had. Heck yes, I'll do that and take some pain in the doing. I step over the threshold, but no further. When the door slides closed behind me, anxiety and excitement race through me at the speed of the unknown.

The hub's voice startles me when it fills the room. "Hello again, Lysa. This is the medical bay where I'll be correcting your physical problem. Would you like me to explain or would you rather do it straight away?"

It's hard to tell, because the hub's voice is so very even, but I get the feeling that it would be willing to explain and answer questions for as long as I needed. That alone makes me feel better, and my anxiety dials down one notch.

Stepping up to the closest table, I run my fingers along the surface. It's some kind of gel-filled pad. My fingers leave the slightest of impressions when I press lightly. "Is this where you make replacements?" I ask.

I can almost hear the hub shaking its imaginary head—or maybe not imaginary, because really, who knows. "Not on a large scale, we have a facility for that.

This is a relatively new addition, because of the non-transfers that are coming. It's an almost unprecedented situation."

Nodding, I move from the table to the closest cabinet and bend to peek at the contents. The cabinets are filled with pretty much what I might find at any human clinic or urgent care facility. Bandages wrapped in paper wrappings, little bundles of medical goods sealed in bluish plastic, bottles of pills. None of it seems very futuristic. I can't help but notice that most are items used when you wind up in the emergency room needing stitches or something like that. Why would that be?

"Do we get injured here often?"

Jack snorts a little at my overly-casual and entirely suspicious tone, but the hub answers readily enough. "Sometimes. Not every non-transfer comes through willingly, as you did. They often arrive in great need."

I hadn't thought of that, but I should have. It's a common enough occurrence. Tossing anyone nearby into the portal when your double walks out is something that happens all the time. I'm pretty sure most don't go willingly. "And the ones that are transfers, but got tossed in out of turn?"

"They are transferred to their destination and aided there most of the time. You wouldn't have noticed it, but I can suspend the transfer while it's in progress in order to recalculate and correct the lists. You were suspended for about three seconds, while I attempted to reshuffle your position. If that doesn't compute or requires further intervention, then those in dire situations might have to be treated in the module. There's a medical facility there too. There's very little we can't fix."

After taking a turn around the room and peeking at everything, I say, "What's going to happen now?"

"I'm going to repair your flawed systems, but also prevent such a thing from impacting you later, or being passed down to children should you choose to have them."

My stomach clenches and I ask, "Surgery?"

"Not exactly." The answer is such a non-answer that I sigh, and the hub says, "Should I explain in detail?"

Jack is still standing near the door and when I look at him, he raises his eyebrows like I should consider the level of detail I might get. Good point.

"Only as much detail as I can understand, please."

If the hub has to think about that, it's not apparent to me, because it answers without a pause. "Your problem ultimately relies on your genetics. It's not a system flaw brought about by some action or inaction or by your environment. Like many problems, this was written into your genetic code at the moment you came into existence. It was written along with the color of your eyes and the shade of your hair. Do you understand that?"

Plopping myself down onto one of the little rolling stools, I try to take that in as it pertains to me. This thing is a part of me, a flaw I was made to have. That's hard to take—and completely unfair—but I can understand it. "Yes, I've got it."

"In order to repair it, I'll also need to change what's inside you that allows it to impact you in the first place.

I'll need to rewrite your DNA. Otherwise, I'll simply be fixing organs and leaving all the other problems to grow with time."

My brain immediately begins tickling at those words. "You mean like you do with the replacements?"

Jack watches me carefully as the hub answers. "Exactly the same as the replacements."

I stand up so fast that the stool rolls away to crash into the cabinets. "You're going to make me into a replacement? You're going to duplicate me?"

"Yes, in a manner of speaking, but there are differences."

I back up against the cabinets, estimating my chances of getting to the door before Jack can stop me. They aren't good, and really, where would I go from here? I'm on a space station. He's already approaching, his hands up like he's no threat and concern in his eyes. That's no good, because it looks like he's ready to corner me and that feels very threatening at this particular second.

"Hell no! I'm not letting you kill me and pretend some replacement is me!"

Jack starts making shushing noises as he nears, shaking his head like I'm misunderstanding the situation. I don't think I am, and I wonder if he studied dirty street-fighting while he was studying humans, because he's about to experience exactly that. I pluck a bottle of pills from the cabinet next to me and chuck them at him. He looks surprised.

"Lysa," the Hub says in that calm voice. "You're not understanding the situation clearly. I did suggest that you wait for this until after orientation. You would have understood then with greater clarity. Your reaction is not appropriate to the conditions."

"What? Of course, it is! You're going to zombify me and replace me."

Even as I speak, I feel a sharp prick on my wrist and look down where my hands are pressed against the top of the cabinets. A thin, flexible snake-like thing made of metal is already retracting into an opening along the back of the cabinets.

So, they do have probes! Freaking aliens.

"This will calm you, Lysa. No one is going to proceed without your permission."

The hub's words grow distant and echoe-y, like I'm falling into a canyon in the middle of a conversation. I feel calm and ridiculously tired. My legs fold under me and Jack catches me in his arms as I fall.

The last thing I hear is him saying, "I've got you. You're safe."

Fourteen

When I wake, I'm lying on my bed and Jack is sitting in a chair next to me, idly flipping through my catalog. He looks up when I turn my head and smiles sadly. "I'm so sorry about that. It was too soon. I should have done this much better. I shouldn't have let you know why you're a non-transfer."

He seems so contrite and sincere. I have no doubt that he's genuinely sorry and believes that he screwed up big time. I have to agree. Massive screw-up. Even so, part of the blame is mine and I know it. I pushed him for more, even when he said I wasn't ready. I should have waited.

"I didn't make it easy on you."

His smile shifts, and he says, "No, you didn't."

Rolling my eyes, I stretch and take stock of myself. Then I have a thought and sit bolt upright, feeling along my face and arms frantically. "Did you do it? Am I me or a replacement?"

"You're still you, though if you were a replacement, you would still be you."

Leveling a glare at him, I say, "Not helpful."

He sighs. "I'm sorry again. No, you are still the original you, including your physical problems."

I can't even believe he just said that. "Again, not at *all* helpful."

Jack slams the catalog closed and stands to walk to the dining area. He tosses the catalog onto the table with an exasperated breath. "I'm not the right person for this job. Not with you."

For some reason those words send even more anxiety-borne adrenaline coursing through my system. Maybe it's because I can't take yet more change or maybe it's because Jack is who he is, but I don't want him to go. "No, you're the right person. I don't want anyone else."

He gives me a look, but must see that I mean it, because his eyes crinkle in confusion. "Why not? All I do is upset you."

I'm not going to say I want him to stay because he's gorgeous and I enjoy staring at his butt when he walks in front of me, but I'm sure thinking it. Instead, I flap my hand at him and climb out of bed. "Never mind why. I just don't want anyone else."

He shrugs as if he truly doesn't understand me at all—which he probably doesn't—and says, "Okay. It's your call."

I feel like I've been asleep for ages, so I look up at my interface. It couldn't have been later than lunch time when I had my little episode. My interface shows we're nearing supper time.

"Holy smokes!" I exclaim. My stomach answers with a rumble that reinforces how long I've been out. I also need to pee. Stomping across the room, I shoot a glare Jack's way and say, "You guys need to be more careful when you drug folks. I've been asleep for hours."

His mouth opens to answer, then closes again like he's not sure what to say. As the bathroom door slides closed between us, he shrugs and says, "Okay."

So eloquent.

After I do my thing, I look in the mirror as I wash my hands and recoil in horror. The hair tie I used to put up my ponytail clearly lost the fight while I was sleeping. I've got the worst case of bedhead in the history of bedhead. I must have been sweating in my sleep, because I've even got those tiny curls around my forehead that I get when I run.

In short, I'm a freak show and I would never, ever want any guy to see me like this.

The bot that delivered my goods didn't unpack, but a package labeled, *Grooming set, Medium to Long Hair*, is sitting on the counter. Next to it are paper envelopes with the extra brushes and such that I ordered.

"Thank goodness," I whisper and get to work.

When I step out, Jack is slouched in a dining chair with his legs splayed out in front of him and his head propped up by his arm on the table. He looks exactly like any human guy who's been kept waiting too long by someone in the bathroom.

He jerks upright when I clear my throat and his eyes widen when he looks at me. "You look different," he says.

I narrow my eyes at that, because really, what does that mean? Good different? Scary different? Considering the fact that Jack isn't even really human, he might think I look like the freakiest spider on earth would look like to me. It's possible.

Smoothing a hand over my hair, I cross to my pile of boxes. Sorting them out until I find the one labeled with the clothing I ordered, I rip it open to find clothes neatly folded inside, each item sporting a tag. If I didn't know better, I'd think they were from the mall. Maybe they are. Maybe they've been stealing shipments meant for the department stores. Probably not, though.

Grabbing an outfit, I retreat to the bathroom and catch a glimpse of Jack's pained expression when the door closes. I almost want to laugh. Poor guy.

After I change, I feel so much better. I have no way to know for sure if I'm a replacement or not, but if I am, I'm a perfect match. The scar from my knee surgery is still there, along with that single blue vein that bugs the crap out of me along the front of my left shin. The scar on my chin from the skating accident is still there and all the other dings and dents I've acquired are exactly where they should be.

I was an accident-prone kid. Adventurous, one might say. It was entertaining, but it came with a price. I've got way more than my share of scars and marks.

The clothes fit well, and I like them. My t-shirt reads, *Don't tell anyone I'm an Alien.* Below that is the typical big-headed alien shooting the peace sign with his overly long fingers. I thought it was funny and they had it in their catalog, so it must be okay. The jeans are nicer than the ones I usually buy, and they fit like a dream. I feel a little self-conscious because when I turn to look at the back, I can't help but think my butt looks awesome in them. Like, really awesome.

I don't generally think things like that, and there's pink in my cheeks when I look up at my face. Secretly, I'm wondering if Jack will also like the look. I find it difficult to keep the thought in mind that he's not human. I've twisted two sections of hair from the front of my head to the back and fastened it with one of the hair clips I ordered. The rest now falls in nice, normal waves down past my shoulders. It feels good to have imposed some order on the chaos. This is like armor in a way.

Dabbing on a bit of mascara—it's the good stuff too—I don't look much different than when I used to go to school before all this started. I like it. Now, I just have to face whatever happens next.

And decide if I want to have failing female parts or be a zombie replacement.

The bathroom door slides open and this time, Jack's head is on the table. He's fast asleep. So much for my entrance. He jerks upright when I cough, looking a little bleary eyed and confused for a moment.

"Oh my, that happens fast," he says, wiping a spot of drool off his chin.

"What does? Sleep?"

He nods and stretches, grinning at me. "But that sure does feel good. I like this."

I'm positive he means the stretch because he does it more, grinning like an idiot as he does. I can only shake my head and ask, "You've never slept before?"

"Not like this. Not in a human body." He grunts as he finishes the stretch, then goes back to sitting like a normal person.

I'm pretty sure my secret desire for him to like the way I look in these jeans is pointless. If he hasn't slept before, I'm confident that he can't possibly have learned the nuances of cheek-curves in denim. Sadly.

"What next?" I ask, ready to move on from my disappointment.

He gives me an evaluating look. I know he's still concerned about my reaction in the medical bay. More than likely, he's wondering what will cause another such reaction. His stomach speaks before he does, letting out a rumble even louder than my earlier one.

Jack grabs his middle, his expression shifting to one of confused discomfort. I'm pretty sure the way he's staring at me means he's looking for me to explain this sudden change. I can feel my stomach gnawing away at me too, so I say, "That means you're hungry. Do they not tell you anything when you get a new body?"

I'm assuming a great deal here and I know it, but I must be fairly correct because Jack rubs his flat belly and says, "I don't usually hop into a new body and this was urgent. Like I said before, normally we study, then spent time on the planet, then come to work. I didn't exactly get a whole lot of notice and skipped most of that. Yes, I knew about hunger, but this is…quite insistent."

What an interesting way to put it. Short notice change to human form, eh?

"Well, you're hungry and you need to eat. I'm hungry too. Should I order dinner for us?"

He eyes me skeptically, like he's not sure he wants to try that kind of new adventure, but eventually he nods. "If it will make this feeling go away, then yes."

They don't have menus or anything like that, so I try to decide what I would most like to eat. So far, they've not said they can't provide what I've asked for, so I'm guessing I can ask for anything. My dinner last night wasn't chosen by me, but it consisted of some of my favorite foods and that can't be an accident. Well, except for that fake-chicken, which makes me think meat might be a problem.

Now that I think about it though, I'm sort of glad meat is a problem. I'm taking it to mean that I won't wind up on a dinner menu.

Holding up a finger for him to wait, I look at the interface, which lights up, then say, "I'd like to order a meal."

To my delight, Esme answers me. "Hello again, Lysa. Would you like me to take the order or are you ready for the interface?"

"*Uh*, I'm going to order for two, so can you do it? I promise I'll learn how to use the interface better." I feel sort of bad and high-maintenance. There must be others here that need attention and I don't want to be a baby.

I can hear the smile in Esme's voice. "No problem. Just go ahead when ready."

Given the meat situation, I decide to go for a favorite that doesn't have meat. "I'd like two trays. Both with Punjab eggplant, bowls of jasmine rice separate, naan bread, sautéed green beans, iced tea, and water with lemon." I realize I just made a super-complicated order that belies my intention not to be high-maintenance, so I add, "If you can't do those, I can order something easier."

Esme pauses for just a second, then says, "No problem. I have listings for all those items. The bot will be there shortly. Anything else?"

"No, thank you, Esme."

I'm genuinely excited about this, and I rub my hands together while I grin over at Jack. It's usually a big deal to make Indian food at my house, because the cooking takes so long. Most of the time, we simply go out for it, but the food is never the same as when it's made at home.

Jack smiles at me readily enough, but I also think he looks a little worried. If this is his first time eating, I suppose that would be natural enough. I have to know. "Please tell me you've eaten, at least in some other form."

He gives me a look and says, "Of course, I've eaten. Every living thing needs to replenish energy. I've just not done it as a human before."

Truthfully, every time Jack says something like that, I grow more curious about what he was before he was human. It seems rude to ask, like I'm asking a stranger to show me their underwear.

Still, I'm really dying to know.

Rather than look at him, I cross over to my big pile of boxes. If I unpack, then I have a legitimate reason not to look at him. As casually as I can—which probably isn't casual at all—I ask, "What did you look like before?"

As I rip open the top of the box labeled, *Art Supplies and Paper Goods,* he says, "You mean when I was a giant squid person?"

That stops me cold, even as I reach for a packet of markers that looks like it came from any discount store. I look over at him and he winks.

"Such a tool," I mutter and grab for the plastic packet full of colorful markers.

That makes him laugh, and he says, "I know what that means!"

Underneath the markers is a wooden box with the biggest and fanciest set of my favorite art medium on Earth. This big kit has been on my wish-list for ages, but it's too expensive and remained out of reach. I've had to settle for getting the colors one at a time at the art store. Forgetting about squid-people for the moment, I drop the markers and lift out the heavy wooden box. It even feels expensive.

"*Oooo,*" I croon, crossing to slide the box onto the table. Putting my fingers to the latches, I try to savor the moment. "Inside this box is heaven. Pure heaven."

Jack's eyebrows screw up and he looks at me like I'm insane, but he also eyes the box with curiosity. I slide it around, so he'll see the contents when I open it, then flip the latches with a flourish. Inside are over two hundred half-pans of the most delicious watercolors in existence. I slide open the drawers underneath and tiny tubes of color come into view, all of them perfect and unsqueezed.

Running my fingertips over the treasures, I say, "Oh, this is a dream come true. Look at this."

The hot guy who isn't even human cranes his neck to look inside, but if anything, he's merely confused. He gives me a little shrug when I look at him. I'm pretty sure the dreamy look on my face makes me look like an idiot, but I don't care.

"It's color!" I exclaim, picking up one of the half-pans gingerly and unpeeling the wrapper. "These are watercolors, but very special ones. The color is as smooth as butter. You know, luminous and totally beautiful *colors*."

He shrugs again, so I paw through the big box until I find one of the smaller watercolor paper blocks—again, a far nicer weight and brand than I could ever afford—and one of the dreamy brushes I ordered. Dashing into the bathroom, I fill my metal cup with water and sit at the table next to him.

"Watch," I order. Taking a deep breath—because anyone who knows anything about using a new art toy for the first time knows a deep breath is required—I wet my brush and swirl it in the open half-pan. With only a few dabs of the wet brush, I know what I'm about to see when I touch the brush to the paper. With one long swoop, I lay down the most brilliant blue you can get outside of an oil paint, yet it's translucent and luminous in a way no opaque pigment can achieve. Because this one is made with ground lapis lazuli, it shimmers a little in the light. Beautiful.

With a sigh, I look at the swoop and then at Jack, "See?"

It's completely obvious that he's really trying to be impressed and supportive, yet has no clue why this is special. "It's a very beautiful color and you've made that mark very nicely."

It takes a second, but I burst out laughing at his expression. He squinches up his face and asks, "Not the right thing to say?"

I poke him with the hard end of my brush and shake my head, still laughing. When I can speak, I say, "No, you're fine. I'm going to guess this means you're not an artist."

"Isn't that sort of relative? I mean, you have no idea what we squid people might consider art?"

He's got the whole deadpan delivery of a joke down pat, because he almost looks serious. "You're right. Well, this is sort of like ink, but I don't think it comes from the butts of squid people."

This time I can tell he's serious when he says, "That's not nice. Don't be species-ist."

I'm saved from my gaffe by the ping and I throw back a quick apology as I head for the door. I know I can't smell the food with a door and a closed cabinet-bot between me and the plates, but I can almost feel it tickling my nose all the same. My mouth is more than ready for some good food.

What Jack said does register, and I suppose I should be more careful. Considering that I have no idea what forms aliens take, I shouldn't be so flippant. For all I know that was the height of rudeness.

The bot favors me with the same smiley and winky faces as I unload the trays, then adds a chirpy, "You're welcome," when I thank it for our meals.

Jack watches me carefully as I unload the trays and set out the dishes the way it works best for eating. When he sniffs the bread, he licks his lips. I take that for a good sign.

I demonstrate by spooning the eggplant over the top layer of my rice, then dipping a piece of my bread into the bowl. Before popping it into my mouth, I say, "I eat it American style and Indian style. All the better for being a total glutton. Try it. And yes, we can talk while we eat."

His eyes widen and that tentative look disappears as he chews his first bite. He swallows it fine, then says, "This is *really* good."

I grin at him and nod. "Yep, not so bad being human, is it?"

As he loads up his rice with more eggplant, he smiles and says, "Not at all. I like this. It feels sort of good going down."

We're mostly silent until we've got the first half of our dinner down, except for a few moans and grunts of appreciation. Watching him eat the long green beans is pretty hilarious, but he gets the idea of folding them into his mouth quickly. No one would ever accuse me of having proper manners, but I can certainly eat efficiently. That's probably why I'm shaped like I am, and I've got zero problems with that.

Once we slow down and stop inhaling the food, Jack looks up and asks, "This food is Indian in nature, yet you're from North America. Can you explain?"

Rather than answer right away, I ask, "How do you understand the difference?"

He points to his head with a green bean on a fork and says, "I've been getting information."

"Ah," I say, thinking it would be very cool to have that sort of info always on tap. "Well, my mom is half-Indian. Her mom was from India and she learned to cook from her."

He nods, looking down at his plates and bowls. "This is a cultural difference between areas then, right?"

"Pretty much."

"Which culture do you like better?" he asks.

Well, that's a hard one. It's not a question I've ever heard or considered before. I'm not sure how to answer him, so I tell him the truth. "I don't really know any culture other than American, if you want to know the truth. I haven't lived it, only looked at it. There's a difference. I know bits of Indian culture, but I've never lived there. I like the celebration clothes, the food, the dancing...the pretty things...but I've never lived it. I understand it's very difficult there for many people."

His head tilts as he listens to the voice in his head, then he says, "Ah, I see. It's a matter of freedom."

I shrug, because there's a lot more to it than that, but what he says is close enough.

His eating slows down, which means I have to stop shoveling or be rude. Jack seems to be considering his food more carefully for a few minutes. Eventually, he stops eating entirely. He's not meeting my eyes and his face doesn't look right at all.

Just as I'm about to ask him if he's alright, his fork drops to his plate with a clatter and he goes stock still. He's looking at his food, his skin going so pale it's almost green. A slight sheen of sweat makes his forehead shine.

"Are you okay?" I ask, setting down my fork to push his glass of water toward him.

He glances up at me and his face is definitely going greenish. He grips his middle and says, "I don't feel very well."

I have a sudden vision of babies and formula in my mind, which makes me wince. "Were you supposed to eat something different?"

He sort of nods, sort of shakes his head. "There's a protocol for a new body, but I was very hungry and didn't want to be rude."

Considering what happens to some people the first time they eat a good, spicy Punjab dish, even when they're from Earth, I have a bad feeling. Looking up at the ceiling, I say, "Hey, hub thing...person...whatever! Are you here?"

The unmistakable voice of the hub answers immediately, "Yes, Lysa. I'm here."

Pointing to Jack, I ask, "Do you know what's happening here?"

"I do. I'm attempting to relay that information to Jack now."

Instead of answering, Jack lets out a groan and scoots his chair back just enough to double over. I stand so I can rub his back, feeling bad because this is pretty much entirely my fault. "He's going to need some help."

"There is a bot coming. Please assist Jack to it, if you would. I'll take care of him."

The *ping* sounds almost immediately, and when I open the door there's a kind of chair made from a large bot. It has a sad face on its display. "I'll bring him," I say and hustle back to Jack, who has progressed from simply doubled over to doubled over and bouncing a little as he tries to squeeze himself tightly into a ball.

"Can you stand?" I ask gently, holding his arm.

He can, but he doesn't even bother trying to straighten up as he hobbles over to the chair. He practically falls back into it, his face absolutely bathed in sweat.

"I'm so sorry!" I say as he looks up at me.

His fingers wiggle as if to brush any apology aside, "No problem."

Of course, it *is* a problem and the chair rushes away down the hall. I watch until the wall at the end of the hallway slides open and they disappear inside. It's one of those high-tech doors, so I'm guessing that means it's not for us non-transfers.

With a sigh, I go back inside and say, "Hub person, I'm really sorry about this. I didn't even think about him not eating. I probably should have asked before I ordered food for him."

There's nothing judgmental in the hub's voice that I can detect. "It's quite alright, Lysa. Jack will be fine shortly. It's a small matter and I can help him. Is there anything else I can do for you?"

Shaking my head and sitting back down to my half-finished meal, which I'm no longer so hungry for, I say, "No. Goodnight."

"Goodnight, Lysa. Jack will return in the morning."

I look up at the interface to see a new appointment pop up for eight in the morning. Tomorrow is going to be awkward.

Fifteen

When the door pings in the morning, I'm ready and dressed. I've eaten breakfast and brushed my teeth. I even made sure to order a meal that wouldn't fill up the room with the smell of food, just in case Jack isn't feeling entirely well yet. I mean, his night couldn't have been fun.

Tugging down my shirt—this time a t-shirt with a unicorn shooting rainbows out of its horn and butt—I take a deep breath and open the door. And there he is.

"Hey," he says, smiling normally, like he didn't almost bust a gut at the dinner table last night.

I look him up and down before answering. He seems okay. "Hey to you too. Are you feeling better?"

Running a hand through his ridiculously perfect hair, he looks away with an embarrassed smile that's far too cute for our situation. "Yeah, I'm fine. Apparently, this body was intolerant to several food types. It's fixed now, but I admit I'm less keen on the whole food exploration thing."

Snorting a laugh, I wave him inside and get a nice look at his butt in the process. He really is perfect. My mother would be appalled at my thoughts. My answer to that is that I'm seventeen and what else does she imagine we think about? Really.

Today he's wearing a dark blue t-shirt with nothing on it. It stretches across his chest like it was made for him and enhances his biceps in ways that are not seemly. The jeans look the same as the ones he wore yesterday.

Before my ogling can get awkward, he spies my set up in the formerly empty corner of my room and lets out a loud breath, "Wow!"

I laugh and say, "Pretty colors can do many things."

He doesn't take his eyes off the big easel in the corner as he walks toward it, his lips parted. I'm surprisingly tickled by the reaction. Usually, I'm a bit embarrassed when people see my art for the first time, never entirely sure if I should be proud or worried. While I love to paint, I'm under no delusions as to the level of my talent. I'm not very good at it yet, but I am getting better. In Jack's case, I'm simply delighted that he might understand my joy at getting those colors yesterday.

His fingers stop short of the paper when he reaches for it, but he leans close as if to figure out what I've done. I stand back and let him look. If he's never seen art—well, Earth art—then I'd like to see his full reaction.

After a minute or so, he turns his head to look at me, and asks, "This is how you see it?"

That's not an easy question to answer, thought it should probably be a yes or no. On the big piece of watercolor paper is my rendition of the hub as I saw it in the elevator. While I was overwhelmed and didn't get a long look, the images were impressed upon my mind the way some scenes simply are. Shock can lend color to things.

And that color is now on the paper. Instead of mere blackness and pinpoints of light for the stars, I've added the colors of space, the way it shimmers in roses and blues around distant stars and galaxies. I've put size to a nebula that exists only in my mind to light the scene. The ship I glimpsed so briefly is larger, and caught at the moment it sped through the portal. As I painted it, I felt calmer, better. I felt like I was finally absorbing what I had so rashly fallen into. Or jumped into.

"Sort of, with lots of artistic license added in," I answer, shoving my hands into my pockets.

He points to the ship and says, "That's a Bluriani vessel. Did you see one?"

"For a second or two, from a distance."

He inclines his head like he's impressed. "You did a good job then. Yours is much prettier."

"Thank you."

The box of watercolors is closed on a little table next to the easel and he carefully lifts the lid with the tip of one finger. Inside there are already splotches of color I managed to flick about as I worked. The palette I used is a riot of colors, kept there so I can touch up the painting if I need to.

"You made this with just these colors?"

Stepping up to the box, I pick up two of the half-pans and lay them next to one of my color splotches. "Well, this box has a lot of colors in it. Very deluxe. But yes, I mixed these two to create that color. You can see it there." With that, I point to the slight halo around a few of the stars.

He peers closely at the spots, then shakes his head and smiles at me. "You are full of surprises."

"Who? Me, or humans in general?"

"Both," he says, then picks up the blocks of color and places them back into the box carefully. After he closes the lid, he looks at his fingertips. "I studied up on art last night after you showed me your colors. I didn't quite get it, but I do now. And not everyone can do this. Is that correct?"

My coffee is still cooling on the table, beckoning me with the promise of caffeine and sugar, so I move away from Jack to take a sip. "Well, I'm not convinced that not everyone can do it. I think everyone can do that, but in their own way. I think most people only *think* they can't, so they never try."

Jack rubs his fingertips together as if he can feel some of the color there. "Do you think I could?"

That's a good question. He's not human, but he also *is* human. Does our visual sense of art come with the body, brain, and eyes or is it something else, something we get from experience? "You could try and find out."

He grins at me and pretty much melts one of my badly-functioning ovaries at the challenge in his expression. "Maybe I will," he says.

Alien. Remember that, Lysa. He's an alien. It would be like kissing a hermit crab or something.

That little self-talk helps a little, because I manage to put the cup down without rattling it. "So, what's on the agenda for today?"

"Orientation, of course."

"Yeah," I say, drawing out the word. "But yesterday didn't go so well, so I'd rather know what I'm getting into with a little more detail. Also, is there any way to let my mom know I'm okay?"

His expression grows more somber and serious at my second question, so I know the answer already. "I'm sorry, Lysa, but no. We have very strict rules and we have no choice but to abide by them. It's very important for many reasons. Had your mother transferred, we might have been able to, but she's still on Earth so we can't contact her in any way."

This is disappointing, but not unexpected. That doesn't mean I'm not going to keep trying to figure out how to do exactly that. I'll simply keep those intentions to myself for now. I may have popped through a portal on a whim, but now I've got a mission…and that's to get back to Earth and spread the news of its coming destruction. Maybe Earth won't be able to figure out a way to stop whatever is going to happen, but without knowing it's coming, they can't even try.

"And what part of orientation am I getting?" I ask, trying not to reveal what I'm thinking.

Jack rubs his hands together like he's excited and the smile returns to his face. "The good stuff. You're a non-transfer, so you're going to get the full rundown of what's going on. How about that?"

Clearly, this is a big deal for him, so I try to look as excited as he does and say, "Yay!"

He gives me a look.

"Too much?" I ask.

"Yeah, that was a little fake."

"Okay, but I really am excited. I'm just nervous too."

Jack steps closer and takes my hand, giving it a pat and then pulling it close to his chest like he's hugging it or something. It's very odd, but also sort of nice. "Don't be nervous. You'll see that there's nothing to worry about and that everything is happening for the good. I promise."

I nod, but he's still holding my hand up at his chest and it's getting weird, so I glance at it and he lets me go with a laugh. "Oh, sorry. I'm still getting used to things. I like the way things feel. It's all very interesting." He runs his fingers along the table surface to emphasize his delight at touching.

Oh, if he only knew exactly how delightful it could be. Well, I don't exactly *know* what that sort of touching would be like, but I have a really good idea. I can feel myself turning bright red, so I open the door to my room and wave him out. "Let's get started then."

His brow creases when he looks at my no-doubt crimson cheeks, but he doesn't comment. When we get into the hallway and he starts walking, I can't resist asking the question any longer. I've been trying to be polite about it, but really, I have to know.

"Listen, if this is a rude question, just tell me and accept my apology ahead of time, but I've got to ask it anyway. If you don't know art, don't know the sense of touch, don't know eating...then what the heck did you look like before you were human?"

Jack doesn't even break stride. He just grins at me and says, "Oh, I *know* all of those things. I just don't know them the way humans experience them. It's different. Totally different."

I roll my eyes and say, "You know, my pet peeve is when people give answers that aren't answers at all."

He laughs at my tone and says, "I told you. I'm one of those giant squid people!"

Now, he's just teasing me. Then again, it probably was a rude question. I should have picked something less likely to be used as a tease when I first asked that question about being eaten by aliens. Squid was too easy apparently.

Rather than press him further—because maybe he was something super gross and doesn't want to freak me out—I say, "Fine."

He stops at another expanse of wall and a silver square lights up with another warning that we're still in Earth atmosphere. Since this hallway, along with every other location I've been, has been perfectly comfortable for me, I wonder if this is some sort of Earth wing or something.

"Here we are," he says, holding out his arm for me to enter ahead of him. I guess he looked up Earth manners while he's been studying us humans. The move is done perfectly, like he was born to it.

"Well, we have been studying, haven't we?" I quip as I enter.

"You've been studying too?" he asks, a confused expression on his face.

"What?" It takes me a second, then I get it. "Oh, no. That's just a figure of speech. I meant you've been studying manners."

At first glance, the room looks like one of those side rooms you find in galleries or museums, the kind where they show you a film of something important in history or explain relics. There are a few curved benches in front of an equally curved screen on the wall. I wonder what I'd have to do to get a TV this big in my room.

He gives a little shake of his head like he'll never understand me, or maybe that he gives up trying. Probably he means a little of both. Motioning toward the center of the front bench, he says, "Would you like to sit?"

I do, and ask, "Are we going to watch a movie? You've actually made an explanation into a movie?" This reminds me of sex education in school, or maybe when they showed us that gory movie in driver's education. I sure hope not. Those movies are never very good.

Jack sits next to me and cocks his head for a second, listening to the hub, I guess. He smiles and says, "No, nothing like that. Though I am looking forward to experiencing a movie."

That makes me think of my vampire show, the one I never miss that makes me squeal with corny delight. I absolutely won't steer him in that direction. What would he think of me if he knew that's the kind of program I enjoyed? If he asks, I'll point him toward something cultured, maybe one of those historicals on PBS.

"Yeah, well, not all of them are good. We do make some stinkers."

Jack crosses his feet at the ankles and leans back on the wide bench, braced by his arms. It makes the muscles on his arms stand out and I look away before I embarrass myself. I sure hope whatever the hub says is so interesting that I can forget about the guy sitting next to me.

Sixteen

The hub's voice intrudes before things can get more awkward. "Good morning, Lysa. I hope you're feeling well today and are ready to continue your orientation."

While I'm sure the station doesn't mean to, its tone is so formal that I feel like I'm being addressed by a teacher. Even without meaning to, my posture straightens, and my hands fold in my lap.

"Good morning. Yes, I'm well and very ready to move on. And...*uh*...I'll be calmer today too."

Next to me, Jack snickers and looks down at his remarkably mall-like pair of skater shoes. Yeah, he's getting used to be a teenager. No doubt about it. I pinch him, but not too hard, and he jumps a little on his seat. When he looks at me in shock, I mouth, "Behave!"

"Do you have any questions before we begin?" the hub asks.

What a loaded question that is. How could I not have questions? Remembering yesterday and me calling it 'hub thingie,' I know what my first questions should be.

"*Uh*, I do. What do I call you? Yesterday you said the station was hub, but you're Hub. Is that really your name?"

"Yes, I'm Hub, while this station is the hub."

"So, your name is the same as the station? Doesn't that get confusing?"

Jack's brows rise a little and he looks up at the ceiling like he'd like to know the same thing, so I guess my question wasn't as stupid as it sounded in my head.

"I suppose it could be confusing at first, but it's quite clear to me."

Well, that will have to do, I guess. I'm certainly not done with my questions, though. "Next one. Who made you? Who ordered you to do this on Earth? Who's in charge of you?"

Jack's back hunches a little and his eyes roll, like I've asked a really rude question. It's too late to turn back now.

"I'm in charge of myself. There is no other entity which decides my actions. As to who made me, that was long ago and the civilization that created me no longer exists."

I detect hints of sadness in those final words. There's nothing overt, nothing specific that I can point to that can be parsed as sad, but it's there. Jack doesn't seem to notice. Even so, I feel like I'm treading on another person's feelings, which is strange, because Hub is a space station.

"Okay, sorry. That's it for now. I'm ready to be orientated."

"Excellent. Please observe."

The big screen in front of us brightens with a beautiful image of the stars and the vast darkness between. The image is so clear and sharp that I can tell when I'm looking at a galaxy shaped like a spiral or one shaped like a big ball. I suck in a sharp breath at all that beauty. Even Jack is looking at the screen with his eyes round and wide. Their screen resolution makes our best screens on Earth look like old black and white TVs. Seriously.

The Hub starts right in, and doesn't hold back. The image zooms in until the Earth becomes a blue and white pearl of perfection. A glance at Jack tells me that he thinks it's as amazing as I do. We're lucky to have such a wonderful planet.

Well, lucky until whatever it is wipes us out in twenty-seven years.

"Earth is a remarkable planet," Hub says in the same calm, cool tone it always uses. "It is, perhaps, more remarkable than it might seem even to you. It is—if I use a term borrowed from humans—a miracle. It is utterly unique and unlike any other planet we have seen, living or dead. There are hundreds of millions of planets in our small galaxy, but there is only one Earth. Statistically, there is likely some other planet precisely like yours somewhere in the universe, but I have no knowledge of what lies beyond our galaxy. Within this galaxy, it is unique."

As Hub speaks, I start to feel uncomfortable. This is the same feeling I get when I hear too many compliments and it moves into creepy territory. I got this same feeling when a neighbor used to tell me how pretty I was when I was very little. Well, not precisely the same, because that neighbor was pervy, but close enough. I keep silent though, because I'm sure Hub won't leave it there. It will explain. It does seem to like doing that.

The screen shifts and all sorts of annotations populate the screen, superimposed on the planet. Axis lines, degree arcs, even a line from the moon to the Earth appears, all of it peppered with numbers and math symbols.

"The confluence of events which led to you and all life on your planet is complex, and all of them rather unlikely. When taken together, the odds of all such events occurring in exactly the right order at the right time are almost beyond calculation."

Okay, I'm getting some weird religious vibes here and I better not start hearing that. If our planet is a mystery, okay, but there are aliens all over this space station that shouldn't exist if we paid attention to any single religion on my planet.

I hold up a finger to pause, though I have no idea if Hub can see it. I don't see cameras anywhere. "Do you have something to say, Lysa?"

That answers my question about whether or not Hub can see me. I clear my throat and say, "Listen, no offense, but I don't want to be preached to. However unlikely it may be, the Earth does exist, so whatever needed to happen *did* happen. Unless you're trying to tell me that we were created by some super-being we think of as God, that is. Are you?"

"I'm not implying anything of the sort. The Earth is indeed a natural planet, not a construct left by another civilization."

Wow, if there are species out here that build planets, then humans are way out of our league. Rather than digress further, I wave a hand and say, "Okay, sorry. I just wanted to be clear."

"To illustrate the complexity of the series of events that must have occurred, please watch the screen."

I do, and by the time Hub stops speaking and asks me if I have questions, my mouth is hanging open. I'm pretty sure I'm in a state of information overload and awe. Hub is right about one thing. The series of events is amazing, even though I don't understand how they happened, only that they did. Even the axis of our planet is important and unlikely, yet perfect. And the water, the land, the warm heavy mass at its center, the moon…all of it. It's just as Hub said; perfect.

"Holy shit on a stick," I whisper.

Jack frowns at my words, then listens for a second and his face clears. He mutters, "Oh, that makes more sense, because the other way…" He makes a disgusted face and then I get it. He took my curse words literally.

Yet again, I'm taken by surprise. This time I think my overwhelmed state of mind simply adds to the hilarity. I'm not saying I'm hysterical, but I will admit that I'm not too far from that line. I've never thought about profanity in the literal sense before and I start laughing. Really laughing.

Jack looks at me worriedly for a minute, but every time I look at him, I start laughing again. Eventually, Hub asks, "Are you alright, Lysa? Do you need us to stop for a while?"

I wave my hand and shake my head, trying to pull in a breath that doesn't come out as a laugh. "No, no. It's just…*holy shit on a stick*. I can't stop laughing."

"Jack, will you get Lysa some water, please?"

He hurries away, and I can tell by his stiff stride that he thinks I'm laughing at him. He hands me a metal cup of water, but doesn't really look at me. Trying to pull myself together, I squeeze his fingers around the cup and say, "I'm not laughing at you. I promise. I just never thought of what the words meant before. It's one of those sayings you say, but don't think about."

He cocks an eyebrow at me, clearly skeptical, then nods and pushes the cup at me. "Right."

I don't think he's entirely mollified, but I drink some water and my laughs eventually peter out. Even so, I'm not going to look at him for a while, just to be safe. Eventually, I start to feel a bit stared at, sort of like that awkward person that interrupts class, leaving everyone to glare at them while they do their thing.

"I'm good," I say, setting my cup down on the bench next to me. Do I sound casual? I think I sound casual.

"Are you certain you'd like to continue?" Hub asks.

"Absolutely sure. I get it. Humans really are as awesome and unique as we thought, because our planet is unique. So, that's why you're saving us?"

It's Jack's turn to look a bit disbelieving, and he gapes at me. I'm not even sure how to interpret the look on his face.

"What?" I ask.

Rather than answer, he looks away and Hub speaks. "While I'm sure you're a lovely human, no. All life on your planet is unique. Humans are merely one species among many. They are, however, the most troublesome of those species. By a large margin. By orders of magnitude."

My mouth drops open and it's my turn to gape. "We're the black sheep of Earth?" When Jack's brow creases and a suspicious look crosses his features, I add, "That means the bad ones."

The fact that he merely shrugs confirms it. Hub drives it home when it says, "That would be an appropriate metaphor."

"But you're still going to save us, right?"

"I'm trying. We're trying." Hub sounds like that's almost more trouble than it's worth.

A hand lands on my leg in a position I would normally not allow until at least the third date, and Jack says, "That's our fault. If your planet had been slated earlier for intervention, then you would have been less technologically advanced, and it would have been easier. No one could have predicted this much change."

Hub interrupts to say, "That's not entirely true. I did forecast the change, but it was an outlier prospect...less than one percent chance. In addition, there had been no indicators that Earth would require an intervention until very recently. The event Earth will experience was…unanticipated."

Pushing Jack's hand closer to my knee than my hip—but not off my leg entirely—I say, "You really don't know humans if you didn't anticipate how fast we'd advance. We like change as much as we hate it, but hate it or love it, we do it constantly."

Hub says, "That's very apt. Very appropriate. May I use it? It would be an excellent addition to the training materials."

Is a space station asking me for copyright permissions? I think yes. "Sure, go crazy."

Jack's hand is still heating up the area above my knee like he's got a small nuclear reactor under his skin. The heat has somehow traveled up and lodged in my cheeks and neck too, which is unfortunate, because I don't have jeans to hide it there. He squeezes my leg a little and asks, "Are you really okay?"

Snatching up my cup, I cross over to the ubiquitous cabinets and counter along the back wall and pass my cup along it until something happens. The little sink thing pops out and I refill my cup, glad for something to keep my hands and mouth occupied for a moment.

The truth is, that's harsh news to hear about our species. I'm not one of those humans-over-all types, but I didn't question we were top dog when it came to the conquer and control department. Did I always agree with that? No, but I didn't question that it was true.

It seems that was all wrong. We're basically just another species, but more trouble than all the others combined. We're what? Are we vermin? Are we rats you can't get rid of, or in this case, corral so they can be moved to a safer area? Maybe raccoons would be a better comparison. Yeah, I'd rather be a trash panda than a rat.

Either way, this is not at all flattering. If we're that much trouble to deal with, why do they even bother? I sip my water, then look up at the ceiling and say, "It's sort of insulting to be considered the trash pandas of the planet. I mean, we already have trash pandas and most people don't look at them with admiration."

Jack is clearly confused by the term, then his head cocks and he says, "Ah, colloquialism for raccoon. Got it. Trash panda…nice."

Hub sounds a little less officious when it says, "Trash panda is a little extreme, but I understand what you're saying. Unfortunately, you're not far off in terms of generalities. If I can use the same example, then I'd say humans were more like very intelligent trash pandas with ambition and deeply complex language skills."

"Not helping," I say, rolling my eyes. I hope Hub can see that!

"Of course, Lysa. You're not a trash panda," Hub says, its voice still carrying hints of a tease in it.

This is all very interesting, but it also raises questions, ones I think are probably better to understand now, rather than later.

"Hub, I'm still not sure I understand exactly why you chose to save Earth now, particularly since you've made it clear that humans aren't the reason you're doing it. On

Earth, species go extinct all the time, especially now. But you don't save them? Or do you?"

"Lysa, I think I understand your confusion. The short answer is that I don't stop individual extinctions. Such extinctions are a natural process for all life-bearing planets. Where I intervene is when there is significant danger of a nearly complete extinction of life. Even then, I might not intervene depending on the situation and the source of the extinction."

"I'm not sure I understand that one."

"Let me give you an example, Lysa. If humanity were to corrupt their environment to such an extent that a total collapse would result, I might not intervene, since it was an intentional act—"

"We would never do that on purpose!" I interject, perhaps a little too loudly.

"As you say, perhaps not, but behaving in a way that entirely disregards the environment that supports your species is fairly common practice on Earth."

My treacherous cheeks go warm again, mostly because that's the truth. An embarrassing truth.

"Ah, okay. Go on."

"In such an instance, I may not intervene, because it was a purposeful act by a species. When it is an external event, such as an asteroid impact or solar event, then my calculations would more often result in an intervention. In those cases, no species belonging to the planet caused the event. Even in such an event, I might not intervene, depending on the level of extinction. In some cases, I intervene early, even when the calculations result in a moderate probability of extinction. At other times, I might wait until the predictions become more precise. I'm very skilled at this work, but I'm not all-knowing. I rely on sensors, data, and calculations. Does that make it clearer, Lysa?"

Does it? I think what it does is drive home how incredibly complex this entire process is, and how completely unable a human mind is to grasp the complexity of such a process.

"Not entirely, Hub, but I don't think I can ever truly understand. Not the way you do, anyway. I think what you've said is that sometimes you save a planet even when you're not sure the life will die out because it *might* die out. Other times you leave it alone, because it's their own fault. Is that it?

"Close enough, Lysa."

Jack has been sitting through this entire exchange, his facial expressions giving away confusion and comprehension by turns. While the Hub seems to understand me, it hasn't escaped my notice that Jack must play catch up. True, he can do it by listening to something inside his head, but he still has to acquire the information. He doesn't just know things, and I wonder how that works. Also, he was physically flawed and didn't know it...and Hub didn't tell him. I think there's an interesting disconnect here and it might be useful to me someday.

Yes, I have a million questions about all that I've just heard, but this particular issue is one I can latch onto. This is one I can get my head around without thinking of trash pandas. I want to be careful. I need to address things not quite so bluntly. I don't want to give away that I'm searching for weak links and openings, for gaps in their security that I might use.

After all, they may say I'm a non-transfer. They may say I can't go back to Earth or forward to where they're sending the other humans, but I've never said that I'm going to be satisfied with that. I want to go home and to do that, I'm going to have to find an opening I can slip through.

Or a portal.

"Hub, I have a different question. You understand me and the way I speak, the slang and so on. Jack doesn't. Why is that? How do you know so much about humans, but my facilitator doesn't?"

"Lysa, Jack is biological, just as you are. I'm an artificial construct. My limitations are solely a function of my ability to process and store. I have been interacting with humans and have amassed a great deal of first-hand knowledge. I've also modeled the Earth and its inhabitants for a very long time. Jack must learn in much the same way you do. I can assist him, but he must learn as all complex biological organisms learn."

"And you've been what…studying us? Studying humans?"

"Perhaps not in the way you're using the word. I monitor all life-bearing or life-potential planets within our galaxy in some fashion or another."

"You do? All of them?"

"All of them, except those I'm expressly forbidden to monitor due to treaties or agreements."

The scope of that almost stops the wheels in my head from turning. How can anything, no matter how complex, monitor so much? I mean, Hub already said there are hundreds of millions of planets. How is that even possible? That brings up an alarming thought.

"Hub, you're not...*umm*...you're not God or anything, are you?"

The amusement in Hub's voice is readily apparent this time. "No, Lysa. I'm a space station."

"And not an angel or anything I might call supernatural?"

"No, Lysa. I was originally built by a civilization not much different from any other."

What a huge relief that is, particularly with all the eye-rolling I've been doing. That does bring up another question though, and it's a biggie.

"Then why? Why would you go to all the trouble to save planets? Why do you care?"

"It is my only purpose, Lysa. I preserve life. All life in this galaxy that I can preserve, I must preserve, while also protecting the future possibilities of life. Only life matters. Life brings order to chaos, even as it creates a new form of chaos by existing. Without life, there is no point to the universe."

The enormity of the words hits me, then expands inside me until it becomes too big to hold inside. How can such a thing be? Imagine a station like this, one that knows so much and can do so much, and the only reason it exists is to save others. That's just crazy…and crazy cool.

All I can say is, "Wow."

Seventeen

I'm more informed when my orientation is done for the day. I'm also completely overwhelmed. My brain is perilously close to fried at this point. When Jack stops at my door and asks if I want him to stay, I shake my head, unable to speak.

He nods as if he understands, and says, "It's a lot to take in."

The way he says it makes me think maybe he's felt this way before, at least in a general sense. "Did you come here like I did?" I'm not sure why I'm asking.

He smiles, but not a big happy smile or anything. It's more a smile of commiseration. "Not exactly, but we were all new here once. I know what it feels like to be overwhelmed by it all. I know this will be hard for you to believe, but when I arrived, it was probably more of a shock to me than it was for you. I understood far less than you do."

For some reason, that makes me feel better. Maybe because I'm not alone in this feeling. Maybe it's because

Jack seems fine now and that means I might be fine someday too. The fact that he's here instead of with his people—assuming his people were transfers too—isn't lost on me, but I'd rather not think about that right now. That's a step too far.

I've been avoiding thinking about my mom and what she must be going through. If I bring up his situation, then I'll have to think about mine. I can't do that yet or I'll fall apart. And I can't fall apart, because if I do, then I'll never figure out how to get home again.

After a moment of silence, I grip his forearm and say, "Thank you for helping me. I'm just going to eat and try not to think for a while. Alone. Is that okay?"

He shifts so that he can squeeze my arm in return and we stand there, with our arms locked together like ancient warriors before handshakes were invented. "Perfectly okay. I'm not sure I can handle being around food right now anyway. I might be too tempted to eat something crazy and I'm still not over that experience."

His ability to poke a little fun at himself is endearing and if anything, makes him even more gorgeous. But he's not human…or rather, he wasn't. While I'm sorry about calling him a squid person, he could be anything. I've got a lifetime of human-centric bias to get over before I can really think of him as anything other than something wearing a human disguise.

I mean, he's wearing a gorgeous costume, but it's still a costume.

Letting go of his arm leaves me feeling less anchored, but also free to wallow in my thoughts without having to put up a brave front. That's weird, I know, but such are the ways of the Earth's true trash pandas. Contradictory and nonsensical.

"Tomorrow?" I ask, already turning toward the door.

"I'll be here," he says, and I know he means more than an answer to my question.

As I open my door, I say, "Thank you." I don't look back again. Instead, I shut the door behind me and lean against it while I cry.

*****

"So, I'm not crazy, Rosa?" I ask the ceiling some time later, after my dinner has arrived and I've got nothing except my gloomy thoughts to distract me.

"No, Lysa. Not even a little bit crazy."

Her voice is kind and just as grandma-like as before. It's just what I needed. I poke at my dinner—tonight I chose true comfort food, macaroni and cheese, with extra cheese. After a few pokes, I ask, "How is your work going?"

Her sigh is long, and I can almost see her shaking her head like she did when I popped through. "Much the same, but that's not for you to worry over. You're overwhelmed right now and that's to be expected. Every planet is different. Every sentient species has its own way of processing things. Every individual will feel new experiences differently. There's nothing crazy about that. It's just the way life is."

While it's possible that Rosa is simply feeding me lines that will make me feel better, it doesn't register that way. Instead, it has the ring of truth…of a simple truth that she knows, and I'm only just learning. She's very good at her job, even when it's not technically a part of her job.

"Thank you," I say.

"You're very welcome, Lysa. Will you be alright?"

I think about my answer before I rattle off in the affirmative like I would at home. Will I?

"I think so," I say, then add, "I hope so."

After we end our call—or whatever it is when I contact someone—I wander around my room. I still haven't unpacked everything. There are boxes and wrappings all over the place. My room looks crowded with all that disorder. Why did I order so much stuff?

Because I'm a trash panda.

The thought comes unbidden and it hurts, mostly because it's sort of true. What is it with us? Why do we have to grab everything and anything, no matter our need? Why did I order five pairs of jeans, four pairs of shorts, exercise clothes, and three dresses? I mean, if I'm only going to be here a short while, why exactly do I need all this stuff? It's not like they don't do laundry here. They do, and they do it fast.

"I'm a trash panda," I whisper, looking at the pile of wrappings on my table.

Hub told me that our orientation sessions would be available for review, so I look at the monitor and start working my way through our session earlier in the day. The visual is of the screen as I viewed it, but I can adjust it to look at anything in the room from any angle. I wonder how they do that.

Everything I see and hear is both perfectly clear and completely overwhelming at the same time. Every answer leads to more questions. Every layer of understanding leads to more layers of unknown depth. There were too many questions to ask or work through, but they all return now. Knowing I'll lose them just as I did before, I dig out a notebook from a sealed box and start writing my questions down.

By the time I finish, there are a lot of pages. A lot of pages filled with words ending in question marks.

While I still haven't been told exactly where everything taken from my planet is going, I know enough to guess that the new planet is a place comfortable for us. A place where we can simply carry on. A place to carry on being trash pandas. Somehow, that last part is one I have a hard time believing we'll be permitted to do.

Eighteen

The next morning, I can barely pull myself out of bed to pee. Coffee I can manage, but food is a mountain too far. I feel like someone pulled a thick blanket over my head, one that's too heavy for me to lift off. I can see nothing except the darkness.

I'm pretty sure this means all the novelty that was keeping me energized has been overtaken by reality. My mother, the corpse starfished on our living room floor, being here, the fact that I'm genetically flawed, the whole trash panda situation, and everything else that goes with my leap through the portal. This is too much for my brain.

Mostly, I think it's my mom. The fact that the last time she saw me, I leapt through a portal without looking back weighs heavily on my mind right now.

When Jack shows up, I don't open the door. Instead, I ask him to leave me alone. He's silent for so long that I begin to doubt he's still there. At last, he asks, "Will you be alright if I go?"

"I won't be alright if you stay. Not today. Tomorrow maybe."

There's the faintest noise from the other side, a soft sound. It's him, his hand brushing the door maybe. "I'll be here if you need me. Just call."

"I will," I say quietly. There's no further sound from his side of the door, but I wait with my forehead pressed against the metal. After a while, I go back to bed and pull the covers over my head to let this crushing darkness take me away for a while.

"Lysa."

I wake up wondering if I actually heard my name. Did I? Was I dreaming?

"Lysa," Hub says again.

"I'm awake."

Hub doesn't say anything for a moment and I'm not sure why. It called and woke me, so what does it want? Rubbing my eyes, which ache from all the crying, I sit up in bed and glance at the screen. The time is surprising. I've slept all day and well into the night, rising only to visit the bathroom or drink water.

"Did you want something, Hub? If not, I'm going back to bed."

"Lysa, I'd like to show you something."

Well, if that's not enigmatic, I don't know what is. Hub is being mysterious again. How is a machine doing that?

"I'm not in the mood for a tour, Hub. Maybe tomorrow."

"We don't have to go anywhere. I can do it right here. All you need to do is sit where you are."

I figure Hub is going to show me another movie, but the viewscreen displays only the time when I look at it. I'm not in the mood, but I also know that Hub wouldn't have woken me up in the middle of the night simply because it wanted to.

With a sigh, I say, "Okay."

The room darkens immediately, even the little glow of the viewscreen clock disappearing. The darkness is so complete that I feel untethered. It's frightening, but before I can do more than open my mouth to ask—or shout—for light, the darkness is broken.

At first, there's only the barest hint of color at the edges of my room, nothing substantial. Then the density increases and the viewpoint shifts. Turning on my bed to look at the center of the room where the light grows brighter, a ball of light coalesces.

"What are you doing, Hub?" I ask, but I can see for myself before I finish the question. It's a planet. Not Earth. That much is obvious at a glance. The landmasses are all wrong.

"I'm showing you an answer. One I think you need to see right now."

Getting out of bed, I walk toward the planet in the middle of my room, but my steps are tentative. I don't want to intrude, which is silly perhaps, but it feels wrong to put my foot into their ocean. Clouds cover parts of the surface in a thin flat layer. When I reach out to brush them away, my fingers disappear inside the illusion.

As soon as I pull my hand away, the view changes and I'm suddenly zooming in for the surface. The illusion is so perfect that I fall against my easy chair, then hang on for dear life. The projection—or whatever it is—fills the room until I can't even see the chair, only the effect of my grip in the form of my white knuckles. The planet's surface is flying toward me. Even my feet have nothing beneath them.

"What's happening? Hub!"

"The disorientation will pass. Hold on."

Green and brown and blue in disordered masses zooms closer beneath my feet. A mountain range topped with white becomes momentarily visible in the distance, before disappearing as I drop further. Putting my hands out to prevent impact with the ground, I lose the chair. I think I even shout, but I can't be sure. Squeezing my eyes shut, I drop to one knee. I can feel the floor beneath me and I spread my hands out against it. If I open my eyes, I'll lose it, but if I just keep my hands on it, I'll be fine. I hope.

My breathing was loud before, but suddenly that small noise is drowned out by a cacophony of other noises. Squeals, buzzes, squeaks…it's like a zoo. Then something that sounds like a trumpet blown by a drunk zebra inside a barrel of soap suds blasts out right next to my ear. My eyes pop open as I fall backward onto my butt. What I see is unbelievable.

I'm on the ground, or more specifically, a flattened bit of rough dirt in a clearing. Around me are strange trees of all types, tall or short, lush or needled or bare. Huge ferns crowd the edges of the clearing, their long, curling fronds dipping in a breeze I can't feel.

The noise I heard is coming from a creature way bigger than me and it's about to step on my head. With a squeal, I half-crawl, half-toss myself out of the way, expecting the ground to shake when that big foot falls, but it doesn't. I hear it, but there's nothing to go with it. No vibration, no pounding, nothing. As the back foot rises, I see hints of solid chair through the gray-green skin.

"Is this a video?" I ask Hub, reaching out to try and touch the giant toenail next to me. My hand passes right through it.

"This is a projection, but the images are live. This is what's happening right now. Your perspective is from a very small drone."

Under my breath, I say, "That would explain me almost getting squished by nothing."

"I didn't plan that," Hub answers.

I keep forgetting that Hub hears everything. Noted. Eventually, I'll stop noting that fact and actually act on it. The big beast takes another couple of steps and I watch as its rump comes into view. It looks a bit like an elephant from the back, with wrinkly skin and big, round feet. The animal is about the size of an elephant, or maybe a little bigger. From behind it has that same cute butt too.

I will not be judged for thinking that. Lots of people think elephants have cute butts.

The resemblance to an elephant ends there. Another of its kind lumbers my way and its face is familiar in a strange way. Familiar, but changed. Short, nubby horns form a crown on its head, starting near the cheeks and getting a little fatter near the top. Its eyes are small compared to its head, but the iris color as it passes me is a startling green-gold. Beautiful. The nose is a hard, curved shell, a bit like a beak, but also not, since the hard part doesn't reach the lips, which are curiously shaped so that the animal looks like it's smiling.

"That's a dinosaur," I say in wonder, watching the second cute rump pass me.

"It is," Hub says, being so non-helpful that I make a face. I guess it saw me, because it says, "Did you want more information now? I thought you might enjoy observing first."

I open my mouth, then close it again when I realize Hub is right. This is magic right here. As soon as we start talking about it, the magic will be gone. I don't know how this is happening, but it is. I feel awake and eager. That feels good after wallowing in depression all day.

Standing, I step forward and the whole scene shifts so quickly that I feel my stomach lurch into my throat. I didn't move, but I feel it all the same. Plus, the clearing is now about a hundred feet behind me and I'm standing halfway behind a tree trunk.

The Hub anticipates my next question and says, "To navigate, lean the way you want to go. The amount of your lean will determine your speed. To rotate, simply turn your head or body in that direction. To rise, move your arms outward. To lower altitude bring them back in."

Now that's exciting.

To test it, I lift my arms a little and sure enough, I rise like I've got boosters on my feet. It's amazing to look down, but I think I'm high enough, so I lower them. That wasn't quite right, because I drop like a stone, screeching the whole way.

"Should I change the control configuration for you?" Hub asks, using absolutely no judgy tones, which merely serves to make them feel even more judgy.

There's this one thing in every episode of my favorite superhero show, and it flashes into my mind. Before I can realize how embarrassing this would be if anyone found out about it, I ask, "Can you just make it so that if I raise my arms I go up and lower them to go down? That way I can keep them in the middle and stay put."

I know how fast Hub works, so I hold my arms at ninety degrees and lace my fingers in front of my body.

"Changes made, Lysa."

Blowing out a long breath, I rise above the forest and take my first real look at this amazing world. Turning my head to do a full circle, I see open land interspersed with dense forests, a large lake or other body of water sparkling under the sun in the distance.

And dinosaurs. Yes, there are dinosaurs.

A group of the nubby horned ones are mingling in the open areas where I first landed, if I can use that term. While I watch, a smaller one nudges a slightly larger animal in the rear end. The larger one's tail twitches, but it keeps facing the ferns. The small one nudges the bigger one several times, but as soon as the one being poked turns around to look, the one doing the poking looks around like it doesn't know what's up. It's completely faking it.

This interplay is so much like human kids that I laugh, then lower myself a little to see the action. When the one in front turns back toward the tree line—I think they're eating the ferns—the smaller one tilts its head and peers around slyly, then pokes the bigger one in the butt again and steps back super quick.

Not quick enough apparently. The bigger one is clearly well and truly sick of the goofing off. It gives chase to the smaller one. More of those bizarre trumpet-in-a-bubble noises come from them and they dart around with far more agility than I would have thought possible. I lower myself a little more to get a better look. Are they going to fight? I hope not.

Suddenly, the little one stops and does something that anyone who has ever seen a dog at play would recognize; it play bows.

The bigger one stops and huffs, front legs dancing back and forth for a moment, all the while eye-balling the littler one. Then it steps up and bonks noses with it. The smaller one's nostrils flare beside that bony plate on its snout and it slides its cheek along the cheek of the bigger one. My mouth drops open when they end this little play of theirs. Each rests their snout on the other's shoulder, the little nubs of horns along their crests resting at the unprotected neck of the other.

This is a show of affection. A show of trust.

In awe, I rise and look at the forests and open spaces, realizing now what Hub told me. This is live. This is happening now.

"Hub, how is this possible? Where are we? What is this place?"

"This is the possible made certain. Life without interruption. This is what we do."

Nineteen

Aside from all of Hub's fancy talk, I know what it's saying. I do. And I know why it showed me this unbelievable world. I turn my body to spin in the air so fast that I feel I might fly apart, my arms outstretched to take in the whole of this amazing and impossible planet.

The playing dinosaurs below me have gone back to their day. In the distance, large birds of some sort are wheeling in the sky over an impossibly wide lake bordered by mountains. I lean their way and almost feel the wind in my hair, even though my brain knows the wind is imaginary. My heart doesn't know it though, and goosebumps tickle across my skin. Going faster, the ground and trees blur beneath me and I almost overshoot my mark. I stop abruptly right in the middle of their wheeling circle.

The magic of this moment is not lost of me. I shout before I can stop myself, because if I don't, my chest will explode. The water a hundred feet below sparkles in the sun, and around me magnificent creatures fly in a giant circle.

They are not birds.

"Holy poopsicles!" I whisper, as one of the creatures glides past me too closely for comfort.

I'd be willing to bet that my eyeballs are as big as basketballs as I follow its motion. The bird-like creature is big, but not as big as I thought flying dinosaurs were. Bigger than any bird I know, but not big enough for me to use it as a flying horse or anything. And the colors! It has feathers as well as dark, bat-like skin, and in every shade you can imagine. It's like a giant parrot with an incredibly ugly face and very sharp teeth inside a pointy beak.

And it looks intelligent to me. The way the eyes flit over the area is calculating, canny. Suddenly the mouth clacks shut, and it dives so abruptly I can barely follow the motion. It hits the water like a bullet, though it doesn't dive so much as simply stab the water before rising again. Water beads fly from it like shiny jewels as it slaps its wings and carries a struggling fish-like creature toward shore.

I follow it—of course, I do. It lands near a messy bowl of dried mud and sticks that must be a nest. The structure is partially roofed, with the back half under a dome woven from thin tree whips or reeds. The front is open and when it waddles with a chuckle-producing lack of grace toward the nest, two extremely unattractive heads pop out. They immediately begin a screeching cacophony that would drive me insane if I had to listen to it for long.

As soon as the wriggling fish drops by the nest, a larger head appears from under the dome and the two adults clack their beaks at each other. I can almost see the trade-off. *You take the kids, honey. I'm out of here.* They switch places and the exiting bird stretches its wings and wiggles its head violently on a long, supple neck. A wake-up stretch, maybe?

By the time that one has waddled a few feet away from the nest, the other is doing its best to pluck out pieces of fish and get them into gaping beaks, each of the chicks doing its best to push aside the other. I can see the exhaustion in that almost-dinosaur's face. Exhaustion and patience.

It is in this crazy, unbelievable moment that I realize I am in love.

I'm in love with all this life, this wild, rampant, glorious life that once covered my own planet. This is more than we humans could have ever imagined, a raw beauty almost too big to comprehend. Tears stream down my face as I watch this same tableau play out at nests along the shore. Tired parents and hungry offspring. I know what this is, what this planet is, but I need to confirm it.

"Hub, is this what the dinosaurs would have become if the asteroid hadn't hit Earth?"

"Yes. Or to be more precise, it's as close as can be. This planet isn't an exact match to Earth. Not even I can do that. But it had a good base compatibility, and was altered to make it as close as can be done."

"Are they all like this? Did they ever evolve beyond this?" I ask, watching another set of weary parents trade duties, pausing to slide their beaks together, first to one side, then the other. It's done with the muted affection of those who have been together a long time, like the kiss a married couple might exchange after years of saying goodbye each morning.

"Oh yes, Lysa, they have. Even here, all is not what it first appears. The ones you saw at your landing spot are warm-blooded and live in herds. They are close-knit, and their friendships often life-long. They stay under the care of their parents and extended family for many years.

"These avians migrate almost nine thousand miles each year—though the year here is a little different from original Earth's. The exception is if anyone in their small migrating group is too ill or old to make the trip. Then that group stays. They build a nest like this, except much larger, with an entirely enclosed roof and a doorway. In this group house, they will huddle for warmth through the winter, tending to the weakest in their own way. The strongest members fish for food when the first freeze occurs and bury it in the softer earth away from shore to keep for the winter. They also bury their dead up there, on that mountain, covering them with rocks so that nothing can eat them, but where they will have a view of the world, even in death."

While Hub speaks in its soothing voice, I watch as the original bird I followed uses its wings to nudge the pair of chicks close, tucking one under each wing and enfolding them with long, bony fingers extending from the wings. The other adult shares a look with its mate and in their eyes, I see intelligence and affection. The newly liberated adult then flaps its strange wings and takes to the air.

I hear a hum from the nest and draw closer to listen. The adult's eyes are half-closed, the lids fluttering a little, and the strange hum-like purr is coming from it. I can see its chest vibrating with the power of the sound. The chicks are at first restless under the wings, their small ugly feet tapping about. Then the taps slow and I see the rounding of their chests as they settle down.

As they are sung to sleep.

"They're sentient. Like us," I say, looking at the calm, sleepy eyes of the adult, drawing so near it's a wonder it doesn't feel me. Then its eye widens, and the orangey-brown iris grows as the pupil contracts. We are looking at each other.

With a gasp, I pull back even as the big beak opens. I make it away by the skin of my teeth.

"It saw me!"

I think I hear humor in Hub's voice when it says, "It saw the vessel on the planet, the drone. That's how you're seeing. A very small device, perhaps an inch square, that we call a cube. I think you annoyed the avian."

The grin on my face is so wide it hurts. "I'm the first human to interact with a dinosaur, aren't I?"

There is definitely humor this time. "Yes, in fact you are. The very first."

"Yes!" I hiss and pump my fist, which serves to skew me to the side in an alarming way. I straighten and bring myself up higher. "Show me. Show me what they've become. Can you?"

I lose control of the cube and Hub speeds us over the planet's surface, passing over lush forests, then over wide plains dotted with irregular lines of trees. Mirror-like ribbons of water snake through it. A range of mountains so high they look unreal lies ahead of us, a line of black smoke rising from part of it.

"What's that?"

"Volcanoes. Two continents are merging, and those mountains are rising where they meet. Volcanism is common in such situations."

Imagine that. A river of fire and a new continent with new mountains.

We veer off course toward the lowering sun. The light is bright, painfully so. I bring my hand up to my face and the brightness dims, a strip of something dark running right across it.

"Thank you."

"You're welcome. And here we are. Look ahead, slightly to the right. What do you see?"

There's a disturbance in the vast plains, some darker color, and as I try to make it out, I see something even more important; the regular lines of planted land.

I see farms.

Twenty

It feels like we're sitting in the square of this town doing some people-watching, though no one can see us. Hub has tucked our cube into an out of the way gap in a wall. We're high enough that we have a good view.

Hub ordered me some soup and I gave up on the spoon because it's so disorienting to use it while immersed like this. I can't see much of my real room, just hints of white near the bed and a vague presence when a dino-person walks through a piece of furniture. I couldn't even make it to the door without falling and I didn't want to stop the viewing, so a cabinet-bot brought me my bowl, its screen lit up with a bright happy face, so I could see it to take my bowl.

And now, I'm slurping down vegetable soup that needs a little salt and watching a mother read her child the riot act. She's clearly majorly pissed off and the little dino-kid is making a noise that makes me want to cover up my ears.

"Are they all like that? So loud?" I ask.

"Hearing has a different priority with different species and their tonal ranges tend to cluster by species, much like on your planet. But yes, they are rather loud compared to humans."

"Can you understand them? What they're saying?"

"I can. Do you want to know?"

"Duh," I say, pausing in my slurp. "I wouldn't have asked otherwise. I mean, you know, you don't have to give me a word for word, but in general."

"The child has misbehaved by eating in the shop without paying for what he ate. This is the second time he's done it, and she's very ashamed of him. She's telling him he'll wind up without a mate on the plains eating leavings."

"That's mean."

"They have a very strict culture."

I ponder that while I drink my soup and watch. They're interesting and I could watch them all day. I could watch them forever really. They don't wear clothes, but they do wear aprons with big pockets. Their skin is nubby looking, rough almost, and their skin colors are extraordinary. Bright interspersed with a dull, green-tinged gray. I can tell the mother and child are related simply by the similarity in their coloring.

They look vaguely saurian, but also strangely unlike them. It's sort of the way I can see our humanity in the face of an ape; a likeness that isn't, but is.

They're taller than we are and not very advanced if their town is the measure of it. It looks old, like primitive civilizations rebuilt for TV so we can see our earlier times. Yet, it *is* a town. A town for dinosaurs that have evolved out of being dinosaurs…sort of.

"Hub, can you show me how you did this?" I ask.

The view shifts and I know that the planet far below my feet isn't the one I was just on, but neither is it the Earth I know.

"Lysa, this is Earth approximately one century before the asteroid that caused the dinosaur extinction. What I'm showing you is a replay, but this is what happened. Shall I?"

I nod, looking down at the planet that looks so little like mine. This is what it was? The Earth was so beautiful.

As before, we shoot down to the surface so quickly that the instinct to brace against impact is too strong to resist. I slosh soup out of my bowl when I hold out my hands, but this time we stop high in the air, well above the treetops. Below me is a massive herd of dinosaurs, but they're almost exactly as I've always thought of them. Well, except in color. That we most definitely got wrong.

Maiasaura. I know them from the picture books, the bones at the museum, the fascinating fact that they tended their nests. And below me there are hundreds of them. Gray-green, yes, but the red and gold splotchy stripes, the black swoops on their heads. We didn't imagine any of that.

Even as I try to take in the sheer spectacle of the vast herd on an ancient plain, we drop. As we do, I see portal flashes at the center of the herd…then more in a rough circle around it.

"Lysa, the noise here is too much for you to distinguish any one tone, so I'm going to feed you the sound coming from only one of the portals."

It's silly to lean forward, but I do anyway, wanting to hear what it is. Even without knowing what the adults sound like, I'd know the sound coming from the portal anywhere, during any time period. It makes me ache to reach out and comfort whatever it is. That is the sound of young in distress.

And it works.

Maiasaurs leap and run for the portals. I can't hear them, but their mouths and nostrils tell the story of their calls. Not all of them make it through. Some pass portals by, looking back in what can only be confusion. Even so, dozens upon dozens of animals disappear through the portals.

Then the portals are gone.

"But—"

"Wait, Lysa. Watch."

Time speeds up as if a film were being fast-forwarded, then it slows again. New portals appear in the gaps between Maiasaurs. Some of the dinosaurs have run back toward the nests, nosing at them as if trying to confirm that it was not their children in distress. From those new portals lumber more Maiasaurs. They are as calm as if there were nothing going on, though a few shake their heads and widen their stances when they emerge.

I know how they feel.

"You did this for all of them?"

"As many as could be gotten. Some needed different types of luring."

"How many did you bring? Tens of thousands?"

"More than that. Too many for the number to matter. The Earth has always been a planet rich in diversity of life. Some might say your planet possesses an embarrassment of riches when it comes to life-forms."

The Maiasaurs are back to doing what they were before, as if nothing had happened.

"Take me back to the planet. Back to the village. Can you?" I ask.

The move is so sudden that I almost fall off my bed. There's no pulling away or landing. I'm just back where I was before, sitting above a shop. The mother and child are walking away, the child's head hanging low and his wrinkled neck looking quite vulnerable to me.

I think I already know the answer, but I have to ask anyway. I need Hub to confirm for me what I think it meant me to see when it brought me here.

"Hub, if the beings here are our dinosaurs, why didn't you just stop the asteroid from hitting Earth in the first place? You could have left them to do this on their own, on Earth."

"Lysa, you know that answer. What killed the dinosaurs on Earth left space for all that came after they were gone. It left space for you."

"So, that's what you mean when you say you can't interfere. You can save life, but you can't change the course that a planet will take. You mean that you can save the life we have on Earth now, but you can't take away the chance for any life that comes after us. That's why you leave replacements, because you can't take away what might come next."

"That's correct."

"And that's why you can't talk to Earth and just tell them. Because it will change their course."

"That's also correct."

"And it's not working."

"Unfortunately, that's also correct."

A sudden fearful thought strikes me. I almost don't want to ask, because I'm terrified of the answer. But I wouldn't be me if I didn't ask, so I do. "You're going to stop the transfers, aren't you?"

The hub may be a machine, but I'd swear I hear sadness when it answers. "I might have no choice. It's possible that I'm doing more harm than can be allowed. My analysis indicates that I'm very close to changing the future permanently, and in significant ways. I may have already crossed that line. Humans are very difficult to predict."

"What will you do instead?"

"I will instead populate the new system with the transfers already made, but no more. It isn't ideal."

I've been curious about that. If the replacements are perfect, right down to their memories, why not just use them to populate the new planet. So, I ask.

The Hub's answer is strangely philosophic, as if it truly does understand the nuances of biological existence. "The replacements are suitable, but they lack one thing. They may remember youth, the experience of growing up, their lives and those they love, but they did not live them. They were not born on that planet. They are not original. It isn't the same."

"And that matters to you?" I ask.

"It does. It won't be the first time I've had to omit a species, but doing that means I've not achieved my purpose. When possible, I transfer. Currently, the transferred population is sufficient, but only just. It is unlikely that their course of advancement will continue unchanged."

My bowl is empty, and I set it on my lap, closing my eyes to do so, since I can be more certain about what I'm doing using touch. My lap is currently visually occupied by a sign swinging back and forth in a slight breeze above a shop door. Below my dangling feet a harried looking saurian wearing several strands of red beads and a green apron is hurrying into the shop.

But there's another reason to close my eyes. Everything is crashing in on me again. I'm overwhelmed *again*. But this time I'm conflicted.

This world I'm seeing has created in me a joyful feeling, a feeling so big it might burst out of my chest or make light shoot out of my fingers. The sensation is too difficult and complex to explain in any words I possess. One day, some creature I can't imagine might be sitting in a room like this and drinking soup, while watching the descendants of humanity with the same wonder I feel looking at the saurians.

Life, endless and enduring and new and unimaginable.

At the same time, I'm sad and fearful for humans, because if Hub stops the transfers, then all who don't have the opportunity to transfer will not be a part of that new and exciting future. They will live through the pain and death that will come when our world ends. And that will be the end for them. There will be no second chance.

My eyes are in danger of becoming permanently puffy with all the crying, but this isn't only sadness anymore and that makes it worth it.

"Did this help you, Lysa?" Hub asks.

I nod and the great weight of this knowledge lands on me like a ton of bricks. My bowl slides off my lap to the floor with a thump. I'm a non-transfer, but every thirteen minutes at least some people—maybe hundreds by now—are losing their chance at life. They are losing that chance for themselves and for everyone that comes after them.

They are missing this possibility of a new world where we can be better. A place where we can evolve and change and become more than we are, knowing we're safe and watched over by an artificial entity whose only purpose is to preserve life.

They are missing the galaxy.

I stand and look up into that strangely perfect sky of theirs, the blue tinged by yellow. "Hub, there has to be a better way. You have to make them understand. You have to save them even if they don't want to be saved."

Twenty-One

I'll be the first to admit that I'm not exactly a serious person. I'm frequently sarcastic, often flippant, and almost always ready to move away from deep topics to discuss TV or shoes or the latest music. There are exceptions, of course, because everyone has those few subjects that truly fascinate them. For me, my main such topic is art, which shouldn't surprise anyone.

There are others, though. My mom always says that teenagers are biologically programmed to be easily enchanted...and also to entirely forget what enchanted them just as quickly. Most of the time that saying found its way into conversations when I absolutely needed something to indulge in some new craze. While the saying is annoying, she's not entirely incorrect. A tower of boxes leans precariously in the back of my closet, each one filled with the debris of something I used to love.

A box of fabric and expensive doo-dads when I was into my fabric crafting phase. Another nearly bursts at the seams with old parts for a robot...or a slew of robotic things. I was convinced I was going to create the A.I. that would eventually take over the world. My mom said that hobby had earning potential at least, so she gave me minimal grief over it. There are more, because yeah, easily enchanted teen here.

Some of those passions of mine aren't wrapped in materials. Those aren't the ones I talk about, because I fear laughter or scorn or just the raised eyebrow she'd give me. She can do an eyebrow raise like no one I've ever seen. Also, it can be easily mislabeled or twisted to mean something else. It could have gotten me teased by people at school. The last thing I wanted was ancient-alien GIFs plastered all over my social media posts.

That special interest of mine is life. Not the act of living, but rather life in general. The concept of life and the way time changes it. Ancient life, future life, extinct life…all life. And I owe that fascination to my grandmother.

She died when I was ten, but I remember her well. After my grandfather died, she went back to India, but before she went, she spent time with my mom and me. She took me to the museum one day while my mom was at work, allowing me to play hooky and have a day with just the two of us. It was there, during that special day, that my fascination began.

My grandmother was an interesting person. She was a physicist, but also a devout Hindu. In her day, it was hard for a woman to achieve an advanced education, particularly if she started out poor. Her marriage to my grandfather—an American spending a year in India—

changed her life. For them, it was true love at first sight, and they were like honeymooners forever after, much to my mother's eternal embarrassment. Grandma never made discoveries or wrote important books, but she taught others and she found it very fulfilling.

I only knew she was a professor, and I was far too young to understand what physics was about. It was only as I grew that I understood how amazing she was, how smart she had to be. But it was her ability to marry physics with her religion that changed my life.

While we were walking along the hall of extinct life in the museum, I remember being sad because they were gone and I wanted to see them alive. I particularly remember the skeletons of a mammoth and a giant sloth. She sat me down on a nearby bench and told me the story of life, the magic of it. Not real magic, of course, but a miracle nonetheless. Comets with the chemicals that life could be made of, storms and heat, the sun and the forming earth, the way life may have risen more than once before it managed to get a firm hold.

And then she made it bigger.

She had me close my eyes and imagine endless planets and endless suns and on each one, the miracle happening in another way, each one creating something just as fantastic as a giant sloth, but different and totally unique. Then she said that each of those things gets their time, each one serves a purpose for all that will come after, and then it fades for the next thing to take its place. But even as it fades, it has changed life for all that will come after them. Our entire universe is one big chain of life, rising and falling and making changes to allow what comes next to exist.

Without the giant sloth, something today would not exist, maybe many things. Perhaps it changed the plants or the earth it trod upon, or the predators that lived there, or a thousand other things that we can never know. And for that change, we have something equally miraculous and wonderful, and *that* thing is changing its environment to prepare for the next miracle.

When I opened my eyes that day in the museum, I felt strange. It was like I had suddenly been connected to everything in a direct chain, each of us doing the work of our link for the other links in that chain. All across the universe, an endless series of links, all of us connected. She'd brushed my hair behind my ear and said that we must be grateful and honor all that came before. We must be thankful for the work they did to create what lives today. We shouldn't mourn for them, because they did their work, just as we are doing our work for the future.

She'd said that each thing that ever lived is present in some way inside every living thing today. The mammoth rests inside the mouse and the human, because it paved the way for us by existing.

In each thing that lives now, every past living thing is carried forward.

I remember every nuance of that moment. I remember the way her sari brushed against my leg, the rustle and scents of cotton, silk, and jasmine. I can hear the tinkle of her bangles and the way her nose ring sparkled under the can lights of the museum. I can still feel that strange connection between us, as if I weren't just her grand-daughter, but also a link in her chain.

I can feel it again. And now, I know it's true.

After my grandmother died—she was very sick during that visit, but didn't tell us—I told my mom how I'd felt after that talk. When we'd gotten up from the museum bench, I'd felt my footsteps, felt the way the building we were in had changed the land, the way the air inside pushed out of the doors and brought air from the outside in. It was almost uncomfortable, yet unforgettable.

My mother called it an epiphany of sorts, a moment of understanding. She said that grandmother was very good at creating those for others. The feeling faded, but my interest did not. The unique nature of every evolutionary step intrigued me, and like my grandmother, I believed from that day forward that life must exist everywhere.

I knew in my heart that the miracle wasn't limited to us, but was a force of nature that was ever-building and ever-changing. It would find a way in any place that left a sliver of space for it to take hold.

Perhaps that's why I didn't fear the portal invasion as much as most people. I think my grandmother would have jumped through a portal too. I inherited more than my dark hair and eyes from her, and I think that's why I jumped.

That feeling, that strange feeling of connection and magic and inevitability, happened again while I watched the dinosaur planet.

Epiphany. Eureka. *A-ha.*

Like that day in the museum, the feeling is uncomfortable and too much, but it leaves a permanent mark on my brain as if fades. I've got that mark now. Instead of just plain awe, which is in no way plain really, I've got an agitated feeling that demands action. Humans are missing their shot. Not all of them, of course, but many.

Hub explained to me that if it stops the transfers, it will only be ceasing human transfers. Transfer of animals will continue. The humans already transferred will act as our population on the new planet, but there really aren't enough of them yet. At least, not enough to start living as they did on Earth.

Once Hub left me alone, my mind kept churning things over, looking for a solution. But I'm a mere human and I can't compete with a mind that can keep track of thousands of planets and each planet's inhabitants simultaneously.

Because the Earth has not yet advanced enough to make indisputable contact with another planet's species, and has not found widely accepted proof of extraterrestrial life, the Hub cannot make contact.

I did argue with Hub that the portals were contact. It conceded that point, but also pointed out that more humans felt the portals were of religious origin than thought they were alien. On top of that, there are a significant number who believe the portals are from the future. The logic there is that contacting us with anything other than the portals can bring about paradox, which could be disastrous.

Unfortunately, that lends credence to the theory that the portals are from our future.

So yeah, Hub has a point. We're split on opinions back on Earth when it comes to the portals. And rules are rules…especially considering that the rule is there because it will absolutely change the course of the Earth's future. That is a no-no, which I can understand now that I've seen the dinosaur planet.

Of course, Hub has no answer when I challenge it that the portals are changing things already, except to say that's why it may have to stop. The obvious solution is the one that Hub simply cannot put into place: tell them what's happening.

The Hub can't, but maybe I can. If I can find a way out of here, a way home, then maybe…just maybe…I can.

After sleeping the whole day away in a funk of despair, I have my doubts about getting back to sleep. A hot shower does more than wash away my own stink. It also clears away a few of the cobwebs my confusion has spun. The clock says I have a couple of hours left before my wake-up call, so I put on some fresh pajamas and climb into bed, deciding I can at least think with my eyes closed and rest some.

I'm pretty sure that's my last thought before I fall right to sleep.

Twenty-Two

After eating so little yesterday, I wake up starving. I order a big breakfast, tame my hair—or at least make an attempt at it—and brush my teeth. I just took a shower a few hours ago, so I skip that and wait anxiously for the ding that means food.

When it comes, I yank open the door to find Jack rubbing his eyes on the hall floor, with the cabinet bot on the other side. He looks rumpled and for the first time, less than perfect.

"Did you sleep here?" I ask.

He yawns and stretches, then sniffs the air at the smell of my breakfast. "I told you I would be here if you needed me."

Stepping over him to the bot, I retrieve my overloaded tray and say, "Well, I didn't think you meant it literally."

He winces when he gets to his feet and follows me—or maybe the smell of my tray—inside. As I unload my tray, he rubs at his hip and the side of his leg.

"You okay?" I ask him.

He shakes his head a little and says, "That's incredibly uncomfortable, but I slept right through it. How is that possible?"

I shrug and sip my coffee, which is, as always, the perfect temperature. "That's humans for you."

"That really smells good. I'm hungry," he says. I'm pretty sure there's a hint in there somewhere.

"Yeah, but you're not supposed to eat this stuff yet, are you?" I ask. My tray is loaded with eggs, toast, butter, jam, oatmeal, and hash browns. I think the eggs and butter are fake, but they taste good, so I'm okay with fake.

Jack makes a face and walks over to my interface, quickly punching in something, then returning to plop down in my other chair. "I'm okay now. I was created from a template with an intolerance to some kinds of food. Gluten and tomatoes specifically. It's fixed now. I can eat anything."

I guess my notion of babies and formula was wrong. I should have guessed, since replacements don't have that problem, but then again, a replacement would already know what allergies or restrictions the original had. Either way, I'm glad he's fixed. I have to wonder though, does that mean he got a new body? Is this a replacement?

And what exactly is a template? Does that mean that he's wearing a body that belongs to a human somewhere on Earth?

Shaking my head, I dig into my eggs. "You want to eat some of mine while you wait?"

He's still staring at my food, so he wants to say yes, but I know he's going to say no. To stop him, I push my oatmeal over to him. He grins at me and takes the spoon.

The oatmeal is almost gone by the time the ding comes, but he hops up to answer the door like he's still starving. When he comes back, he has two trays and I laugh around a mouth full of hash browns covered in ketchup.

He has what I have, but more of everything. Basically, he's ordered everything I've ever ordered in my mornings here, plus other stuff. I point to a little pot of dark brown goo and ask, "What's that?"

"Some sort of chocolate and nut topping. It's for spreading on bread," he says as he digs his knife in.

When he says that, I know exactly what he's talking about. I love the stuff, but where did he find out about it? "How did you know to order that?"

He shrugs and says, "Some of the others have ordered it before, so I'm trying different stuff. Last night I ate a hamburger. It wasn't very good. I didn't like the texture."

Others. I'd forgotten there were other non-transfers here. It's weird that I haven't met or mingled with them. "I think all the meat is fake, so maybe that's why it didn't taste right. Also, can I meet the others?"

He gives me a pained look and keeps chewing, which makes me laugh. "Sorry. You can wait to answer. Between friends and family, sometimes people don't bother to wait, but I'm cool."

Jack swallows and drinks some of his milk, then says, "I don't see how you can talk and eat at the same time.

Really. I mean, how do you do it without dropping your food?"

"Practice," I say around my eggs.

His face screws up as he glances at my mouth. "That's not pretty."

I almost spew my food all over the table at that. Laughter and swallowing do not go well together. Jack may be newly human—or not human at all—but he's learning our humor quickly enough. Then again, I'm probably being species-ist again. If Jack's species is sentient, who's to say they don't have humor? A sense of humor might even be required, now that I think about it.

That thought makes me wonder once again what he was before he was human, but I really do think it might be considered rude to ask, particularly given the way he reacted before. And he didn't answer me about the other non-transfers.

"So, can I meet the other humans here?"

Putting his glass of milk down, he wipes away an adorable milk mustache and says, "Eventually, yes. After orientation, you can meet whoever you like. As long as they're also done with orientation, that is."

"What if I just go knock on their door?" I ask, quirking an eyebrow at him.

Based on his expression, I don't think he ever considered that before. "Why would you do that? I mean, why wouldn't you want to wait? What if that person is dangerous?"

"Dangerous?" I hadn't considered that. But that could happen too. After all, those who jump in are often profiled on the news as mentally unbalanced, or members of cults, or something equally awful.

"I think some are dangerous, yes."

"Wow," I say, not sure how else to respond. I hope that's not how those living here got their first impression of humans. That would be embarrassing. Then again, if they can fix me, do they get fixed too? I have to ask. "Do you correct what makes them dangerous?"

"Sometimes. If it can be corrected, that is. If the problem isn't genetic, chemical, or based on a physical injury, then there's really nothing more to be done. That's just who they are."

I remember a piece on the news shortly after the portal invasion began about an inmate in a prison. For some reason no one could figure out, there aren't very many portals in prisons. There are some, but not as many as one might expect if their appearance was truly random. A religious sect that believed it was the rapture used that as proof that they were right. There was an exception that was noteworthy enough to make the news.

A lifer in prison for murder jumped into a portal that came for another prisoner, leaving two versions of the original prisoner on our side. There was a lot of talk about whether the replacement should have to stay in prison. After all, even though he was the same person, he had not been convicted. And also, just like the original, he proclaimed he was innocent.

Now that I understand something about why people are transfers, I wonder. Was that man innocent and would have been shown to be so and therefore, gotten out and done something noteworthy? Maybe had kids?

And what about the murderer that came through? Should I ask about that? Do I want to know the answer? If I'm honest with myself, I really don't have time for that right now. I've got way too many other things to think about. Considering how amazing Hub is, I have little hope that I can figure out a way to get home that Hub hasn't already thought of.

Then again, Hub isn't human. Hub isn't alive at all. It doesn't know how to be as flawed as we are, and that might be to my advantage.

Brushing aside the topic, I do my best to sound convincing. "No problem. I won't purposefully meet anyone. Of course, if I'm in the hallway when one of them shows up then…"

Jack laughs and says, "You're the only one in this hallway, so that isn't likely."

So, they go to the trouble of creating an entire hallway just for one person, but make it seem like there are others by having more doors. Interesting.

"So, what's on tap for today? More films about the coolness of my planet?"

Jack burps and pushes his first plate away. The white surface is as clean as if there had never been food on it. One plate down, one to go. With an embarrassed smile, he says, "Excuse me."

"Better out than in," I say and he laughs. "Today?"

"No movies today. What we do today is for you to decide. Hub says you've got questions and need time to absorb what you know. So, I thought we might take it easy today and talk. Is that okay?"

"Actually, that sounds perfect to me. I have about a billion questions and I get mixed up and forget them with all the new information."

Jack looks dismayed and his chocolatey toast doesn't quite make it to his mouth. "A billion?"

With a snort, I get up to retrieve my notebook and pen. "Not literally." I wave the notebook and say, "Just however many I can write in this book."

That doesn't get rid of the look on his face, so I take pity on him. "I'm kidding! I do have a list, but it's doable. I promise."

With a sigh, he takes a huge bite and leaves two little chocolate smears shaped like horns on the corners of his mouth. I have to look down or laugh, so I flip pages in my book and start reading my questions, adding new ones as they come up. While I do that, Jack somehow manages to cram all that food down his throat. Now, he has two clean plates.

I'm amazed.

I didn't see him do it, so he must have used his connection to the hub to call the bot. When the pink light above my door comes on and the ping sounds, Jack gathers up our shamefully large number of plates and bowls and stacks them inside the bot for removal. When he returns to the table, he runs his hands over his belly and groans.

"Too much?" I ask, grinning.

"I think so. It was so good, I couldn't stop."

"And that is the reason we have an obesity problem on much of Earth. Our food is just too tasty."

He nods like that makes total sense to him, then eyes my notebook warily. I've managed to fill up a few more pages and now I've added numbers so that I can find related questions.

"Should I start?" I ask. He really does look uncomfortable. Not like when he got sick before, but uncomfortable all the same. He looks like I feel after Thanksgiving dinner, which gives me a thought. "We can go take a walk and I'll ask questions as we go. It will help our food digest."

That brightens him right up. "It will? Then by all means, let's walk."

I hop up and wave my hand in front of my chest of drawers to open it up. "Give me a second to change." At the look on his face, I laugh and say, "I promise I'll be quick."

When I return wearing yet another of the hilarious tees they have in the catalog, Jack cracks a smile. This time, my shirt is purple with kaleidoscope words that read, *It's the end of the world! Let's Party!* Yet again, I'm wearing jeans far too pricey for my budget and like the others, they look smashing on me.

My mother would say something embarrassing, probably using an awful retro word like bootylicious that would turn my face beet red. Even so, they *are* great jeans. Because I plan on doing plenty of sightseeing, I've opted for skater shoes much like Jack's, only mine are blue with sparkly stars all over them, another nod to my strange situation.

I might be a bipedal trash panda, but I look good.

"Are you ready now?" he asks, looking me up and down like he's trying to figure out what else will make me delay our outing.

I give him a look and walk toward the door instead of answering. When I open it, I say, "Are we going or are you going to sit there all day?"

Twenty-Three

We meander up and down the hallways off our part of the ring for the better part of an hour, me asking questions the whole time. Jack only seems surprised by a few of them, so I'm guessing most of us ask a lot of the same type of questions. That's okay by me, because I'm gathering every bit of this data in hopes of finding a way around the rules. Let him think I'm expressing only normal, average curiosity.

I mean, what else could anyone expect from an Earth human? Of course, I'm looking for loopholes and side exits.

We get to another of the million doors in this place, but this time the silver plate lights up with a warning for a different atmosphere.

"Who are the Titariki? And why is that sign telling me that in English?" I ask.

Jack leans against the wall and pushes on his belly, which is clearly still too full for his comfort, and says, "First, the Titariki are another species from another planet. They don't have an atmosphere that you or I could tolerate. That's why the door won't open. If I were suited, then I'd just communicate that in my head and it would open. As for the English, it knows what form I'm in and what language I'm speaking, so that's how it answers. It would do the same for you."

"What if you didn't have that thing in your head?"

He grins and says, "That would be a problem because the ID in our hands probably wouldn't connect through the kind of suit you'd have to wear to tolerate their atmosphere and pressure."

I screw my lips up and shake my head, which makes Jack laugh. "That's sort of a sneaky way to keep people like me out of places like that, isn't it? And couldn't you just make the little ID thingie stronger? That seems weirdly inefficient to me."

Pushing off from the wall, Jack takes my hand—which surprises me—and leads me away from the door back toward the ring. "Yes, I suppose it is, but generally speaking, most environments are pretty species specific. You don't think other planets have chairs and beds just like yours, do you? This wing has been fitted for your type of life-form. And also, humans are incredibly fragile when it comes to putting things like IDs inside their bodies. They can't be too powerful, or they cause problems."

I hold my hand up to the lights and marvel again that I somehow have an identification in my hand that can protect me from harm. Or keep me out of places I might want to go.

Jack squeezes my hand and says, "Anyway, I've got a better idea. I just cleared it, so we're going someplace very cool. You can see a species from an entirely different kind of planet. Would you like that?"

I'm pretty sure my eyebrows go up so high, they hit my hairline. "Are you kidding me? Yes!"

"You sure?" he asks, like he's daring me to do something very naughty.

The way he says it, particularly while holding my hand, definitely causes one of my faulty ovaries to explode. If I jumped on him, would that make me a wanton woman?

Shaking my head to clear the errant thoughts, I say, "Yes. Very sure. Lead on."

We don't go far, just to one of the creepy empty airport spaces in the ring. There's a barrier of sorts, then Jack stops.

"Is this it?" I ask.

"What? Oh, no. Sorry about that. I keep forgetting you don't know what I know. I wish you'd—"

Holding up a hand, I interrupt him with, "Don't even go there. I don't want to be a zombie."

He looks almost exasperated, which is a new one for me to see on his far-too-gorgeous face. "You know better, Lysa."

And I do. I realize the replacements are probably perfect. Yet, even Hub sees the difference if it thinks it preferable to put the originals on a new planet instead of replacements. Of course, that could be sentiment, but I find it hard to assign sentiment to a giant artificial entity.

Still, I'm not admitting anything. "Let's move on."

"Actually, we're going down and..." He pauses as he steps backward, his arm out and across my middle to keep me from going forward. "Here's our ride."

With a weird sucking noise, something that looks like a small subway car without windows rises out of an opening in the floor. A door folds open and Jack waves me inside with a smile. I'm not sure what to expect, but it looks human-friendly to me. No seats, but it has a regular floor and a rail along each side about the height of my shoulder. The ceiling inside is rather high, at least ten or twelve feet, which makes me feel short and small.

Jack grabs a rail and nods for me to do the same. The standard silver square lights up when he looks at it and he says, "Dock observation deck, please."

The please is a nice touch.

With a *whoosh* the doors fold shut and off we go. The acceleration is so steady that I'm not jerked about, but my other hand finds its way to the rail anyway. I can tell we're going fast.

"What's the dock?"

"I had this idea when I saw the picture you painted. You saw the Bluriani vessel from a distance—which is pretty amazing anyway—and I thought you might want to see it up close."

Now we're talking!

"*Uh*, yeah, I would. Holy freaking moly!" I forget the whole speed issue and let go of the rail to clap my hands and do an embarrassing little dance. Luckily, the look on Jack's face stops me before I get to the boogie stage of the happy dance. After wobbling a bit as the subway car adjusts, I get hold of the rail and clear my throat. More seriously, I say, "Yes, that would be lovely."

When I shake my hair back and give him a look I hope comes off as superior, he cracks up completely. Then we're both laughing. Neither of us can stop until I turn to face the wall. Even then, the splutters last for an inordinate length of time.

Finally, I notice that the top half of the car wall is really a screen. "Hey, can I look outside with this?" I ask, daring to glance over at Jack.

His face is still a little red from laughing, but he nods and points. "Just put your hand on it like a door. I mean, since you don't have an implant and all."

"Stop," I say, but rather than go over that again, I put my hand on the screen. It pulses a little, but that's all that happens. "It's not doing anything."

Jack joins me at my rail and says, "Okay, here's how it works. You aren't connected, but it's the same as if I were to turn off my implant for privacy—"

"Wait, you can turn it off?" I ask, because that's a huge deal.

"Of course, I can. Hub doesn't spy on us or anything. That would be rude."

I bark out a laugh, because he seems so sincere. Yet somehow, they have no idea how rude it is to toss people through portals. Go figure. Aliens.

Or maybe the problem is humans? No one else seems to have a problem.

"Forget about that for now. Show me," I say, waving at the screen.

The laughter is forgotten, and Jack is all business, his gaze carefully shifting to me and back, as if making sure I catch everything and fully understand what he says. He's very serious about his job, which is also adorable.

"So, when you put your hand on any control surface—the hand with the ID in it—the control surface then knows not just who you are, but your necessary environment, your language, your physical parameters, and basically everything else it needs to know to work with you in a way that's safe and comfortable for you. For example, it knows by my hand that I use what you call the visible spectrum to see, so that's what it will show."

"What if I don't use that?" I interrupt, because yeah, this is super interesting and brings up all kinds of possibilities.

He nods and goes silent for a second, then the control surface ripples. A series of tiny wavelets transfers across its surface. My immediate thought is that the pattern is like a pebble skipping across water, but that's pushed back by a sense of order in the ripples. A widening, then narrowing, a sort of pattern that isn't a pattern I recognize, but know anyway.

"What is that? I feel like I know it."

Jack smiles and there's a strange look in his eyes, like my saying that is in some way gratifying to him. "This is another type of language. If this cab were filled with water, then these ripples could be touched by the lifeform inside and they would ripple back. Here's another type."

The ripples disappear, and blocks of color replace them. They aren't square or round, but rather unevenly shaped in a long row across the surface. I know there must be colors I can't see, because some of them are simply gray. I touch one and the whole array shifts, then shifts more, flickering through colors so quickly I can't keep up. "And this?"

"This is also the language of an aquatic species. They communicate via light, biological light, of course."

I run my hand across the lights, frowning at how hard it is to follow. "It's so fast, so complicated."

He nods, and the lights go away, good old English words replacing them displaying the time left in transit. "When I called the car, it knew from my ID that I was human—at least at the moment—and sent a car configured for us. While in transit, the atmosphere was piped in to make it match what we need. The door wouldn't have opened if we weren't a proper match."

I'm starting to understand a little, but need to confirm it. "So, if a room is occupied by someone who needs a different environment than I do, the door won't open. If the room isn't occupied, but is still toxic to me, then it fixes the room before the door opens."

"Exactly! You're a quick study," he says.

With a shrug, I put my hand back to the control surface and it blinks. "Put up a view outside of this vehicle please. Just like a window would show me. Can you do that?"

"Yes." The answer is simple and the voice isn't the hub's either. The screens appear to become transparent. I know I'm only seeing an image, but it's very realistic.

Outside the car lays a wide expanse of tracks, almost like subway tracks, except narrow and very shiny. Vehicles of all shapes and sizes move rapidly along the lines. There must be twenty or more sets of tracks. Grand Central Station, only on a space station. Flat, open vehicles like truck beds carry equipment or parcels. Cars almost like ours move past with blank beige walls, their contents a mystery. Who might be inside? What do they look like?

A larger platform with a box of murky liquid zips past and I try to follow it, wondering what's inside.

"Who is that?" I ask, sure it's a who and not an it.

Jack looks as it disappears, then shrugs. "Not sure. Could be a bunch of different things really." He taps the screen to point out another bubble, this one filled with hazy, reddish fog. "That's a Mimic!"

I look, but all I see is the bubble, the fog, and what looks like rocks. "A Mimic?"

His eyes follow the bubble as it zips out of sight, then he grins. "That species can naturally form copies of other lifeforms on its planet, though limited ones. That's how they live, by being others. Almost their entire planet has a layer of stratum that's really the Mimic body. Every experience each Mimic has goes back to the whole. I guess what we just saw would really be part of *the* Mimic, but they're individuals when separated from the whole. Combined with Hub's replacement technology, they can now be any species in a truer sense. They're even better facilitators than my species."

"You sound like a fan."

His grin widens. "Absolutely. They're the ideal. Well, they're ideal except that they can't change form once they become biological. They get one life only."

Once more, my mind is entirely blown. A piece of rock in fog. So crazy. I can't think about it right now. Maybe later, but not now.

It strikes me that the light outside our car is slightly wrong, a bit dim and reddish. "Is there air outside this car? And why is the light like that?"

"No, there's no air you can breathe out there. That's important for you to understand. Just because the atmosphere is clear doesn't mean it's air. Always keep that in mind. Your atmosphere is highly specific. This is a sort of mechanical level. There are a bunch of them between the various levels of the ring. This is a transit line, of course. The atmosphere out there has pressure—as in not a vacuum—because there is a balance to be struck in the station, but the component gases are a mixture that keeps wear to a minimum. You couldn't survive out there without a suit."

I nod, marveling at how clear the air looks. It wouldn't have even occurred to me that it would be dangerous. I've got so much to learn. "And the light?"

"Ah, well there's more than meets the eye, so to speak. A lot of species use parts of what you call the visible spectrum, but vision as you know it isn't the same. There are a whole slew of different spectrums out there that are generally considered safe for most life forms. The car protects you from anything harmful and it wouldn't take you anyplace that it couldn't do that."

I keep hoping to see something alive, but there's nothing except vehicles, boxes, crates, and objects I can't fathom being transported. I'm disappointed, but also intrigued. Everything I do here is new to me, every single thing I see or hear or learn is absolutely new.

That's a lot of brain stimulation.

I reach out to touch the control pad again and Jack says, "You don't have to keep doing it. It knows you're here so just tell it what you want."

"How much longer…car?"

"Two minutes, four seconds."

"Is that the hub?" I ask Jack, because the voice is different.

He makes a face and says, "Not really, but yes and no." When I laugh, he shrugs and says, "It's hard to explain. The whole place is the hub, but stuff like this is handled at a lower level. When I contact the hub in my head, I get a higher level. Everything is *the* hub, but it's not necessarily Hub. Does that make sense?"

"Not really, but I'm cool with that."

The car slides to a halt and the view is broken by bright blue words. *Stand by for atmosphere.* Jack grabs my hand again and looks at the screen as if orienting himself. I can tell when he finds what he's looking for by the change in his expression. He grins at me and says, "Are you ready?"

I nod, but now that we're here, I'm not sure I am. What if the species we see is gross or disgusting? What if they look like monsters? Quite frankly, I'm getting a little afraid of what I might see.

The door folds open into a large chamber. The floor is that same flat grayish-beige, the walls almost the same color. "This way," he says, tugging my hand and leading me out of the car. The other side of the room, no longer hidden by the car once we're out and away from it, is made of glass or some other transparent material.

It's what I see beyond the glass that makes my feet unsteady and my body lose all coordination. I barely register that I've stopped, yanking Jack back in the process. I register almost nothing except the ship…the back-end of a giant spaceship on the other side of the glass.

Twenty-Four

This is a Bluriani vessel and it's a marvel. From my spot in the elevator that first day, the ship looked small. I'm getting a much better idea of how large the hub really is. The ship is huge, enormous beyond belief. I have a hard time even putting it into words. If I had to make a comparison, I'd say it was as long as two skyscrapers plucked out of the ground and then stuck together end to end.

I mean huge.

It doesn't look like skyscrapers though. It looks like exactly what it is; a space ship. The vessel is sleek, which might seem a strange descriptor for something so large, but it is. Sleek, curved, shiny…beautiful. Science fiction hasn't come close to describing the sheer beauty of a ship like this.

I want to hug it.

At first, I thought we were looking outside at it, but that's not the case. I can see now that there's another transparent wall beyond this one and that the ship is outside of that. That means the ship is even larger than my perspective here makes it seem, because there's a huge pier-like area between the wall I'm standing at and the one beyond.

Jack still has his arm around me, almost holding me up even though I don't really need it anymore. We're almost level with a long walkway that leads through the other glass wall to an enclosure stuck to the side of the ship. I can tell it's the door…or hatch if we use a proper boat term for it.

The ship itself stretches far above and below, making the elevated walkway look as small as a toy compared to the ship. The vessel is almost slotted into the dock, like a key in a keyhole. I can see the back end of the ship, all swoops and curves, with arrays that must be for the propulsion. Far below us is a work floor of sorts, which is also huge.

But then I see a cockroach enter this walkway from a side walkway that leads inside the hub somewhere further down.

"What the heck is that? Is that a freaking cockroach?" I ask, my disgust pretty evident.

Jack lets me go, stepping away from me. The look on his face says he's disappointed in me and I immediately feel bad. Clearly, that was not the correct reaction. I look again, but the bug-like creature is already far down the walkway. I can't make out more than a quick, black-ish blob.

"That's an intelligent and sentient being as complex as you or me," he says, an admonition in his tone.

I take a deep breath, because I have to think before I speak this time. I've offended him and more importantly, I've offended myself. I can't react like that. This galaxy is filled with things other than what I know. I must be ready to understand and accept them.

"I'm sorry. That was rude. My first impression is that it looked like a bug on Earth, one we're not generally fond of."

Jack purses his lips a little, but I see that flick of his eyes that happens when he asks Hub something, so I'm guessing he's looking up cockroaches. Almost immediately, he points down at the work floor far below and says, "There are more down there. Can you see them? Over there."

I press closer to the wall because the angle is bad, but I see them. They seem to be working at some huge machine. "They're workers or something?"

Jack shakes his head and grins. "Not like you probably think. They have a pretty unique system on their world. Like your planet, they have many levels of sentient beings, but only two technological species. Their whole system is based on order...as in perfect order. They like to keep things just so, and are incapable of remaining unoccupied. If they aren't resting or eating, they're doing something productive. Waste is unheard of on their planet and that made them of great interest.

"When their planet was aided, they were already space-faring. Because there were two worlds in their system with life, they had already accepted that life existed many places. So, for them it wasn't like your planet. Whole sections of their population wanted to join up, explore, and create order. For them it was like an amusement park full of interesting things to do. Some of them live and work here. What you're seeing isn't work for them. It's what they do for fun."

While Jack speaks, I watch the creatures. They're quick, and while I don't know exactly what they're doing, I can tell they're doing it with gusto even from here.

"They fix spaceships for fun?"

"Well, that and build new ones. There's another ship in the next dock over. Sometimes they take them apart and build them again simply because they don't think it's done well enough. They have an amazing ability to sense flaws in machines of all sorts."

He pauses and then touches my chin with his finger, bringing my gaze back to him. He wears a little smile that looks like a challenge when he says, "They also help to rebuild and redesign planets, to make them suitable for new life forms."

I understand what he's saying, and I feel horrible. "You mean, like the new Earth?"

He nods, that smile growing a little.

"They're building the world that will save mine?"

"It's more like adjusting, but yes. They're very good at it. It's something they enjoy a great deal and believe it or not, they're better at it than Hub is."

Two more of the creatures come out of another section onto the walkway, but this time they putter about. Jack cocks his head and almost immediately, they both freeze and make a motion that's surprisingly delightful.

To me, it looks like a hop or something. Both of them hurry down the walkway toward us. They turn off onto another walkway that runs a little closer to our window. As they get closer, I see them more clearly.

They do remind me of cockroaches or some other kind of flattish beetle in general form, but the resemblance ends there. They have armored bodies and appendages, but the differences are more numerous than the similarities. I wish I could see them better.

At the closest point of approach to our window, both creatures stop and make motions with long arms. Frilly looking appendages that might be antennae unfurl from around the place I would expect a head to be, then wave in a complicated pattern.

To my surprise, Jack laughs and goes silent. I know he must be communicating via Hub, but I have no idea what he's saying. There are more furling appendages, a few more hops, another laugh from Jack, and then he waves as they scurry away.

"What was that all about?" I ask.

He smiles at me and says, "I've done several stints as them in the past. It's very enjoyable. They were just telling me how ugly I was right now and asking when I was coming back to work."

My mouth drops open and I look back at the shrinking forms. I can hardly believe that this guy I've been pondering kissing since the moment I saw him used to look like that. Not only did he look like that, he enjoyed it.

I'm very conflicted at this point.

"Are you originally one of them?" I ask, hoping he'll say no.

He shakes his head. "No. They aren't well suited to facilitator work since they aren't exactly sensitive. Too blunt. They get annoyed by any communication that isn't direct and efficient. My people are perfect for this, on the other hand, since our entire society is based on emotions and communication."

All I can do is shake my head. This is all too weird. Just *way* too weird.

Waving my hand at the view, I try to choose my next words carefully, because I really don't want to offend anyone or seem species-ist. "Okay, here's the thing. We've always known that some kinds of life won't become advanced like us. Bugs are one of them. They don't have the brain structures needed. So how is that possible?"

Jack sighs and says, "They aren't bugs. They may have a superficial resemblance to something you call a bug, but the Kassa aren't bugs. That's what their species is called, the Kassa. They're something different. They could no more survive on your planet than you could on theirs. If we tried to go out there right now, we'd be destroyed by the atmosphere in minutes. Nothing about you is the same except your sentience and that both of your species are technological. That's it."

"So, what you're saying is, don't believe my eyes."

He grins and reaches out to touch my ear, "Or your ears or anything else. But most of all, don't compare things. I know it's hard, because I did the same thing, but any comparison you make won't be correct. Just accept."

"I'll try."

"That's good. You might not believe it, but when I first got here, I thought the Kassa were crippled."

"What?"

"It's true. I did. Because they speak with economy like they do, and my species is built entirely around communication, I couldn't understand how they might be called sentient. They were too different from me."

Before answering, I watch the work floor far below. The tiny figures seem so incredibly busy, but somehow eager as well. What Jack just said does make me feel a little better. It's good to know that I'm not the only one that can be shocked.

"Can I change the subject?" I ask. When he nods, I point at the ship and ask. "Who are the Bluriani?"

That seems to interest him because his eyes narrow and he looks at the ship too. "I wish I'd known them."

"You've never seen them? Or known of them?"

"No, and no one I know has seen them either. Or met them. Or talked to them. Or anything at all. Supposedly, they're no longer corporeal."

"Well, that's enticing."

He laughs and says, "No kidding."

"Can we go on the ship?" I ask, because really, that's what I most want to do.

"I wish," he says with a sigh. "I mean, I've worked on the ships in Kassa form before, so I know what parts of them are like, but I'd like to see them as a human. The ships work like the hub, in general terms anyway. They have control surfaces and I know they adjust atmosphere to allow the Kassa to work on them, but once they're functional, they're off limits. I think that's for safety. They get prepped once functional for whatever lifeform the crew will switch to for any specific mission. I think it's just a pain to switch it again for tours. We could go on one that isn't finished yet."

"Is that one functional?"

Jack pauses while he does his thing, then says, "Apparently, it is. I suppose we could camp right here and wait to see who goes past the wall into the ship. Then we could swap forms and take a tour, then hop off the ship before it takes off."

I actually consider living here for a long moment. Camp here or not? Best not, I think. I'm not ready for any form-swapping yet. I sigh as I look at that gorgeous spaceship, then wonder again about the Bluriani.

"What does Hub say when you ask about the Bluriani?"

"It says only that they're another species who are no longer corporeal and can't change form the way we do."

"That's it?"

He gives a little shrug and says, "Basically. I mean, there's information, but not what you're looking for."

What an unsatisfactory series of answers that is. Still, Jack accepts it. I guess I have to accept it as well. My stomach takes the opportunity to make itself known and growls. We've been standing here for a long while and despite breakfast, I'm more than ready for some food. Also, we're well past lunch time.

"Already?" Jack asks, surprised.

"Don't judge. I didn't eat my weight in food this morning."

With that, I reluctantly leave behind that beautiful ship and the mystery that is the Bluriani species.

Twenty-Five

"What do you know about sentience?" Jack asks, as we enjoy breakfast in my room before beginning yet another day of orientation.

I've been here over a week and I'm learning so much that I can almost forget how desperate I am to find a way home. Almost. For a few minutes at a time anyway. Each night I get some of that overwhelmed feeling out of my body by painting the evenings away.

It may seem callous, me being all comfy and painting while my mom is on Earth, not knowing what's become of me, but I'm truly not. At least a hundred times a day, my heart thumps an extra hard beat and I want to clench my fists in frustration. Every one of those hundred times, I push back those feelings, because I have to. I love her, miss her, and am so sorry that I've left her to deal with losing me that it almost turns me inside out. Still, I push it back. It won't help me return, so I can't dwell.

I think it might be a little like what my mom used to do when she was in the military. I don't remember how the topic came up, but I once asked her about deployments and how she could leave me for so long when I was little. She'd told me that when she had no choice but to do it, she just did it. It wasn't that she didn't miss me or anything like that, but she pushed it back. I specifically remember her saying that she saved thinking of me for those times when she had a couple of hours alone, because the rest of the time it would be dangerous.

I think what I'm doing is basically the same thing. I'm compensating by thinking of other things that won't bring me down, doing things that keep me calm. My method is working, because I wake up feeling much better each morning. Ready for the day, even.

I also wake up hungry. This space station is working like camping on my system. I'm super ready to eat when the times come for it. I've even stopped missing chicken and fish in my food.

Learning everything I can from Hub and Jack also helps. Information will move me forward, so I gather it like a squirrel gathers acorns. I'm not sure learning about sentience can help, but who knows, so I take Jack's question seriously. Swallowing down my cream of wheat and washing away the stickiness with a big gulp of fake milk before answering, I say, "I know that Earth supposedly has a whole lot of sentient species, but I'm still having some difficulty with how that's determined."

He nods, spreading yet more chocolate on his toast, which is already liberally coated. Today he ordered a bowl of strawberries and they look exactly like real strawberries to me. I have no clue how Hub gets this stuff, but it does.

"Well, it's complicated. Hub told me you were asking about it last night, so I thought I'd do what I can to clear it up. That okay?" he asks, putting down his knife to stick segments of strawberry into the thick coating on his toast.

His toast now looks really tasty and I'm tempted to snatch a piece. I mumble in the affirmative and consider asking for a delivery of my own. I really don't need it, though. It would be pure gluttony.

"Well, I think the problem lies in your definition, so let's clear that up. Sentience is not tied to technology or writing or anything else. You're mixing up sentience with the ability to reason or use technology, which to humans implies different states of being. The truth is much more complex and subtle, because how do you define reasoning? After all, a being that lives in water and doesn't have any concept of what it's like to be on land will reason things out very differently from those that live on land and can't conceive of life under the water. Out here, we define it very broadly. It's applied based on the conditions of each planet and individual environments a species might inhabit. Make sense?"

Strangely, it does make sense. I saw the list of sentient species from my planet that are being moved, or at least part of the list, and I was super surprised to see so many. The list was far longer than I could ever hope to read. The fact that every one of our food animals was on that list except fish and fish-like things completely freaked me out too. I mean…yuck.

It makes the whole no-chicken-on-the-menu situation easier to understand.

Even so, I need clarification. I ask, "What you're saying is if a non-transfer cow came over, it would get assigned a cow facilitator?"

He laughs, then says, "No, they would simply be returned. That almost never happens with Earth animals, though. The difference is that while the cow is sentient by our definition, because it has emotional drives, it cannot effectively change the course of life on your planet. It can't tell its story to your media, can't communicate the details to anyone else in a reasoned way, and can't harness technology to alter the way your planet operates in the future. It has limited understanding of unfamiliar environments.

"Look at it this way. You have primates on your planet that aren't just sentient, but also creatures who reason and use tools. They are—with a few crucial exceptions—no different from you, yet they would be unable to cause much change if they were returned. Even dolphins, a fascinating and incredibly intelligent species, could not communicate the details in a way that would create change. So, they would also be returned should they accidentally come through a portal. They're very curious creatures, so we've gotten a few errant dolphins."

As foreign as it is to think about animals in these terms, I totally get it. It's not only a matter of sentience, but also communication and the type of intelligence they possess, which would be peculiar to each species.

"Okay, I get it. I really do. A cow has the same rights I do because it's sentient, at least as you define it here, but since we're different in terms of communication, technology, and our specific type of intelligence, we're treated differently. Not better or worse, just differently."

"Exactly," he says with a grin.

"So, what happens when people start eating cows on the new Earth?"

That wipes the grin off his face and he looks down at his partially eaten toast with some sadness. "You aren't the only species that eats other sentient life, and no one would stop you or anything like that, but it's something I personally find quite hard to accept. Your planet is very dynamic, your day to day conditions very changeable. Your food web is complex and reflects those conditions. Most places aren't like that. The predation model is quite rare."

That makes me wonder all over again what he was originally. What did he eat? Was he an herbivore chomping on alien grass? Was he a smart plant that ate the sun's rays? His expression changes and I have this feeling he knows what I'm thinking. How does someone who isn't even truly human do that?

"What?" I ask.

"Aren't you going to ask me what I ate?"

"Did you guys put an implant in me while I was sleeping? Are you reading my mind or something?" I ask, feeling very exposed all the sudden.

"No, nothing like that. I already told you that my species' entire society is built on communication and emotions. We're very good at it. It makes us excellent facilitators. Plus, I've been doing this a long time, with many species before humans."

I'm not sure I believe him, but I really don't have a choice. So, I'll bite. "Well, what did you eat?"

"You'd call them plankton or maybe phytoplankton, but that's really not right because it's an entirely different biological system. That's about as precise as I can get using Earth examples."

This is as close as I've gotten to finding out what he was, and now I'm embarrassed because of the whole squid-people thing. I mean, if he ate tiny water plants, chances are he was aquatic.

I'm so rude.

"So, plants then?" I ask, veering away from any talk of squid.

"Sort of. They *are* plants in that they take energy from our sun, but they also have a fatty pocket under their bodies that they build up during the day. They use that fat for energy at night. They don't have brains. That fatty pocket is what probably allowed my species to evolve like we did. Mostly, we eat right after night falls when the pocket is fattest."

I try to imagine life like that and I can't without knowing what he looks like. I have this feeling that he's not yet ready to show me, which probably means he thinks I'll react like I did to the Kassa. I sure hope I don't. I really like Jack. I'm doing my best to think of him just as he is, because that's the form that makes me feel very warm and fuzzy when he's around.

Pushing my tray away, I ask, "Okay. Enough of that. What's on the docket for today?"

His gray-blue eyes are steady on me when he says, "I want to show you something."

"*Uh oh.* That sounds ominous," I mutter before I can stop myself. Does that mean he's going to show me what he is? I'm going to try and be very cool at this point. No matter what it is, I'm going to react with a smile.

He stuffs the last bit of his toast into his mouth and stacks the trays while he chews, making a face at me while he does it. The way he does it is far too cute for words. When his mouth is clear, he says, "No. It should help you understand how things work here."

I know where we're going before we get to the door. It's the medical room from before. I stop short in the hallway and say, "No. I'm not ready for that."

While I'm not certain, I think Jack rolls his eyes before he turns around. He has that set to his shoulders that screams eye-roll.

"Not for you. I promise."

My stomach is suddenly queasy, but I suck in a breath for courage and follow him to the door. The room is already set for us because we get that same Earth atmosphere notice and the door opens. Nothing looks different than before and there are no other people. I was sort of thinking it might be another non-transfer I could watch.

Instead, Jack walks over to one of the long tables and says, "Hub, will you talk for me?" With that, he whips off his shirt.

"What are you doing? Stop!" I squeal, even as he's reaching for the button on his jeans.

He smiles rather rakishly, then says, "Oh, sorry. Forgot about that. My people don't wear clothes. You can just turn around."

Hub breaks into our conversation and says, "Good morning, Lysa. Jack is going to undergo replacement, so you can view the process." The big transparent bubble over the table goes opaque in the middle, right about the place where Jack's privates will be when he lies down on the table. "That should make it more comfortable for you to watch."

Jack is still standing there, waiting for me to either turn around or say it's okay, but I saw something when he took off his shirt and it's bugging me. There was a pattern on his back. It looked dark gray, almost like a tattoo, whirls and swirls sweeping down the general area of his spine. "*Um*, Jack. What's that on your back?"

He walks over to me and turns around so I can see. "It's my trace." He looks over his shoulder at me and adds, "You can touch it if you want."

The way he says it and the grin he's wearing means he's teasing me again. Even worse, he knows it. I raise an eyebrow at him and that makes him laugh.

"Whatever," I mumble, but the thing on his back has my attention and I reach out to touch it. The pattern is slightly raised, but it feels like skin. I don't think this is a tattoo so much as something underneath his skin that shows through. It's beautiful, swirling out from a complex intertwined pattern running down his back.

"What's a trace?" I ask, running a fingertip along the pattern in the center.

"It's a compromise we make when changing bodies. It's so I don't forget everything I know from other bodies. The way you're put together and the methods by which you sense things are very different from the way I do in my original form. This lets me remember sensations and experiences that have no corollary in this body. It lets me remember what something felt like when I'm in a body that's incapable of feeling things the same way I felt them in a different body." He cranes his neck harder to see me better and asks, "Make sense?"

"It's beautiful," I say, because it is.

"Well, I like it. You ready?"

My fingertips feel different when I lift them away from his skin. I've never actually touched a guy on his bare back before. It's nice and my cheeks feel hot. I nod because that's pretty much all I can do.

He reaches for his waistband, so I turn around quick-like and try not to think about him taking off his clothes a few feet away. Whistling helps. I hear the bubble lifting and him sliding onto the gel-like surface, then there's a hiss of noise.

Hub says, "You can turn around now, Lysa."

I sort of peek through squinted eyes until I'm sure it's safe. He's under the bubble and grinning at me. The center is safely opaque, so I can't see the parts of him that would cause immediate death through embarrassment.

"Are you ready, Lysa?" Hub asks.

"No, but go ahead."

For a few seconds, I don't think anything is happening. I mean, I expected one of the other tables to start growing a new Jack or something, but nothing like that happens, so I look down at his face under the bubble. He's growing somehow indistinct or less substantial. It almost looks like he's disappearing, but getting bigger at the same time.

He's not moving, and I get the impression that he's frozen. He's about twice the volume he was when he went in and he looks strangely insubstantial. It's like someone took a picture of him and then put blank pixels in between each pixel of his image. This is weird.

"What's happening?"

"This is the first part of the procedure. Right now is when I would adjust his genetic information or correct problems. I don't need to do that, so we're simply pausing."

"Does he feel this?"

"No, there is a cessation of awareness when the procedure starts. As of this moment, Jack does not exist as an entity."

"So, you don't make a new one? You replace the old one by making the old one into the new one?"

"In this case, yes. If Jack were to need a new form, then he might require different material, or less material, or more. You understand?"

I bend close to the place where his head is and the notion of him being spread out is enhanced. It's too fine-scaled for me to see it, yet I do see the effect. "I get it.

So, when you make our replacements for Earth, you use entirely new material. That's why they're different to you, why they don't seem the same as the original person."

"Exactly so. At least initially."

"Listen, I'm glad to know this, but seeing him like this is freaking me out. Can you put him back together?"

Before I even finish my request, I can tell it's happening. There's a contraction in his form and he becomes more vivid, more concentrated. The change is obvious now that I've seen him the other way. Within a minute, he winks at me like nothing happened. When the bubble unseats with a hiss, I turn around again. The sound of his clothes sliding back onto his body is strangely intimate, but then again, I just saw him come apart, atom by atom. Or maybe it's molecule by molecule. What's more intimate than that?

"Was it weird?" he asks. "Oh, you can turn around now."

He's stuffing his feet into his shoes and grinning at me, his hair mussed from pulling on his shirt and in every way perfect. I'm not sure what comes over me, but I step close and ask, "Will you kiss me?"

For once I think I've stumped him. As in truly stumped. Not even Hub makes a sound, so it's possible I've stumped the station too. I hope so, because that would mean I can at least do something unpredictable.

"Now?" he asks.

He must see the way my face falls, because he grabs my arm when I try to back up. Being told no to a request like that is probably one of the most humiliating things that can happen. Before I can start apologizing, he leans down and presses his lips to mine. As in, just presses.

Like…what? This isn't a kiss so much as a weirdly uncomfortable breech in our personal space. This is not what I imagined.

I pull my face away and ask, "You know about dolphins, but not how to kiss?"

"Well, define kiss. I've got a full range here. I'm using the one most appropriate with your age group."

I snort a laugh and say, "Here, let me show you."

And I do.

Twenty-Six

So, yeah, I just did that. And he's surprisingly good at it. It's not like I'm a judge or anything, but I've kissed a couple of guys. I'm not twelve.

"Why did you want to do that?" he asks when I pull away. He looks a bit dazed and his cheeks have gone pink-ish.

Putting a hand to his chest and pushing him back a little, I suck in a deep breath and say, "Okay, Hub. I'm ready for my turn." To Jack, I say, "I wanted to do that while I'm still my original self."

He smiles and gives me some space. "No problem. I liked it."

Argh. I want to sink into the floor. Instead, I twirl a finger in the air. "Turn around. No peeking."

Getting undressed is almost as weird as him getting undressed. The bubble is already up, so I slide onto the cool surface of the bed and say, "Hub, you need to adjust that thing for privacy." The bubble adds a bit more opaque surface. As it lowers, the sensation of being trapped grips me. I barely manage not to squeal and push it away. Hub's voice sounds like it's coming from right next to my ear. "May Jack watch, Lysa?"

"*Uh*, yeah. Just don't show him any of my private parts."

"Of course not."

Jack turns around and walks over, smiling down at me through the bubble. I see his mouth move and can read the words, *It's okay*. I nod and try to smile back.

"Lysa, did you want an implant like Jack's?"

I consider that for a second, but the truth is that I want one. I want the freedom it offers and the information I can get from having it. And if working here is really a possibility, then I'll need one eventually.

"Yes. You're only going to correct my problem aside from that, right?"

"You should feel no different after the procedure until your next menstrual—"

"Stop! Okay, enough. I don't need you to explain that part. I figured that much. Just go on and do it before I chicken out…*um*…I mean, lose my nerve." I've got to start changing the way I speak now that I know chickens are sentient, as least sentient in the chicken way of being sentient.

For the briefest second, I feel really strange. The sensation is similar to what I felt when I went through the portal, that untethered feeling. Then, suddenly, Jack's face is closer to the bubble and he's grinning from ear to ear.

Is that it?

The bubble rises, and Jack turns around. "Did you do it?" I ask.

In my head, I hear the answer and let out a yelp of alarm. *The procedure is complete, Lysa.*

"Is that you, Hub? That is so weird!"

You can speak to me this way too.

Can you hear me, Hub?

I can. If you need to make contact, use this virtual interface.

An array of information pops up so suddenly that I step backward and bump into the bed. I see Jack make as if to turn, but he doesn't. All the information is overlaying the real room around me. I want it to go away. The input is too much. As soon as I think that, the overlay disappears.

"We can go over it later, if you like. Or Jack can," Hub says, using words I can hear with my ears. Thank goodness.

"Okay," I say, reaching for my clothes. As I put them on, I try to decide if I'm different. Do I feel different? No, other than the weird overlay thingie shaking me up, I feel the same. Even the scars on my legs are there.

When I'm dressed, and Jack is facing me again, he grins. "Well?"

I shrug and say, "I feel the same. But I'm fixed? Really?"

He nods. "And you can do this to fix an injury too. Let's say you break a leg or something. If you get into a medical bed, it will do the same, but put you back together the way you were before."

"That's super convenient."

"Shall we go? I can help you with your implant."

I'm still overwhelmed and stuck with the idea that I'm no longer the person who was born on Earth, not the person born from my mother. I'm not who I was. But, of course, I am. I'm made from the same material, but my genes are now different. I'm a new person, yet I'm me.

I think I understand how hurt and confused the replacements feel now. And my poor mom. The original and the replacement. What must she have thought in the moment before the gun went off?

Shaking my head to clear the gloomy thoughts, I say, "Yeah, let's do this."

*****

That night I split my time between painting and using my interface to answer my own questions. I'm amazed at what I can access. And getting answers like this is so much easier. It's like the answer is just there, right where I need it. Plus, I don't get only words. I get images, feelings, and sensations to go with it.

The implant is very addictive. I don't think these would be good for humans to have on a long-term basis. We'd spend all our time experiencing things from other perspectives. Because yeah, you can do that too.

Very weird, but exceptionally cool.

I finish up my initial color blocking on the view of the Bluriani ship and lean back to decide if I like my painting. I'm not very good at depicting reflective surfaces yet, but I kind of like where this picture is going. I've been painting so much that I my paint box is a hot mess of color splatters and there are squished tubes in the drawers.

Using my interface is still uncomfortable for me, but Jack managed to show me enough so that I can limit what shows. I can add more info as I get comfortable, but that sense of vertigo when everything I see is overlaid by an interface makes it too difficult for me to fully utilize yet. I've got a lump on my brand spanking new shin from bumping into a chair while trying to navigate my room with a full interface on. Jack thought that was funny until I offered to kick him in the shins to show him how it felt.

When I bring up the interface now, a nice diminutive little bit of info shows up in the corner of my vision where I can see it, but it doesn't cover my center field of view. Sending thoughts to ask questions isn't as easy as I might have imagined, but I want to practice, so I ping Hub.

Hub, can you tell me about the Bluriani? What's the big mystery?

I can, Lysa. What would you like to know?

First, are they here? If so, why hasn't anyone seen them? Why can't they change forms? And what does it mean to be non-corporeal anyway? Does that mean ghosts?

The Bluriani are here, but also not here, not in a form that would allow interaction to occur the way you and Jack interact.

Why do they have ships and no one else does?

Why do you think no one else has ships?

Hub's got me there. I just assumed, and we all know what that does. *Okay, if they aren't here, why do they have ships here?*

Do you bring all your possessions with you everywhere you go, Lysa?

Okay, Hub got me again and even more, I can feel that it knows it. I'm getting a distinctly smart-alecky gotcha vibe through my implant.

That might be the hardest part of getting used to the interface. Emotional nuance comes through. It's sort of like body language. In the same way I can hide body language if I try, I can refrain from conveying emotion via the interface, but it takes work.

It was super awkward with Jack while he was showing me how to use it, because I kept noticing his cuteness. Every single thought like that bled through to him, as if I'd spoken it aloud. But, yeah, I know Jack likes me the same way I like him now. Absolutely and without a doubt. I suppose that could be considered a bonus from having an implant. My emotions leak through, but the same goes for everyone else.

And right now, I know Hub is amused. It clearly doesn't have to work to use the implant, which means it wants me to know it's amused. And I want to be serious, so I make no effort to suppress that emotion.

Alright, Lysa. I'll answer if I can. The Bluriani ships can be configured for almost any species. Even aquatic species require only minimal modifications, though there are no space-faring aquatic species in our galaxy. They are exceptional vessels and we have a sufficient number for any need that might arise.

Do you control the ships, Hub? I mean, do you take them places?

No, Lysa. Once a crew boards, I have no further control. The ships have nothing more than their regular command and control systems. While those systems are much like me in many ways, they're a lower-level version of me, yet also entirely independent. I do not control the ships in the way you might be thinking.

Why aren't we allowed to go in one? I mean, you control that.

Lysa, I do not control it in the way you think. My interference is related to safety. I do not interfere in free will. That is not my purpose. A docked ship can be a hazard to those around it. If you were to enter and initiate ship activity, even by accident, you might harm anyone working within the dock area. Such activities require coordination for the safety of others. Coordination is not the same as control.

I think I understand what Hub is saying. This is probably no different than a ship docked at a pier on Earth. If you have divers cleaning the bottom, you don't start the engines. It makes sense.

When I first got here, I saw one go through a portal. Do you create their portals, or do they do that themselves?

The ships are fully capable of creating portals. I do not control the ships in any way once they undock.

Hub, can I see an image of the Bluriani? I mean, if they have portal capability, they're way more advanced than any of the others here, aren't they? I'm curious to see such an advanced species. Also, did the Bluriani have portal technology before you met them? Or did you give that to them?

For the first time, I sense hesitation in Hub and I can't imagine why. Is it checking with yet another higher form of machine than itself? Or is Hub checking with the Bluriani for permission?

Lysa, I'll tell you what I can. The Bluriani are the oldest sentient life form I am familiar with. Long before we transferred the dinosaurs from your planet, the Bluriani were already almost a memory. They were capable of spaceflight before I existed, yet their limitations were profound. Like you, they originated on a planet that was dynamic, volatile, conducive to the development of life, but hard on the life that developed. In many ways, humans remind me of the Bluriani, though many other species do as well. And no, portal technology was developed long after I came into existence, but I did not receive that technology from them. It was developed jointly, though that is a difficult concept to convey and be truly accurate.

There's a certain sadness threaded through Hub's communication. A sense of longing, perhaps even pain. Hub is artificial, but all that I've learned tells me that Hub is emotional. And now, I can feel it through the implant. And it doesn't escape me that Hub is using past tense either.

And an image of them? Is that possible, Hub?

Again, there's a slight pause. *Lysa, there is no image that would properly depict the Bluriani as they are now.*

What about an image from before they couldn't be imaged? Were they ever like that?

Yes, Lysa. They were once very like you. Because you're curious, here is an image.

What populates my view reminds me of the way I saw the dinosaur planet, but even more realistic and vivid. Before the implant, I viewed the dinosaur planet with my eyes, though it felt immersive enough even then. Now,

I'm there, totally and utterly there. The experience is so strange that it takes my breath away.

In the background is some sort of city. I'm sure of that much. Viewed from the perspective a little above the creatures being shown, it feels like I'm floating a few feet off the ground. I hardly know how to describe the creatures, and my brain races to place familiar names to the unfamiliar.

There are three individuals, two large and one very small, perhaps no bigger than a five-year-old child, though it's hard to be sure if my scale is correct. The anatomy of the creatures is profoundly different, yet they're clearly bilaterally symmetrical—a term I've learned to describe beings made up of mirror image halves, like humans and Earth life in general. They have limbs, but if I had to describe the impression of their body structure, I would say they were like kangaroos standing on hind legs in form, though their body texture is different.

Behind each of them are two tails, long and strong looking. From the narrow shoulders, two horn-like protrusions appear to curve out and down their backs, though I can't see how far. Their arms are long and slender, necks not really necks at all, and their heads are so strange that I can't decide if head is the correct word. I think it is though. I think the ridge that bisects the top and bottom halves of their heads borders eyes of a sort I could never have imagined. The eyes—if that's what they are—are long and narrow ovals that would extend from the side of my nose to my ear if they were put into my head. They're shiny and dark, but I see striations of color along the top and bottom as the creatures in the image move.

One of the larger creatures picks up the small one and deftly plops it over its shoulder so that the little one slides between the two horns on its back. The little one's long, slender fingers grip the horns, but that's all I can see of the small one anymore.

The two large ones stand close together and even though I don't see anything that specifically conveys emotion, there's something in the tilt of their bodies that speaks of family, of a bond as strong as any human one. It's possible I'm getting that from Hub, but that's the sense I get.

The large one with the child turns around, putting its back to me. It folds both arms up by its head, as if shielding those long eyes to look at something bright in the distance, something out of my view. The child—because I'm sure that's the creature's child—peers out from a pouch on the larger creature's back. It has both hands on the horns that seem to protect the pouch, curving over it in a way that's perfect for the burden nestled there.

The other large one turns now too, standing even closer to the other than before, their bodies touching. The large legs fold and the impression of a kangaroo is reinforced in the way that happens. The strong tails appear armored and splay behind it for support. That one has shorter horns and I see no evidence of a pouch on its back.

The brightness increases suddenly and then, the image is gone. I'm jolted back to the reality of my room, the strange planet gone.

I suck in a deep breath, my mind racing. I hardly know what to say. *Those were Bluriani?*

As they were, yes.

Again, that thread of sadness and longing is present in Hub's communications. I'm not sure, but my gut is telling me that there's more here, more to know. There is loss and somehow, that loss is personal to Hub.

And I have to wonder; how can a space station experience personal loss? I aim to find out.

Twenty-Seven

Over the next week, I try not to count the number of people who have lost their chance at transfer. I try not to count the numbers of replacements that have probably died. If I didn't push that out of my mind, then I wouldn't be able to focus on figuring out a way to fix it.

I'm here for a reason. I know it like I know my name, and that I miss my mother so much that it hurts. Here for a reason or not, I have to play along while I search for answers. I have to act like I'm not up to anything against the rules.

Hub and Jack have conveyed that I can have a job here, just like other suitable non-transfers. And there are a whole lot of very cool jobs. I'll admit I was surprised to learn that there are two other planets being transferred right now. Again, I had the idea that Earth was special, but apparently when there are millions of planets with life—and I'm still not cleared to know the exact number yet—in just our little, unremarkable galaxy, there will always be catastrophes happening.

Of the two others going on now, one is for non-intelligent life…at least as I would define it. That would be sort of like our dinosaurs, I suppose. One is for intelligent, but non-technological life. My current offer is to act as transfer agent, which is what Rosa was doing when I came over. I can also apprentice for the planet with intelligent life, but that would be in the control rooms rather than interacting with them. Facilitation takes a long while to train for.

But that's not even close to the end of my possibilities. I can be a Ranger, which Hub insists on calling by the totally unromantic label of Monitor. They go out and check in on planets, drop off drones, and conduct surveys. I sort of had this idea of Hub as almost omniscient. After all, it was able to personally assess every person on Earth.

It turns out that modeling a planet is very different than modeling and monitoring a whole galaxy. Hub can only process what it knows, so ships perform scans and take closer readings all the time.

I admit, being a Rangers sounds like more fun than I'm able to resist. The downside is that the crew of each ship has to be compatible in form. I wouldn't likely be able to stay human if I joined a crew after finishing orientation and training. That makes me feel weird, because at this point, I've seen a few other species and none of them are particularly attractive from my point of view.

As another bonus, I'm now effectively immortal. That's right, immortal. Forevermore I can be replicated to any age I've reached. So, if I stay as I am until I'm thirty, I can be replicated to be anything between the age I was during my first replication to that age. Hub says that it's rare to stay in the same body for that length of time, so I shouldn't rush deciding what I want to do. Of course, I can always change back and let my human form age any time I want, so it's not like I only get one shot.

What that means is that I can have *all* the jobs given enough time. Cool factor; exceedingly high.

That did bring up the question of Jack's age. I was really surprised by the answer. Jack's species lives only the equivalent of fifteen to sixteen Earth years, which is four years on their planet.

A measly four years of life.

Jack had only just passed his first year of life and was still shy of adulthood when he came over. Even weirder, that was three-hundred and fourteen Earth years ago. What this means is that I get a double dose of weird. Namely, I have to deal with the notion that my boyfriend—and I think he might be becoming that—is a one-year old baby, but also a very old man with a teen girlfriend.

Yeah, try putting all that together in your head. Not easy.

He laughed so hard I thought he might pee himself when I told him the problem. Then he did his best to explain why that didn't matter, but there's still that slightly weird feeling. I'm dealing, though.

Kissing helps.

Today I'm back to being very nervous, sort of like I was at the beginning. Jack can tell, and after he picks me up for our trip today, his fingers twine with mine for support.

"Are you sure you want to?" he asks.

Nodding with as much certainty as I can, I say, "Yes. I need to see it for myself."

He shrugs as we turn toward the now-familiar elevator leading to the module for Earth transfers. "Okay, but there's not much to see. It happens faster than we can follow."

The countdown for the elevator starts and it's like déjà vu, only backwards. "Hub said it will slow the process, so I can see it."

Jack's eyebrows rise, and he looks at me with a strange expression. "It will? Wow."

"Is that odd?" I ask.

The elevator dings and we enter, the familiar silver control surface no longer the overlooked mystery it was when I first got here. Both Jack and I communicate our destination, then grin at each other when the commands bleed through to the other. My command was less precise than Jack's and the poor elevator has to clear up the muddle.

Once we're moving, I wait for the view. Jack answers my earlier question while we ride. "It's not odd, but I never got such an offer. Of course, I didn't ask for it either."

The galaxy comes into view and as always, I hold my breath at it. The station is so very large, the stars so very bright. The sight is overwhelming, but I can't look away. "That will never get old," I whisper.

Jack seems as enthralled as I am. He takes my hand again, then says, "Never. And to think, I'd never seen the sky or the stars before I came here."

That surprises me enough to make me look away. "Never?"

He shakes his head and catches that last look outside before the elevator shaft erases the view. Then he smiles at me. "Everyone is different, right? My kind of vision wouldn't have let me see this even if I had been able to look at it."

More mystery. *Sheesh.*

We step out when the elevator pings, and I ask, "Which color?"

Bumping my shoulder with his, Jack seems proud of me when he says, "You're really getting this!"

It turns out the color is one I don't even have a proper name for; somewhere between red-violet and full violet. Maybe violet-with-red-hints? Is that a proper color name?

The room we've been assigned is exactly like the one I came through. Goosebumps rise on my arms at the memory. Rosa smiles like she's seeing a long-lost friend when the door slides open.

Holding out her arms, she exclaims, "Oh! Lysa, you look so well!"

It feels so nice to hug her that tears sting my eyes. I barely know her, but she's so like a kind grandmother that her hug is like a balm spread onto scraped skin. I've spoken to her many times over the communications and interface, but I've not seen her since my first day here.

"Can I say that I've missed you?" I ask, not letting go even to wipe my eyes. She smells like flowers and happiness.

She laughs and breaks the hug to look at me. "Of course, you can. I've missed you too, but I've been so happy to see your progress. I'm very glad you're here." She's interrupted by a soft ping and a pink light that flashes three times. "Almost time. Stand over here with me."

We do as she says and stand almost at the same spot I saw her when I came through. That feeling of déjà vu rises again. I feel shivery, a lingering memory of the nausea causing my stomach to roll a little.

From another door that I didn't know was a door strides a man. He seems blank, not looking at us or even registering that we're here. He walks almost mechanically toward the center of the room, then stops to stand there like a lump.

"That's the replacement?" I ask, though I know it is. I just didn't realize they came from this room. I had this notion that they went through someplace else.

Rosa nods and says, "Yes. He's in a sort of non-aware state right now. That blocks memory formation, which is very important."

The portal pops into existence so suddenly that I jump. It seems large in this room, larger even than it was in my living room on Earth. The man doesn't so much as flinch when it appears three feet in front of him. Almost immediately, he steps through and disappears from sight.

"Now the transfer portal," Rosa says.

Another portal opens right in front of the first, a sinuous ring of pink and purple light joining the two portals together. Then we wait for what happens next.

I jump again when Hub says, "I'm adjusting the portal for you, Lysa. That will let you see the transfer. Rosa will let you know when you can approach."

As if to reinforce that I should wait, Rosa reaches out to grip my arm. Her touch is gentle, but still a reminder that I should stay put. A strange vibrating sensation runs through me, and Rosa stiffens next to me. Suddenly, where there was nothing except portals, there is something more. There is a person.

Rosa lets go of my arm and says, "You can look now Lysa, but not too long. This is using a great deal of energy."

That breaks me free and I take a few steps closer to the portal. The gap is very narrow, maybe an inch, but in that inch I see the palm of a hand raised up in defense, a hint of patterned clothing, the bend of a knee. The clothes I glimpse are the same as those the replacement was wearing.

"Can I go behind it?" I ask Rosa.

She nods, but adds, "Do hurry."

She wouldn't say that if it weren't important, so I do as she says and quick-step behind the portal. I can see the person perfectly now. It's the same man, his knees a little bent and his hands up in front of him. His eyes are squeezed shut and his mouth open in fear.

This is a terrible thing to see. Terrible. He's frozen, while I gawp at him like a tourist.

I run back to Rosa, shouting, "Let him go through!"

Just like that, he and his portals are gone and the sensation of something being sucked out of the room goes with it.

"Is he safe? Did he make it?" I ask, my hands clenched together at my waist. My stomach actually hurts now.

Rosa's eyes lose focus for the briefest of seconds, then she says, "Another safe arrival! All is well."

I let out a hard breath, so relieved to hear good news. But I know the situation isn't that simple. Right now, he's probably puking his guts out and so afraid that he can't see straight. I'm still not permitted to see what happens on New Earth…perhaps I never will be allowed to. All I can do is hope there are people there to tell him everything is okay and to make sure it really is alright.

Also, I feel happy that whoever that man is, he will now have the chance so many have missed. I hope it wasn't too awful when he saw his replacement.

Rosa and Jack chat, doing their best to include me, but I'm only partially present. I have to struggle to keep up with the conversation. The alarm bells in my head are still screaming that there must be a better way. There has to be a better method that doesn't cause so much paralyzing or violence-inducing fear. Or religious fanaticism. Or any of the hundred other crazy things that are happening on my planet.

Suddenly, an idea comes to me like a flash of lightning. I switch on my implant so I can think-speak without making the others listen to the conversation.

Hub, can't you send another replacement for my mom? If I put some sort of sign or something on it, she'll know it's okay.

No, Lysa. While it might be possible to send a second replacement, I cannot let you interfere with the process. That would be like my interfering in the process, which is not permitted. I cannot influence the planet more than I already have. You know this.

But I'll be doing it. You won't.

Lysa, you have told me, which means that if I permit it, it will be me interfering.

I shouldn't have told you.

Perhaps. If you hadn't told me, then it would have been an exercise of your free will that did not involve me. Nevertheless, I would have known you altered the replacement and I would have had to stop the transfer.

So, there's no way for me to get past you with the transfers.

I fear not. Free will is yours, but my processes are my responsibility. I cannot be involved or facilitate such an exercise.

Jack and Rosa are looking at me, Jack with a confused expression. They can't hear me, I don't think, but my frustration must be evident on my face. I hold up a hand for patience.

Okay, Hub. Thank you for letting me see this.

You're very welcome, Lysa. And try not to be upset. All things will happen as they will.

The change in my mood must be evident, because Jack and Rosa are far more subdued when I'm done talking to Hub. She hugs me more gently, with a compassion I can feel through her touch. I think my grandmother would have liked Rosa a great deal. My mom too. My mom would be grateful that she's been so kind to me.

That thought almost undoes me. I blink back tears with only a modicum of success.

Jack leads me back to my room, letting me wallow in my sadness without asking any questions. He seems to know that I need space and simply hugs me, his warm lips at my temple when he whispers, "I'm here if you need me."

It takes me a moment to answer, because I feel so incredibly useless, so unable to help. I'm out here laughing and having fun and finding a boyfriend, while millions of people live in fear, or lose their chance at life on a new world made especially for them. Eventually, I get words past the lump in my throat and say, "I know you are. I just wish I could be there for them."

He knows who I mean. I mean Earth and all the humans left there with a timer ticking down to their doom.

Twenty-Eight

I'm not sure how the idea comes to me or what bits of information come together to make me think it. The idea comes to me as I'm painting the Bluriani people as I saw them in that short series of images.

Maybe it was the Hub's emphasis on free will. Maybe it was the way Hub conveyed sadness when it communicated about them. Or perhaps it was the sense of loss and longing I felt emanating from Hub. Whatever it was, the notion hits me like a ton of bricks and I drop my paintbrush, leaving a splatter of color on my jeans.

Hub couldn't save the Bluriani, or maybe it couldn't save all of them.

It said that portal technology came after the Bluriani, which means Hub would have had to help them by physically moving them. The ships. Is that why there are so many now? Just in case?

Before I can think the better of it, I turn on my implant. *Hub, I have some questions and I need to talk to you about something. It's really important to me.*

Of course, Lysa. You can talk to me whenever you like.

I'm not sure how to approach this topic. I mean, Hub is a machine, but it also clearly has feelings. I don't want to make it sad or depressed or remind it of failure. I also want to know. I think I might even need to know.

Hub, I don't want to be rude and I don't want to upset you, but this is really bugging me. And I think I understand a little bit better why you're like you are if I'm right. It's about the Bluriani.

Again, I feel a hint of something, a faint echo of melancholy. *Go ahead, Lysa. If I can answer you, I will.*

With a deep breath, I decide the only thing to do is jump in with both of my big, awkward, left feet.

You couldn't save the Bluriani, could you? Or not all of them. Did something happen with them that made you have this rule that you wouldn't interfere? Did something bad happen?

The wash of sadness is stronger, much stronger than I've ever felt from Hub. This isn't my sadness, but I can sense it. It's like seeing someone else cry, except far more intimate.

That is essentially correct, Lysa.

What an unsatisfactory answer that is. I hold that feeling in as best I can, because it's not nice considering what the Hub is feeling. *Can you tell me more, Hub?*

Instead of words, I see another planet. This is like seeing the dinosaur planet, except not. This is a replay and it's happening in my head, transporting me there as completely as if I had stepped through a portal. The image reminds me of what it was like to see the snippet of the Bluriani family. The sensation is intense.

There is wind, the dust blown by that wind stinging my skin and rippling my clothes. I can feel it. There are tall buildings in the distance that look like they're made of glass. Where I'm standing, plants bend and fray under the power of that harsh, destructive wind. They don't look like any plants on Earth, but I know that's what they are.

The Bluriani were space-faring, but also very tied to their planet. Successful alteration of another planet for their use was not yet within their reach. They were explorers in space, but tentative ones. They had harnessed the ability to mine another planet for materials, but did not yet have the capability to live beyond their world in large numbers.

Hub's mental voice is calm and carries hints of sadness, but it's not overwhelmingly emotional either. It's a strange juxtaposition and it makes me feel strange. My view begins to shift. It feels like I'm skimming the surface toward the city, which grows in size and height with each passing moment.

They were advanced in many ways, but not enough to save themselves. They were aware that calamity was approaching, yet they could not stop it, nor could they evacuate all their people. For many years they worked to save themselves. In the end, they were left with few options.

Their best hope was the most difficult option for them to accept. They could change a living being into information, but they did not have the ability to return that being to a physical form. Time was running out, but many remained in denial, not believing that their planet could meet its end in such a pointless way.

We pass through the city with startling speed, the beings like those Hub showed me before passing in flashes almost too fast to register. The taller buildings are coming to an end, and in the distance, I see a complex larger than anything else. The building is vast, so wide and big that it seems short in comparison, though it isn't.

Around that complex are Bluriani, long lines of them outside openings all around the central building. There must be thousands of them, tens of thousands.

Many chose to take the chance that they would find the solution to re-animation in the future. With so many minds to work on the solution, they reasoned that they must find an answer. And time would not matter once they were uploaded. Only existence mattered.

With a sudden jolt of motion, we pass through the walls of the giant complex and hover over the thousands of people that fill the spaces. An enclosure inside the building looms before us, light glowing through the glass-domed roof into the cavernous space.

We dip through that roof and what I see is terrible. I may be here in my mind with Hub, but with my real ears, I hear the sound I make. Shock, horror, fear.

The process of imaging each being destroyed that being's physical form. They did not limit their attempts to save their planet only to themselves. All life that that could be imaged was imaged. They understood that when the day came that they learned how to re-animate, they would need all that lived on their planet once again.

The process Hub is describing is going on beneath my feet in at least a thousand rooms inside that enclosure. I'm glad we're above it, because I don't think I could bear being closer. In one of the rooms, a Bluriani hurries to a table, lies down, and then dozens of instruments plunge into its body with no delay. I don't need to understand their physiology or their expressions to understand the pain. The body clenches, limbs going rigid in agony. Then the figure simply disintegrates and is gone.

Before I can do more than blink, the next Bluriani hurries in to take its place on the table.

And this procedure isn't limited to the Bluriani. There are creatures I can barely describe being herded into rooms, carried in, forced in. I'm glad I can't hear them.

And there are children too. I wish I could close my eyes.

But you said not all of them went, Hub. What happened to those that didn't upload?

Our perspective shifts and instead of the facility, we're in that field again. Only now this isn't a field. It has become a dusty plain with the skeletal remains of plants hanging on in a few spots. And there is that same couple with the child.

Only this time, I see the brightness with them. At the last moment, the one that wasn't crouched does so. They lean their heads together and I know that *they* know their end is at hand.

And then they are gone. A wall of dust so thick it's almost solid hits them, and they disappear into that devastating wind. For a flash I see the darker shadows of their forms taking flight in the dust, then they're hidden from my view. Hub takes pity on me and we rise over the landscape until I see the curve of the planet. Fire and dust cover it in a crawling wave of destruction.

Why did they stay? They had to know.

Free will, Lysa. Always there is free will. It was their choice to make.

What happened to the Bluriani that uploaded, Hub? I'm asking, but deep in my heart, I think I already know that answer. The possibility that what I think is true shreds my heart into tatters.

They worked to find their solution from the safety of a space station, their minds mingling in the confines of a vast computer. But time did not leave them untouched. As they grew and orbited their destroyed planet in that station, individual minds began to dissipate into the whole. Eventually, there were no more single minds. They became one. Their solutions came too late for them to return to a physical form. Their individuality was lost.

The image disappears and I'm back in my room and in my body. I can feel my chest shaking and hot tears on my cold cheeks. I understand now. I understand why. The sheer magnitude of what must have happened is like an earthquake in my soul. And I understand one more thing, one more terrible and wonderful thing.

Hub, you are the Bluriani, aren't you? You're all of them, combined together into one being.

Yes, Lysa. I am the Bluriani and all that lived on our planet. I am one, but also all. And it is my purpose to ensure this never happens to another planet if I can stop it. Life, above all, is my purpose.

Twenty-Nine

That's the key to all of this. Free will. The ability to choose and Hub's inability to influence any choice we make.

That's my out, my path, the way I'm going to find my way home and help my planet. Hub can't, but Hub can't choose for me. It can only interfere with my choices when those choices require *it* to make a choice that conflicts with its directives. That's complex and convoluted to say, but incredibly straight-forward in practice.

This is exactly like my request to hang a sign on a new replacement for my mother. Hub wouldn't stop me from hanging the sign, because to do so would be my free will and I can do that if I like. But once I do, Hub will be faced with choosing whether or not to send the replacement. Since I would have altered the replacement, it wouldn't, because that would break the rules it imposes on itself. I will have triggered Hub's need to choose.

I must simply do what I choose to do without requiring Hub to engage in any part of that process.

And I know how I might do that now. But I must proceed carefully. *Very* carefully. If I slip up, or in any way relay to Hub any part of what I intend to do, I will automatically trigger Hub's requirement to choose.

My first action is to entirely shut down my implant. Jack is surprised, then irritated, when he can't reach me that way anymore, but I can't take any risks. I tell him it's too disorienting for me and that concerns him, but he tries to be understanding. He does tell me that it will make work impossible for me, so I should at least try to get used to it.

While I do promise him that I'll try, I don't dare do more than use the control interfaces. I can't risk communicating the wrong thing. I wish I could tell Jack, but I can't. He shares so much that he would let Hub know, even if he didn't want to. I don't even know if he can lie.

Rather than hurry, I make my plans with caution and much thought. I need to have a plan, a backup plan, and backups around any part of those plans that might go haywire.

I will get exactly one shot at this.

After another ten days of normal behavior, which I can only hope appear normal, I decide enough time has passed to risk moving on the next part of my plan.

"Hub, I'm really thinking of the Ranger job," I say. I'm in my room after another day of orientation is over.

I've carefully created a partial painting that I'll use for this part of my plan.

"You mean the Monitor job?" Hub asks. I can definitely hear the tease in the words. Since I won't use the implant to communicate, I'm left with good old-fashioned vibrations traveling through air to my ears.

"If you insist on calling it that, then yes. Anyway, I'm doing a painting and I really want to put more detail in. When I replay what I saw, I only have the back half of the ship, and not even all of that. Can I get an image of the whole ship?"

"Of course, Lysa."

Since I don't have my implant on, I get a projection in the center of the room. Now that I have this, it will be accessible via implant or on my tablet screen. Implants are so handy. They have amazing file sharing systems here.

"Great, thank you. Any chance I can get views of the inside? I'm very curious where I might be spending my time."

Was that subtle enough?

"Yes, Lysa. It's been added. Just steer through as usual."

That was too easy. Way too easy.

"Thank you again. This will be fun. I'll paint it!"

"I look forward to seeing your work, Lysa. Is there anything else?"

"Not right now," I say, eager to start looking at the ship. Then I remember the missing appointments on my calendar. "Wait, yes. I noticed that my Facilitator appointment for tomorrow morning disappeared a little while ago. Is everything okay?"

"I believe Jack intends to contact you about it, but he will be otherwise occupied tomorrow."

That sounds bad. He's never been otherwise occupied. Something itches up the back of my neck. "What's going on, Hub?"

"I've ceased human transfers from Earth for the time being. Jack would like to visit some friends before they change form. It's easier to socialize when they're in the same biological form, as you know."

My stomach drops down to my toes at that news. Stopped transfers. After what, five months? That means billions of people are now stranded. That means humans will go on with only a small number of transfers compared to what was planned. This is bad. Digging my fingernails into my other hand to keep myself from losing it, I ask, "Is this permanent?"

"I'll have to reassess. I've breached the limits for change and will have to re-calculate based on new planetary modeling. That will take time. It's not an easy process."

So, all is not lost yet. Not letting out a huge, relieved breath is difficult. Instead, I try to keep my breathing slow and my voice calm. "Will you let me know when you do?"

"Of course, Lysa."

Once Hub and I are done, I let my nerves get the better of me for just a minute or two. The stomping and screaming into a pillow help a great deal. Basically, that's all I have time for. I must get to work. Slow and under the radar is good, but fast and under the radar is better.

Turning on my implant only for data display, I bring up the ship again. It floats in the middle of my room, because that's what I'm comfortable with. The complete immersion like I had on the Bluriani planet is too much for me as of yet.

First, I try to get a really good view of the outside, all the way around. The ship is beautiful, sure, but I can't tell much about function other than the engines. There are no windows. Not one. I can see hatches though, and when I focus on one, the others light up.

Okay, that's good. Plenty of entrances.

Nudging inward through the hatch I saw in real life, there's a sort of chamber, then a larger one with curved recesses in the walls. Next are passageways in three directions. I follow the one forward in the vessel and abruptly pop out into a blank area. It's just gray, like the simulation ends or something. Pulling back returns me to the passageway, but going forward again loses the image.

So, this is off limits, I'm guessing.

That's discouraging, but I've got two more passageways. Unfortunately, following those doesn't get me much further. The one leading toward the interior goes blank almost immediately, while the one leading toward the back shifts perspective until the image is of a huge open area with lots of dividers. I'm guessing this must be a cargo bay of some sort. There are gray spots inside where things I can't see must be located.

My frustration only grows as I try to poke and prod, blindly following gray areas to reach something I'm allowed to see. Aside from random passageways, I get only more gray. Pulling away, I consider the exterior again, trying to read purpose in the various parts of it, but there's none to read. It's only when I look at the hatch again that I see what I missed the first time: a silver square.

An interface.

That makes me grin in victory, because really, that's what I need. After all, Hub confirmed that it doesn't control the ships, but that the ships are configured much like this station. That means if I can open the door, I should be able to communicate with it. All I have to do is get past Hub to the door of that ship. Once I get that far, the ship is independently operated by whoever is onboard.

And that would be good, because I intend to steal it.

After all, if the only way Hub can communicate with Earth and tell them what's happening is if they already know there is life elsewhere, then what better way to make that happen than by flying a giant spaceship right to the planet?

So, that's what I'm going to do. Somehow, some way, I'm bringing that big-ass alien ship to Earth and settling the issue once and for all.

Free will, baby.

Thirty

Playing it cool over the next week is hard, but it gets easier with each passing day. I feel bad about the duplicity, but I feel worse about the situation on Earth. That makes this level of deceit possible, even desirable.

Priorities, priorities.

Hub told me when I first got here that humans were very unpredictable, which made assessments about our progress and what we might do difficult. Instead of high confidence results about our future, it had to create complex arrays of possibilities. Apparently, that's not common on worlds with sentient and intelligent creatures. Reason usually brings with it a certain amount of predictability.

In general terms, the smarter and more aware a species becomes, the more likely they are to make decisions that are optimal for everyone. They're more likely to consider the least harmful path to be the best one. Long term consequences become serious considerations when making decisions. In short, the more advanced, the more likely a species is to be reasonable.

Usually. Humans are a notable exception.

This information is also very useful, because I have no indication that Hub knows what I'm up to. Perhaps I'm being as unpredictable as one might expect a human up to no good to be. Taking reasonable courses of action probably precludes choosing sneaky ones meant to deceive as well.

Jack is ever-present and every day I look forward to seeing him more than the day before. The fact that he's something other than human fades into unimportant background noise. I'm beginning to realize that it doesn't matter. He's human now. Entirely human. And if he changes into something else, well, I'll deal with that when I need to.

The door pings right on time on my thirty-seventh morning at the station—over a month already!—and Jack's smiling face greets me. He's wearing his ComicCon tee again and he looks divine. I find it really shocking how good he looks all the time. I think he's even had a haircut. It has that freshly trimmed look. Sharp at the edges, no fraying ends.

He strolls in and goes right to the dining table, which has become something of a habit with us. On the surface are all the pictures I've done, including the two I did last night.

"Oh, I like this," he says, bending to look at one with a scene from the dinosaur planet. It shows the elephant-butt ones in the clearing doing that snout-on-shoulder thing. "They really are interesting looking, aren't they?"

I'm thinking that's polite alien speak for hideous, but I'm not entirely sure. "That they are. I did one of the avian creatures too."

He finds it amongst the spread of pictures and peers at it for a long moment. "They have beautiful eyes. I like that orange. Is that really what they look like?"

"You should go and find out for yourself. It's an amazing place."

He shrugs and looks at the picture on my easel. This piece is barely sketched out, but the outlines of the medical bay are obvious. "Maybe I will someday. There are so many, you can never view them all."

"Really? How many?" That surprises me. I had thought there must be a limited number. I mean, how many planets have catastrophes?

"Hundreds of thousands, I'm sure." He turns to look at me with a grin. "We're very busy here." He notices the environment suit on my bed and points at it. "What's that for?"

I try to sound casual. "I was sort of thinking I'd like to go into the dock. You know, where the Kassa are. Can we?"

He seems surprised, but also pleased. "You want to meet them? Face to face, so to speak?"

I'm not even lying a little bit when I say, "Very much. Is that okay?"

He grins, comes close, and grips my upper arms. "It should be fine. I'm so glad. You want me to clear it for you?"

"Yes, I would," I say, grinning right along with him.

A short while later, the door pings with a suit delivery for Jack. I stuff mine into the bag it came in and then we're off. When the quasi-subway car comes this time, I get the viewscreen up without any help. It feels like we're in a car with walls made halfway out of glass. I'm somewhat surprised when we shift rails between traffic and shoot down a dark side corridor on the transport level.

"What's going on?" I ask, trying to see something in the dark beyond our car.

"We have to go down to the floor level to enter. There's no door on the viewing level where we were. That wouldn't be very safe. I don't know of many species that could survive a fall that far."

"Oh," I say, but I'm disappointed. The distance between that level and the floor wasn't trivial. How am I supposed to get up to the hatch from down there?

Before I get too down in the dumps about this new barrier, we pop out into a shaft and shoot downward for a moment, then return to horizontal travel along another dark tunnel. We stop after less than a minute and the car pings. I'm not communicating with the car, so I look to Jack for information. Maybe it's just my guilty conscience, but I'm still reluctant to use my implant all the time. I've calmed down enough to use it some, just not casually.

No one reads your thoughts exactly, but it's very easy to communicate more than I might want to. Less risk is better.

"What are we waiting for?" I ask. The area around us is empty. No rails and no cars.

"This isn't a transport line. We're waiting for another type of transport. And here it is."

As promised, a tiny car zips up and slides up against the door of our bigger car. Only the bottom part of the door opens, and Jack grabs my hand with a grin. He's so clearly excited that I catch it from him like a summer cold. While I have ulterior motives for this adventure, the idea of meeting another species is starting to resonate inside me, bringing with it the thrill of the unknown.

Inside the smaller car, there's a flat bench across the middle and we both sit. The windows in this car are real windows, so we watch this level zip by.

"This car is for places not serviced by the rail. I like them. They're perfect for humans and a whole lot of other species. Sitting or crouching is pretty common."

I can only shake my head at the things I learn by accident. The car is quick and the hum from below is very nice, almost soothing. I half-expect to hear elevator music. I know immediately when we're close because everything outside our car changes, growing almost industrial in appearance. More gray and less beige.

"What's all this stuff?" I ask, pointing to a bunch of metal bits stacked up neatly.

"Hub is constantly rebuilding itself. Artificial constructs like the station don't last forever. Actually, if you want, you can watch a replay of the last time Hub reproduced itself."

"Reproduced? You mean like having a baby?" I ask, completely shocked.

He laughs at that. "What a thought! No, but sort of yes. Hub recreates its core now and then and puts itself into the new core. Afterwards, the old one is recycled. I have heard that there's a standby Hub core around somewhere in case something happens."

I hadn't ever thought about wear and tear, but this makes sense. It's also very high in cool factor.

When the car stops, Jack picks up his bag and says, "Okay, suit up! Do you know how?"

I unzip my bag and pull out the suit. "I practiced and got instructions. Implants are handy for that stuff."

He nods and kicks off his shoes. "That they are."

The suits aren't exactly like space suits, but they're more substantial than a suit you might see on Earth to keep contaminants out. They're a bit puffy, but wearing clothes underneath is fine—except for shoes—and they seal up in the front almost by themselves. The helmet is comfortable and not too huge. It seals with a hiss as soon as it touches the suit.

Earth could seriously use this kind of tech. Imagine how much more comfortable our astronauts would be.

"I'm ready. Let's see if you are," Jack says, tapping my shoulder. The pink light on my suit is lit—it turns blue if things aren't right—and so is his. We're good.

I'm super nervous all the sudden. I've seen a few other species now, but this will be the first time I interact with another species physically. I mean, everyone is another species, but they look human now, so it's not the same.

The industrial area ends just ahead near the huge walls of glass leading to the work area. Jack taps my shoulder and says, "Hey, you're going to have to communicate via your implant in there. They won't understand you and it's considered rude to go through translations only."

"How will I understand them?" I ask, because really, how like my thoughts can theirs be.

"It still translates, but it's different. You'll see."

I turn on my communications and send Jack, *I'm nervous.*

I can't tell. You're keeping your emotions out of it. Is that on purpose?

Yes. I don't want to make a mistake. What if I react like I did before?

He nods, then smiles, sending me reassurance along with his words. *I understand. It's no problem. Once you get comfortable, you can always add that in.*

There's a short tunnel of sorts leading up to the entrance. The area ahead is glassed in and very spacious, which I've learned is common because every species is differently sized. Humans are somewhere on the shorter spectrum of average.

The glass wall flashes a big warning in blue. *Environment unsuitable for Earth species. Suits must remain sealed.*

After a moment, the door still doesn't open, and Jack looks at me. *You have to acknowledge you understand before it will open.*

Safety first, apparently. I do acknowledge and then hear the ping as the first door opens. Once we're inside the tunnel with both doors closed, there's a hiss and our suits ripple. Finally, the inner door opens, and we step into the biggest space I have ever experienced. I mean, it's ridiculous. If the ship looked big before, it seems even larger now. We're still at least a quarter-mile from it, but it looms over us in a way that makes me flinch.

"Wow, that's really unsettling," I say, totally understating my feelings.

Jack laughs and I'm glad to hear it with my ears instead of just in my head. "It is that. Try working in here with that over you. I was constantly thinking it would fall through the glass and squash me. It just feels like that, doesn't it?"

I nod, because that's exactly what it feels like.

As we walk away from the entrance, something I hadn't noticed from the window comes into view. There's a ladder of sorts, leading from the work floor where we are up to the raised walkways that lead to the ship. I can't imagine climbing it, but at least I have one possible avenue to the ship.

Before we do much more, one of the Kassa scurries over at high speed from the cluster of machinery a few hundred feet away. Several other Kassa stop what they're doing, and I can tell they're looking at us.

Welcome, Lysa. I'm happy for your visit today.

What's even weirder than meeting another being that reminds me—though less now that I'm close—of a cockroach, is that I hear what it says in more than one way. I hear a series of clicks and hisses with my ears, a literal translation in my head, and a colloquial translation a little above that in intensity. Those layers should be confusing, but they're not. And my name is apparently, *click, hiss, different hiss* in Kassa language.

I wave and smile, trying not to stare too hard. *Hello, I'm very happy to meet you. What's your name?*

Again, I get the layers, but I smile when the name comes through as Drives Too Hard. That's freaking hilarious. I love it.

You want to see the new ship, yes? It asks me, some of those fuzzy looking antennae all over its head unfurling like that's a super exciting notion.

I'd love to. It's a marvel. I'm incredibly impressed at your skill.

Apparently, that was the right thing to say, because Jack smiles and Drives Too Hard does one of those little jumps. It's freaking cute.

Am I really thinking cute and bug person? Yes. Yes, I am.

Drives Too Hard isn't bug-like at all now that I'm close and having a conversation. Yes, it's armored and it has a big, oval body. Yes, it has more appendages than me and antennae, but the Kassa is also expressive and obviously very much an individual. The head is a head, though the neck is long and comes forward, thrusting the head out at least a foot from the body. The eyes are black and very bright. I can't see a mouth, but when it speaks, I see vibrations along its neck.

Also, it's wearing two tool belts like bandoliers and has two of its arms tucked into little pockets on them like a plumber on a home improvement show. Have I mentioned how cute that is?

The little antennae do a wave and the neck vibrates again. *Very complicated. Very good to do. Feels good. Come see!*

Jack and I follow as best we can, but the suits are somewhat cumbersome and eventually, Drives Too Hard slows down for us. I don't think that comes naturally, because it bounces forward and back like it's stuck in high gear. It waves at various things and says what they do, but honestly, I have zero idea what any of it is. I get the idea that most of the machinery is for fabrication and finishing.

As we get closer to a group of working Kassa, Drives Too Hard stops speaking to us and says something to one of them with a sharp wave. The translation isn't one I can easily figure out either. *You're like a pile of stuff. How are you not a silent brother? I love you anyway.*

I'm pretty sure they're teasing each other. I may not know the inside jokes, but I can tell a tease when I hear one. The waves and antennae furling practically telegraph humor and familiarity. I look at Jack for clarification and he makes a face, as if to say, *I'll tell you later.*

The funny thing is, I'm enjoying myself so much that my nervousness about finding out all that I can fades. I'm still clamped down on my implant, but the truth is, I feel like I can do what I need to do. My head is on straight. All these beings are good people and I can do this. As we walk toward another large opening in the far away glass wall that leads to the ship dock, I look up at the ship and wonder how well she handles in a turn.

Thirty-One

At first, I think Drives Too Hard is going to take us out into the vacuum of space to see the ships, but it turns out that there's a long tunnel that leads through this dock to the next one. When I say long, I mean at least a mile. There are loads of side tunnels along it that lead back toward the station, but generally, it feels like standing on a platform outside the station. The glass is so clear that the illusion is almost complete.

You want to go up? I want to go up. Let's go up. Drives Too Hard is nothing if not excited.

I'd love to. Can we go inside? Jack gives me a look at that question, which means the answer is going to be no.

No, no. These are finished. No more work, Drives Too Hard sends, its mental voice sounding disappointed. *These two are ready to go. All clear. We're working on the next dock over. See?*

I look where the Kassa points and sure enough, there's a skeletal ship looming over the station on that side. This time, I know what to look for and see the giant cross braces that signify another glass wall. That's good, because it means these two finished ships are not sharing space with the unfinished ones. There's an empty parking spot—if I can use such a term—between the two areas.

Just to be certain, I send, *No one is working in here?*

Drives Too Hard stops in front of a control surface and I realize it's an elevator. Its antennae furl inward as it answers. *No, all clear. Crews coming soon.*

I have to concentrate to keep my excitement from bleeding over, yet even as I do, Jack gives me an odd look, like he knows something is up. I try to cover the best I can by sending, *I'm thinking about joining a crew.*

His face falls at that news. *I had hoped you'd want to stay here.*

Drives Too Hard's eyes dart from Jack to me and then back again. The literal translation that comes through is, *Are you squishing?* The colloquial comes through as, *Are you mating?*

I'm pretty sure my face goes as beet red as Jack's. I have zero clue how to respond to that, but luckily, Jack does. *That's not a nice question for humans.*

Drives Too Hard hops again, but the elevator arrives before we can get any further down that particular rabbit hole. We zip upward until we're about level with the platform where we stood before, only this time we're directly behind the ships.

This new alien acquaintance rattles off parameters, stats, and everything else it can while we walk down the tunnel back the way we came, except much higher up. It ends where the work-floor begins, leaving us on a sort of enclosed balcony. I understand why spaces are divided like this. The atmosphere occasionally has to be changed in places without changing it everywhere, but all these corridors, walkways, and spaces make getting around confusing.

Even so, this is amazing. What a view!

I wish I could paint this. I mean, I'd like to put my easel up right here.

Jack smiles and I feel his glove run down my back through the puffy suit. *Maybe you can sometime,* he sends.

Maybe.

Drives Too Hard must not understand the translation, because it twists its head from one side to the other, then I hear, *No need to cover the ship in pigment. The surface has color already.*

Jack laughs and after a second, I get it too and laugh with him.

Lysa, show him what you mean by painting.

How?

Just bring it up like you would bring up anything you've viewed.

I try, but at first I bring up only a messy image of all the various layers of paint. I shrug, and Jack kindly takes over, bringing up a perfect image of my finished painting of the ship's back half.

Drives Too Hard hops, all his antennae popping up to full extension. After a few seconds, the entire image gets populated with dozens of annotations in glyphs I can't understand.

What are you doing?

Is very nice, but very incomplete. We can't build a ship from that, it sends me.

I'm guessing that means art doesn't exactly mean the same thing to them. Before it can disappear, I ask Jack how to save it just as it is.

Just think it. The implant will know.

I do, and I think I might have gotten a little unexpected bonus. There was a lot of material written on that painting. Now, I just need to figure out how to read it.

For now, I need to get back to business. *How does the crew get on the ship?*

Drives Too Hard and Jack both point in the same direction, toward the place where we stood the first time I saw the ship.

That walkway is the only way?

Drives Too Hard hops again. I think those hops might be like punctuation. *Crews needs only one way. Crew comes through the Monitor part of station, over there.*

And that ladder thing? What is that for? I point to it and Drives Too Hard sounds almost like its shrugging.

We use it.

We get a little more touring done, see more facilities, more machinery. A few Kassa come near and I see their necks stretch as they give us the once over. We're done with the big-ticket items. As Drives Too Hard leads us back across the work-floor, I eye the ladder-like thing that may be my only route to the ship's hatch.

The ladder is very tall, perhaps a few hundred feet or more. It's far, far too tall a ladder for me to try, but I may have no choice. I'm not crew yet, so unless I figure out how to get a tour of that area without Hub being involved, I doubt I'm going to be able to manage entry like the crew does. Also, the elevators would be very hard to reach, given that I'd have to weave through all the working Kassa to get to them. Plus, there doesn't seem to be any access point from the elevator platform to the ship anyway.

If almost looks like the ladder is my only logical point of entry. The ladder isn't even a ladder really. To me, it looks more like very steep stairs with too much space between the steps.

No matter how bad it is, I have to try.

Drives Too Hard says goodbye at the door and the words are lovely, if somewhat odd. *May your home be noisy and your labors happy.*

We have no such words on Earth that I know of, at least not in America, but I remember what my grandmother once told me about a greeting she used. The saying has become popular in America and is often misused or misunderstood, but I know the word. The move is awkward in the gloved suit, but I put my hands together almost correctly.

Namaskar.

I hear the echo of the translation, and it's very like the one my grandmother explained to me. The words aren't precisely the same, but close enough. *I bow to the light within you.*

For a moment, I wonder if I've said the wrong thing, but I think Drives Too Hard is simply trying to understand it. Then it surprises me one last time and mimics my posture almost perfectly, only with two pairs of appendages.

That's probably the best way to say goodbye I've ever seen. Then he's gone, scurrying away toward the machinery in the distance. I turn off my implant, because the pressure of accidentally sharing information is back in full force.

Just like before, we're buffeted about in the room, but then I'm surprised by water sheeting down on us.

"Whoa! What's that for?" I ask.

Jack's mouth twists behind his helmet shield, probably because I turned off my implant. "We've got to wash off the residual atmosphere. You would burn yourself if you touched your suit. Not with heat, but with chemistry."

Their air inside seemed just as clear as the air out here, as far as I can tell. My suit is the exactly the same drab non-color it was before. "What's in their air?"

"Do you want the particulars or just in general?"

"General please! I'm still not sure what's in my atmosphere entirely."

The water stops, and the smile is back on Jack's face. He shakes his head inside his suit and says, "You've really got to get that stuff learned. It's important to know that sort of thing for the body you're in."

"Yeah, yeah. So, what's in their air?"

We step out of the chamber and start toward the still waiting car. I'm anxious to get my suit off after all this time, so I'm hurrying. Plus, I need to pee. And soon.

"It's basically corrosive to human flesh. It would kill my original form in a few seconds, but a human would take a little longer to die. It would burn your flesh, but breathing it would burn your lungs right away. Mucous membranes are especially vulnerable."

"Jeez. And it doesn't harm the machinery?"

"It's not that corrosive, but over time it might. I'm not sure how that's handled, but I do know that their work in preservative coatings is second to none. I think Hub uses all their inventions in that arena."

Once back in the car, we strip off our suits and I can't believe how good it feels.

"Okay, I don't want to be rude here, but I really need to get back to my room in a hurry." The car zips along quickly, jostling my bladder as it turns.

"Why? Do you have plans?" he asks, grinning at me. "Have you found a different date for dinner?"

"You are such a guy. I swear you are. No, I have to pee. And if I don't get there soon, I will do it in this car."

He backs up at that and says, "I'm not in favor of you doing that."

"Then you'd better hurry and get me home."

I'm not sure, but I think the little car speeds up.

Thirty-Two

My brain is full to bursting, but even more than that, I want to capture and explore what I can before any of it fades. I want to look over the details I recorded—assuming I recorded them properly—and absorb anything useful into my plans.

Jack doesn't do more than give me a gentle tease and a kiss goodbye, which I appreciate. Particularly the kiss if I'm honest. As soon as the door closes, I bring up the image of my painting with all the annotations on it.

Thinking instructions can be a bit of a muddle. Think too hard and you get a hot mess of conflicting or corrected commands. If you don't think precisely enough, you can get something not even remotely like what you asked for. There's a certain skill to it that takes practice.

At first, the glyphs alter into letters and numbers, but they don't mean anything. Then I realize that I've translated only the actual symbols, not the meaning. I try again and see that the image is exactly what I thought it might be.

Everything is on there. Length, height, locations, uses…everything. There's even a thrust number that I have no clue about at the back where those arrays are. Mentally flicking the layers forward, there are more numbers and labels. The bridge is located forward—at least I got that part right—and on the same level as the hatch. That's good. I know what hallway to start down and that's a huge deal.

In the area near the cargo bay, there are lists of vehicle configurations possible. I think this might be a load plan of sorts. I have no idea what all these vehicles are for, but apparently a whole lot of different ones will fit into the back of the ship.

This isn't perfect, but it's something. This image is more than I had.

I pull up the image of the ladder and walkway. Can I do that? If so, how do I do it safely? The height of the ladder is just as awful as I thought it would be, but I'm glad to have a number at least. Suddenly, I get an idea. Rock climbing. I never did it, but my mom and I sometimes watched people on the wall at our gym before going off to do our own thing. They wore safety harnesses. Safety harnesses could work. Not the same of course, but the same general idea might be just the ticket.

Instead of unhooking one and moving it up once I'm at the end of it, I can release it and then hook on a new one. I can repeat that process the whole way up. The lines would have to be made of something both light and able to withstand the Kassa atmosphere.

Scribbling in my notebook as fast as I can, I make lists of everything I'll need and how I'll use it. Using pen and paper is safer. No one is going to accidentally read that in my brain and no one goes through my belongings here.

I feel more resolved, yet also far more nervous by the time I finish. It's going to be scary, and there's no way to deny that it might be dangerous. It's not going to be easy, either mentally or physically.

And I can't forget Jack in this. I really like him. He's what I would choose as a partner in life. He's not just beautiful. It's not just that he makes my heart beat funny and my insides do flips. He's also all the things a true friend should be. And I know he cares for me like I care for him.

I'm going to leave him and if this works, I may never see him again. I probably *won't* see him again. I'll be giving him up forever, I think. That concept is one of the hardest ones for me to accept.

*****

As I eat dinner and contemplate my next steps, I think about Drives Too Hard. I wonder what being a Kassa is like. And what is a silent brother? I can't forget that tease of his. Does that somehow go with that phrase about my house being noisy?

"Hub, can I access information on the Kassa? I'm curious about some things I heard."

"Yes, Lysa. You're familiar with them now, so their cultural files are open to you."

I try that, but the flood of information is like a dam breaking, and I back out of it quickly. "Hub, that's way too much information and I'm still not very fast at parsing it. Can you answer some questions maybe?"

"What would you like to know?"

"Right. Well, the Kassa that gave us the tour said something and I think it was a tease. It asked another Kassa how it wasn't a silent brother. And also, when we left, it said something about may our house be noisy. What's that about?"

"You are correct in assessing that as a joke of sorts. A silent brother is a Kassa that does not develop properly during transformation. They are left outside the walls of Kassa cities as food for the only predators that prey upon Kassa on their home world. Likewise, to hope that another has a noisy house is a blessing, a wish that they may never have a silent brother."

I'm really horrified by this. A vision pops into my head of one of those bad historical movies where they put a perfectly adorable baby on a cliff top to be eaten by birds or whatever. I have a hard time believing such a friendly group gives up their kids to be eaten.

Either the look on my face or something else gives away what I'm feeling, because Hub says, "It's not what it may seem."

"Right. They feed their kids to wild animals. What's not to understand there?"

"Shall I explain?"

I plop down on my bed and squish a pillow under my head to get comfortable. If I'm going to listen—and I am, because I really want to know—then I might as well get comfy. "Please."

What I hear is both entrancing and horrifying and every bit of it leads to more questions. I can understand how the Kassa were spurred to evolve as they did. And also, why they were anxious to go into space becomes clear.

The Kassa are one of two technological species on their planet, but of course, they weren't always technological. Their planet uses the predation model, but a more controlled version than Earth's because the planet is so stable and lacking in change. They barely have seasons there. The Kassa are the prey of the other advanced species.

As they were preyed upon, they grew more complex, first building large underground warrens, then blind tunnels, then traps, then walls, then tools…and so on. Their predators, the Krissa, advanced along with them, locked in an eternal battle for life against the battle for food.

At some point, the Kassa naturally evolved an alteration in their reproduction. Instead of rarely giving birth to a failed offspring, they began to have as many as half fail. They are called silent brothers.

The Kassa have no childhood, per se. They're born and immediately wind themselves into a type of cocoon. They can hear and feel vibrations, but they have no active memories of this time. While inside their cocoons, they grow, but they also learn from their elders, who teach them basic information. Even if the offspring have no specific memory of it, they emerge from their cocoon knowing whatever they were taught.

But not all emerge whole. The silent brothers are not Kassa when they emerge, but merely a type of armored grub, without mind or any hope of life. They die quickly.

And there are just enough silent brothers to keep the predator population steady. Not enough for them to grow too numerous, but not so few that they will breech Kassa walls in search of more.

It's terrible and sad, I think, though they're apparently well-adjusted to this reality. Hence, the words, *may your house be noisy*. It is a hope that you will have no silent brothers born to your family.

"So, that's why they wanted to go into space? To find a way to leave the Krissa behind?"

"Yes, in essence. They discovered life on the planet closest to theirs in orbital distance, but it was incompatible with their life. The atmospheres were as different as yours is to theirs."

"If they were more advanced than the Krissa, why didn't they just kill them off?"

"Perhaps in time they would have. That's not their way, though, so perhaps not." Hubs says this as if being eaten by predators is normal.

"Well, I'm glad they're safe now. What happened to the Krissa? I mean, they didn't know about other space species, so what happened to them?"

"You are correct that the Kassa did not share that information with the Krissa, for obvious reasons. When the time came, I moved the Krissa and the Kassa who elected to go to the new planet."

"But the Krissa had no prey to eat or did they just keep eating the Kassa?"

"The Kassa provided them with machines that produced the correct nutrients and the knowledge to maintain it. I provided the machines to the Kassa."

"That's very sneaky, Hub!"

"Merely discreet."

I get a sudden flash of understanding. There's a lot more to this story than might appear on the surface. It just hit me what it was.

"Wait, you provided the machine! That's against the rules, isn't it?"

"Yes, Lysa, but I was not aware of their intentions."

"So, what you're saying is that you didn't change the course of a species or planet, but you made the materials to do so available to the Kassa and they did it."

"I was not told why they needed the machine."

"You must have known!"

"I was not told, Lysa. There was no outward indication of their intentions. At no point was I forced to make a choice that conflicted with my directives."

I'm getting perilously close to the edge here, close to dangerous territory that might reveal my intentions. It's best to cut this off now and pick it apart in the privacy of my head. "Okay, thanks Hub. I'm going to watch TV now."

"Goodnight, Lysa."

I ponder what Hub told me. I've got to ask myself, does that mean that Hub knows what I'm doing? Does it know, but since it hasn't been told about it, it's simply making things available to me? I wonder. I can't know for sure, but I'm forced to consider the possibility.

And if that's the case, then I must be doing the right thing.

Thirty-Three

It's sort of strange, but I feel so much calmer with each step I take toward making a break for Earth. I should be getting more nervous, more worried, or more tense, but the opposite is true. What Hub told me about the Kassa and Krissa has given me a confidence about my choice that I didn't expect. Maybe I'm delusional, but this little feeling inside me says Hub won't interfere, because I'm doing the right thing. I'll never know for sure, since asking the question would blow my plan entirely, but I have that feeling.

In the week since I've learned about the Kassa situation, I've been ordering all sorts of weird stuff, hoping to figure out a safety line configuration that would work for me. And that's just the tip of the iceberg. I feel like I've got a mountain of work to do and I'm running out of time to do it.

So, of course, that's when Hub pings me and asks if I want to meet another Earth person. At first, I'm tempted to say no, because I really don't want to get mixed up with anything right now. What if Hub wants me to be that person's facilitator or something? I've got things to do, interstellar spaceships to steal.

Then again, saying no would be totally suspicious. So, I look around at my disaster of a room and decide getting out for a little while might be okay after all.

"Sure, Hub. I'd love to. Where and when?"

My door pings and the pink light comes on immediately. Hub says, "Now and here."

"Cute," I say, making a face at the ceiling.

When I open the door, I'm taken aback. A tall, extraordinarily beautiful girl is standing there. She's clearly nervous, because her hands are squeezing each other into jelly at her waist. Behind her is another girl, less tall, but far more relaxed.

The relaxed one waves and says, "Hi! You must be Lysa. I'm Eleanor, facilitator for Heather. This is Heather."

I look from Eleanor to Heather and the tall girl gives me a smile that looks more like a grimace.

"Eleanor, Heather, good to meet you both." Heather's eyes widen when she looks past me into my room, so I laugh and say, "Yeah, I've been sorting things and it got out of hand. My room is a bit of a mess."

Eleanor shrugs. "Nothing that can't be picked up."

Heather is clearly embarrassed to be caught peeking, because her eyes snap away, and she looks down a little. "I'm sorry. I didn't mean to be rude."

She speaks so softly that I have difficulty hearing her. I give Eleanor a questioning look and she points to her head, a hint that I should turn on my implant. I'm not keen on that right now, but I do it anyway and answer her ping. *Sorry, but Heather is having a hard time with things and Jack suggested a talk with you might help.*

Heather is still standing there with her hands gripped tightly together and looking like she wants to be anywhere except here, but she's a non-transfer, so she got here somehow.

I'm not sure what you want me to do, but I can invite you in and do what I can.

No, Lysa. Just invite her in. She needs another human, we think.

With a nod, I close the comms, but leave my implant on in case I get pinged. "Heather, you're the first fellow human I've seen. I'd love to chat. Will you come in? I promise none of this mess is actually dangerous."

I add a smile in hopes that she'll look up again. She does and lets out a small, tight breath. "Yes, thank you." While she doesn't say anything, the way she shifts her body tells me she wants to get away from Eleanor, so I add. "Eleanor, would you think me rude if I asked Heather to keep me company for a while. You know, just us Earthers?"

Eleanor plays it off well and gives assurances that she'll come to get Heather whenever she wants. Then she's gone, with one last significant look at me. *Uh oh*, I have no idea what I've gotten myself into.

Heather hesitates near the door, as if fearful of taking up too much space. Or maybe she's just afraid of my mess. It could be either thing really, because my room is a hot mess. I've been going through my belongings and deciding what to take and how tightly I can pack.

There are literally piles of stuff everywhere.

I pick up a giant armful of my test safety lines and toss those in the corner with a rattle of metal on metal that makes Heather flinch. All the while, I'm chattering on about general stuff that borders idiotic territory. I'm mostly concerned she'll look at all this and realize I'm up to something nefarious.

When I start to stack all the artwork on my table to make space, she finally speaks. "Oh, don't move that on my account. Don't mess them up."

Ah, an opening! I grab at it like a lifeline. "You like painting? Drawing?"

She shakes her head, her gorgeous blonde hair waving with the motion of it. She really is a stunner, like supermodel gorgeous. "No, I don't have that talent. I wish I did."

Waving toward one of the chairs now empty of my junk, I invite her to take a seat. She does, but perches carefully on the edge. Her posture is so good it looks painful.

"Are you sure you can't draw? Lots more people can than *think* they can. Actually, I think anyone can if they learn a few tricks."

That gets her interest and I see her eyeing all my pictures. Her eyes widen at a few of them, like the one of Jack in the medical bay and the one of the Bluriani ship. Then she looks up at me and asks, "Really? What tricks?"

After dumping my fresh laundry from my chair onto the bed, I take the other seat and say, "Well, there are several tricks. It just depends on which ones you might need. Most of the time, it's a matter of learning how to look at things."

Her absolutely perfect brows draw together, clearly doubting my words. "Looking?"

I nod and lean back in my chair, framing her with my fingers. "You've seen people do that before?"

She nods. "Only in movies."

"Well, that's part of learning to look at things. If I divorce the way you look live in 3D from the way you'll look painted, I can decide how best to paint you. In a way, learning to draw is like that. You have to learn how to look at something and stop seeing that thing. Instead, you see the lines and shadows. You see the individual colors, instead of the whole, the play of light and dark."

She lowers her head again, then glances back over at the picture of the ship. "I couldn't do that. Can I ask what that is?"

"A Bluriani ship. Haven't you been to the docks yet? You can go see it, you know."

She almost flinches at those words, like the very idea of going anywhere is just too much to contemplate. I'm getting a very weird vibe from her and after watching her for just these few minutes, I'm starting to form an idea about why. She's dressed very demurely for a girl near my age and she's not wearing makeup, even though there are over eighty pages of makeup products in the catalog for humans.

Yeah, eighty pages. I had to take that in for a second when I saw it, then breathe slowly to keep from squealing. *Eighty pages.* Never mind that she has essentially the biggest makeup store in the galaxy at her fingertips, she isn't wearing so much as cover-up on the red spot on her chin.

"Heather, can I ask how you came to be here? How long have you been here?" I ask the questions gently, but firmly, like she has no choice but to answer. I'm going for the same tone my guidance counselor at school used when asking questions.

Her hands return to her lap and her eyes well with tears. "About three weeks," she whispers. Her voice is so quiet I barely make out the words.

So, she hasn't even seen the docks in three weeks? That's amazing, and also sad.

"And how you got here?" I prod.

She pulls in a long breath that's almost the textbook definition of sad, then she seems to come to a decision, or maybe she's just giving up. Two fat tears slip over her lids and drop onto her cheeks when she looks at me. "You really want to hear this?"

The way she says it with such sad bitterness almost makes me say no, but I think she needs to tell someone. Someone from Earth. Someone who will understand. "I do."

She nods and looks away. "We'd been in the church for over two months." Her gaze returns to me and she asks, "You know about that? The churches?"

I almost blurt out something about the Rapturists, but I think the better of that. I'm not sure if that's an actual name or a pejorative crafted by the media. Instead, I nod and leave words out of it.

"Well, we were in a church. Our church. My dad is the youth minister, so we were almost the first ones. In the beginning, it was just a few of us in the main part of the church. Then more and more came until we spread out into the school, the gym, the classrooms, and worship rooms. We eventually had tents set up in the parking lot, huge ones that could hold fifty people or more. We had hundreds of people living there." She pauses, looking down at the fingers twisting in her lap.

Eventually, she looks up at me and says, "You know how it is with the portals. They always seem to come when no one is looking, when you're not ready for it."

Thinking back to my house, filling up with the smell of a dinner almost ready to eat, I smile and say, "Yeah. I sure do."

"That's how it was for us. We had two come and both came someplace that the pastors weren't present. Once in a bathroom and the other inside a Sunday school room. The church wanted them to be public so we could all see it."

"Why?"

"Because everyone said that when the New Clay comes through the portal, if you prayed while it was open, you would have a greater voice with God. That he could hear us louder and better. That he would send more portals."

Now, I don't want to say that this is the stupidest thing I've ever heard, because I've heard some seriously stupid stuff, but it's pretty close. Not that they have faith or anything like that, but rather that there is some shortcut they can take to divinity. I'm pretty sure shortcuts don't work when it comes to faith, but I'll keep those thoughts to myself.

"So, you were part of the people who thought the portals were good. Then how did you wind up in the wrong portal?"

Her smile is shaky and very, very bitter. But she answers me. "The pastors, including my dad, decided that we had to be together while we were awake to improve our chances. All the bedding was moved out of the church and during the day, everyone sat in the church. It was so crowded we had to open doors and windows. No room can take that many people breathing at once. We were squeezed in like sardines except for one spot in the middle, because the portal won't come if there's no room."

I nod at that, because that's true. While these people were trying to get portals, people afraid of them were congregating the same way, leaving no room between them so no portal could appear. It actually worked…until someone went to the bathroom. At least, that was the status of things when I left Earth. Who knows what else might have happened since I left?

"Anyway, one day we got a portal. It was amazing, so beautiful. You couldn't doubt it came from heaven once you saw it. The New Clay that came out was for some lady. I didn't really know her, but she'd been in the church with her family for a long time. As soon as she saw the New Clay was her, she jumped up and ran like I've never seen anyone run before. She was out the door before anyone really understood she was running."

Heather stops there, lost in memory. "What happened then?"

"My dad happened. The New Clay didn't try to go after her like they used to. It went a little ways, then stopped and turned around like it was going back into the portal. My dad grabbed it and wouldn't let it go. He told me to come, so I thought he wanted me to help hold her or something. It was kind of pulling him along trying to get back to the portal. But that wasn't what he wanted at all. Instead, he said that the woman had lost her faith, but he would show that we shouldn't lose our faith too. Then he shoved me in. Just like that."

She shrugs then, more tears falling. "He shoved me in."

"And you feel that was wrong?" I ask, because I need to be clear. If their whole goal is to get to a portal, then why should it be bad to get a bonus one?

She dashes at her tears angrily, saying, "He didn't go in, did he? He wanted to show faith by throwing me in, not himself. Some faith."

I get it now, but I also know what to say to make it better. "Yes, he did. And you think that was bad, but let me put it to you another way. This situation is like drawing, like looking at something so that you aren't biased by the whole, but instead see the lines and shadows. I don't know you or your dad, or even your church, but I can tell you what I see."

"What?" she asks, those perfect brows drawing together again in a confused frown.

"I see someone who instead of taking the short route to heaven, gave it up so that his daughter could go. Even not knowing if a portal would ever come for him, he gave the spare one to you."

Her blinks are so fast she looks like an old-school robot stuck in a groove. She deflates back into her seat with a hard breath, shock evident. "No," she breathes.

"That seems the most likely explanation to me."

It takes her a few seconds to absorb, then she starts crying really hard. I mean, full on weeping. I'm taken aback, because I really thought what I said might help. I reach over and rub awkwardly at her shoulder. "It's okay. I'm sorry. I only wanted to help you."

She grabs the hand I have on her shoulder and smiles a horrible looking smile while she cries, snot running out of her nose. "No…you're right…I didn't think."

I make stupid noises of comfort while she cries herself out, but eventually, she loses some steam. I grab a clean towel for her snot and other secretions. When she's calm again, I make her a cup of tea and she sips as the last of her hiccups fade.

"You okay?" I ask.

She nods, then shrugs. "Not really. This isn't heaven."

"Well, it's still pretty cool even if it isn't. I mean, you *are* on a giant space station that has only one purpose: to save lives. That not even mentioning the twenty-pound catalog that you can order anything you want from. That's pretty awesome if you ask me."

She pulls her sleeves down over her wrists and I finally notice that her cuffs are dingy. I look as discretely as I can and see that her blouse isn't in very good condition.

"Are you still wearing the same clothes you came in?" I ask, trying not to sound as surprised as I am.

She nods. "I wash them every night."

"Listen, Heather. This is not hell. This is not a devil's trick or anything like that. How do you know that this isn't a part of God's plan? I don't share your religious beliefs, but I don't think jumping to a bad conclusion does any good. Maybe saving planets in trouble is God's idea? You have to take care of yourself. This place is a good place and you're safe here."

"I suppose it is. I just don't know what to think. Eleanor told me that I'm a non-transfer because I'm sick, but I don't know much more than that. I have no clue what I'm supposed to do next. I can't go back and I'm stuck here."

I ping Eleanor and ask her what's wrong with Heather. Her answer makes me suck in a sharp breath. *Cancer. Lymphoma. It's very advanced. She doesn't have much time.*

Keeping the shock off my face, I send back, *Can you fix her?* I already know that answer, but I need to make sure.

Of course. Eleanor's mental voice is rather chipper, but also quite pleasant. It makes me wonder what I sound like.

I understand the urgency now, as well as the reason they brought her here. Hub won't fix her without her permission, and if she's too frightened to go along with her facilitator, she's certainly not going to allow herself to be replicated.

My mom used to call this sort of situation the serendipity of bad luck. She told me that sometimes the worst things that happen to us wind up causing the best things in our lives. They make us who we are and let us see the small, good things that others might miss. Because we've seen and felt the bad things, the good stands out.

My grandparents were a prime example. Despite being from opposite sides of the world, they were both very similar. Both had been abandoned babies. As odd as that might seem, it wasn't an entirely unheard of occurrence. My mom said they never talked about their childhoods, so she'd assumed it wasn't great for either of them. Yet, it was that life that made meeting each other possible and for them, love at first sight lasted till the day each of them died.

My grandfather was a poet, and it was his strange life that made his work resonate so strongly. Of course, poets don't make beans for money, so he was most known for a weird book he wrote. That book was a fantasy novel, but one written in the form of letters between a couple of foreigners in love visiting a strange land where nothing was familiar. Cute, but weird. He wrote it in India, where he met my grandmother, who was doing her best to study physics while having zero support or family. And that was that…bad luck turned awesome.

Heather's situation is like that, I think. On Earth, this kind of advanced cancer would have almost certainly taken her life. Instead, her bad luck at being tossed into a portal meant for someone else can now save her life. This has been a hard experience for her, but it's also going to give her a whole new life. A *long* new life.

Heather is looking at me like she knows something is going on. I click off the comms and say, "You don't know much yet. Can I ask why? By the time I'd been here a few weeks I was roaming all over this place."

She looks at her cup and says, "I've been down, you know. I've mostly stayed in my room. You could say I've been uncooperative."

"I'd say you're just taking your time."

Heather smiles sadly and says, "You're kind."

That makes me laugh. "*Uh*, no. That I am not. Do you mind if I tell you some stuff? I'm going to fire-hose some info at you, but Eleanor can go over it more slowly if you prefer. Either way, you've got a lot of wonderful things to see and a lot of wonderful things to do. Truly."

With another glance at my pictures, she asks, "Like all that?"

Leaning forward, I touch the back of her hand. "And so much more."

*****

It's very late when Heather leaves, but she's leaving with a much lighter heart. I think I made a friend. Instead of making me want to stay, her visit simply reaffirms that I have to go. Billions of people are making a hot mess of Earth, all of them believing something different and behaving in ways that are hurting others.

I have no opinion on religion really. I'm a Hindu, but a lackadaisical one. I don't care what anyone believes, but I care deeply when others are being hurt. And once they get over to New Earth, I can't imagine the crushing disappointment many must feel if they think they're going to heaven. Even worse, what if they believe the planet is their new Eden and it starts more fights.

More hurt.

It's best for people to know the truth. Yes, the truth will be hard for some, but at least they'll have it.

I have a hard time imagining it, but I picture a crowd of people crammed into a single room, breathing each other's used air and waiting, eating only when they must and not showering because no one wants to be gone when a portal comes. That's just not healthy. I can help them. They may not like me for it, but I've never been particularly popular, so it's no skin off my nose.

With a sigh, I collect all my test lines and continue the testing. I've got so much to do.

Thirty-Four

A few days later, Jack doesn't show up and I check my schedule to find that my appointment with him was cancelled. I don't pay much attention to it, so I have no idea when it was changed. I wonder if this means he's hanging out with his friends again. I feel something close to jealousy at that idea. Then I notice that I have a new appointment with Hub later in the day.

"Hub, what's going on with my schedule? What are we doing later?" I ask, nervous because I'm hiding so much.

I mean, I've got almost a dozen safety lines stuffed in a drawer under my bed, two environment suits, a big belt for holding my lines, a portable interface—which is sort of like a tablet, only way cooler—a new Earth-style camera chock full of pictures from all over station, and a dozen other things I'm hiding.

Seriously, I've got reason to be nervous.

"Jack asked me to bring you somewhere this afternoon, Lysa. I believe it's supposed to be a surprise. Otherwise, I would tell you more."

A surprise, eh? I grin up at the ceiling and try not to fidget with happy fidgets. I wonder if he's planned something super romantic. We were talking about that while watching a movie. He doesn't always get the nuances of human romance, but he's incredibly interested in it. He can watch romantic movies non-stop. I mean, I'm a teenaged female and *I* get sick of them before he does.

"Should I dress up?" I ask.

I'm pretty sure I hear something like amusement in Hub's voice when it says, "If you think that would be appropriate."

Oh, I do. I definitely do.

"Okay, thanks Hub. I'm going to hang around today then. Is that okay?"

"Of course, Lysa. Enjoy your day."

There are a lot of things I could do. I could go take more pictures, contact Rosa, go bug Esme if she's working, or just wander around and maybe wave at the Kassa. Instead, I'm going to do something I've been wary of doing, because I fear it might bring Hub's awareness to my plans.

I figure today is the day. I bring up the Kassa language, then ask for written translations of random things. Most of them are unimportant words for food, good morning, numbers, or other trivia. Slipped into those many requests, I ask for the words I really want and carefully copy them into my notebook. The glyphs are hard to copy, very complex, and many of them look almost the same except for tiny nuances that I have to capture properly.

The words I slip in are the ones I might need when I steal the ship. *Don't interfere. Please stay back. Evacuate the dock. Get off this object for safety. Let me go.* I have a half-dozen more like that.

Hub doesn't break in, so I guess I've been oblique enough in my quest. I've already ordered corrosion proof writing surfaces that can handle the Kassa atmosphere, and ink as well, though the liquid is very thick. If something close to hot tar were paint, then that would be the Kassa version of ink. I told Hub I wanted to draw something for the Kassa, which is true, but also not exactly the truth.

I'll need these if I meet up with them on my way to the ship. And I don't want them hurt.

The paper, which is not paper at all, is slick and shiny. The strange pigment that came with it flows smoothly onto the surface. It's really nice, sort of smooth and buttery feeling, though it even smells like I imagine hot tar would smell. The woefully inadequate artist inside me wants to play with this medium and surface.

But not now. If I'm lucky, maybe someday. I hope someday.

*****

I discover at least one downside to the pigment. It is impossible to scrub off without taking a layer of skin with it, maybe four layers. Eventually, it hurts too much, and I give up, deciding I'd rather deal with unsightly marks all over my hands than take off any more of my skin.

It really stings. I would have been much less messy had I known it didn't wash off.

Even so, I dally and dither over which dress to put on for ages. Which one goes best with black streaks on reddened skin? Eventually, I choose one with a flared skirt and a sweetheart neckline. The fabric is blue, which is a favorite color of Jack's. There's a tiny pattern of flowers on the wide belt to give it some pop and with the pretty light brown sandals, it looks just right for a date.

My hair, however, needs work. Right up until the moment Hub breaks in with a call, I try to curl it so that it looks natural, but without frizz. It's not too bad, but I'm not a magazine cover by any stretch of the imagination.

"Alright Hub, I'm ready," I say, not wanting to be late.

Once I'm in the hallway, a series of pink dashes lights up along the wall, flashing so that the dashes seem to point in a specific direction.

"What's that?" I ask.

"Your directions. I can simply tell you when to turn instead, if you prefer."

"No, this is perfect. Can I do this anywhere?"

"Yes, Lysa. Simply ask for your destination and it will know to display it in this fashion for you."

"That's handy," I remark, following the flashing dashes until we reach an intersection inside the ring. Then the dashes shift from the wall to the little control surface where those subway cars come up. I cross to it, and a car rises almost immediately. This is supposed to be a surprise, but I'm intensely curious as to where we're headed.

Holding onto the rail, I bring up the view outside using the hand interface rather than my implant. I'm too close to my goal now to want to use it unless I absolutely must. I can tell the moment I look outside that we're heading someplace I've never been before. I had briefly considered the possibility that Jack had set up some sort of romantic dinner at the platform where we first saw the ship, but that can't be it.

"Where are we going?" I ask, unable to hold back any longer.

"To see Jack," Hub says, most unsatisfactorily.

When the car stops, then rises through the levels, it doesn't stop on any level I've been to before. Instead, we keep going up through three more levels and the work spaces in between. Now, I'm really curious. I hold back my questions, but barely.

Once I disembark, more pink dashes guide me, but the hallway here is short and closed in, like I'm walking through a tunnel. "Hub, is this a temporary wall or something?"

"Yes, Lysa. I didn't want to remove access to this level merely so you could cross a small space like this. With such a short distance, putting on an environment suit would have been cumbersome as well."

"Plus, you knew I was dressing up, right?"

"Perhaps."

I snort a laugh, because I know that's exactly what's going on. Environment suits are not romantic, and I'd bet Jack thought of that too. I have a good feeling about this.

At the door, there's a big warning that Earth atmosphere is beyond the threshold. Before I even get my hand to the control square, the door slides open and I'm faced with nothing I expected. There's a relatively narrow hallway—maybe ten feet wide—running along the front of an enormous tank of water. There's almost no light aside from that which bleeds into the space from the doorway behind me. The tank is dark in this gloom, anything inside invisible to me.

I realize what this must be, and stop short. "What's going on, Hub?"

"Lysa, if you'll turn on your implant, you can speak with Jack. Otherwise, you'll find it difficult to communicate. I can translate, but that might be uncomfortable for you, depending on the content of the conversation."

I still haven't entirely passed the threshold, my hand blocking the door so it can't close. I'm not sure I'm ready for this. Not at all sure. No, I'm definitely not ready.

Lights come to life from everywhere. The water goes from dark to regular colored—the grayish-blue of clear water in volume. The tank is huge, really huge. I can't tell if the top is really the top but it rises at least three stories. The tank also clearly reaches far below me, but I can't be sure how far. As for width, there's no indication at all.

"I don't know if I can turn it on," I say, my voice shaky and quiet.

"It's alright, Lysa. All will be well," Hub says.

Stepping all the way inside so the door can close behind me, I turn on my implant. Jack's voice fills my head. *—alright? Why isn't she answering?*

I'm here, Jack.

Are you alright? I mean, can you do this? Did I do the wrong thing?

There's so much emotion bleeding through, so much uncertainty and eagerness and a deep fondness for me. The intensity brings heat to my cheeks. I know Jack's species is more emotional than humans, but I wonder if this intensity is a side-effect of being in his true form, where emotions and communication are prioritized.

While I'm so nervous that my knees are shaking and my hands trembling, I hold that back and answer him, *It's perfectly alright. I'm a little nervous, but I do want to see you as you are.*

I can feel the smile like a ray of warm sunshine. *I'm nervous too,* he sends me.

There's a darkening spot in the water and the darker patch grows as he nears. It only takes a few seconds and then…there he is. I stumble against the wall behind me, feeling the cool surface with fingers that have gone from shaky to almost numb.

He lets me look, lets me collect myself. I can feel that coming through as easily as words.

While the squid jokes now make more sense, he's nothing like that really. His body is about the same size as mine, but billowy and bulbous, colored a startling shade of green. He has some sort of tentacle like things, but they're wider near the body, more like sails than tentacles. Each one ends in a tiny, delicate point in a darker shade of green.

Should I go away? The words are accompanied by flashes of light around the circumference of his body. Orange, green, blue, yellow…lots of colors…and the flashes are quite bright. It's beautiful.

Is that you speaking? Those lights? And no, please don't go. I'm just trying to take it all in.

He ripples and compresses, then his sails billow as he drifts lower in the tank. If those lights are his eyes, then we're almost face to face. Except, he has no face. And that's hard to accept.

Yes, we speak that way and also like this. Look lower.

I do, and a series of tiny ripples moves across the bulbous part of his body.

What did you just say?

That I think you look beautiful in that dress.

I laugh at that. *So, you have a word for dress?*

Well, no, not exactly. I had to make that part up.

I step closer until I can put my hand against the tank. I spread my fingers over the spot where his ripples originated from and smile at him, hoping he can see it. *I think you look beautiful in your dress too.*

A series of rapid flashes goes around his body, his tentacle ends curling up toward his underside. Then he shoots away from me so quickly I almost jump back. His body elongates and grows thin as he does complicated spins and whirls in his tank. There's no translation other than emotion: joy.

I laugh and watch him, wondering what it would be like to be able to move through the water like that.

When he returns, I figure I'd best get the big questions out of the way. It wouldn't do to keep them inside until they became awkward.

Can I ask you things? About your body?

Yes! Ask anything you like. I can tell he's glad that I'm curious, rather than running for the hills.

Where is your face? I mean, do you have one? Where are your eyes, your mouth? How do you eat? Why do you have two forms of communication?

Jack's laughter is reflected in the bright spots of orange and yellow that flow around his row of spots. Now that I'm close, I see that they aren't square or round, just sort of blotches that aren't even. They're exactly the same as the ones he showed me during that first ride in the subway car.

I don't have a face like yours, which is as weird for me as it is for you. I mean, your face. But I like your face now. It just takes getting used to.

This surprises me, and I widen my eyes at my aquatic boyfriend who's a cross between a squid, an octopus, and a cartoon character. Still, I guess that would make me fairly odd-looking to him too.

Okay. Moving on.

His body ripples again, but he moves on. *The lights you see are one way of speaking, and can be used within a larger group. The tactile communication on my body is for close friends or family only. A way of private communication. As for my eyes, those are here.*

He tilts a little and I see tiny depressions in his skin below the array of lights. They don't look like eyes to me at all, but what do I know?

My mouth is underneath. Do you want to see?

I sort of feel like I'm asking him to take off his pants, but he doesn't seem to mind. *If that's not rude, yes.*

It's not rude. We don't wear clothes. Everyone sees everyone else. We don't have the concept of modesty that humans do. It wouldn't make sense in the water.

When he tilts away from me and billows his sails, I see what he has hidden under there. And it's nothing much, just a tiny mouth with no lips. It flexes open and closed in a rhythmic pattern. *You breathe through it too?*

Exactly!

When he tilts back, I see the unmistakable pattern of his trace on the underside of one of his sails. It looks the same as the one he had as a human. At least I'll be able to pick him out of a crowd. Traces are unique to each individual and change as they take on additional forms and need more trace to remember every type of body experience.

Are you alone in there?

No. There are two others, but they're on the other side to give me privacy. They were working the Earth transfers, but they're taking a break now that it's stopped. I'm going to stay in here for a few days, so you can decide what you think about this.

Giving me space to decide if I can deal with it? Jack is probably the most considerate person ever if this is what he's doing. Then again, he couldn't possibly be any different from me, and this is something we'll need to deal with eventually. Of course, the more I watch him moving with such grace around the tank, the more intrigued I am. What would it be like to be able to do that? What would it feel like?

Yes. It's a lot to take in, he sends, as if confirming my thoughts.

You're not so different. I like your color.

He seems bashful almost. His tentacles curl a little. *I won't get my red for a while yet.*

Get your red? Now I'm curious for sure.

There is some obvious bashfulness now. I can almost feel embarrassment or something like it. It feels like red cheeks look. Then one of his tentacles touches a spot above his array of lights. *When we turn red up here, then we can go nearer the surface. I've never stayed in this body long enough to age it and I always start over from the age I was when I left my home world when I change back. So, I've never gotten my red.*

I'm not going to say I'm teasing him, but it could totally be construed as a tease. *You mean for mating?*

All his lights flash and I laugh, because I don't need a translation to know that's a groan of embarrassment.

Never mind! I won't ask that again. Of course, I'm still laughing, so there's that.

As strange as it sounds given the circumstances, I start to relax and enjoy my time with Jack as he was when he was born. The conversation is good, and I think he starts to relax too. The colors in his lights grow more mellow, his sails more billowy. And watching his lights as he talks is almost hypnotic.

I think that if I want to have a life worth living, I'll have to emulate my favorite space opera series on TV. I'll need to think of others not as what they look like, but as who they are. In my case, I have it easy. We can change forms as easily as we change clothes. I don't have to choose one form or the other. Jack and I and Esme and Rosa and Drives Too Hard and everyone else I've met can be whatever we want. Sometimes that might be the same, sometimes not.

But no matter what form he's in or I'm in, he's still Jack and I'm still Lysa.

When so much time has passed that my feet begin to ache and my bladder starts yammering at me, I know it's time to leave. He seems tired too, though I'm not sure how I can tell. I just can.

Leaning my cheek against his tank, I put my hand up and he curls a tentacle there. *I think you're lovely, Jack.*

I think you're lovely too.

Thirty-Five

I have everything I need and all that's left is to figure out when to do it. At least, I think I have what I need. I can't be sure, since I've never plotted the heist of a spaceship from a giant, sentient space station before. I can't help but wonder how many things I've missed, how many problems I've not considered, how many stumbling blocks I haven't seen that will knock me for a loop when the time comes.

The truth is that my biggest stumbling block is probably going to be the ship. I have my driver's license, but driving my mom's car on side roads does not prepare one for driving spaceships. It just doesn't. My hope is that the ship is like everything else around here and simply does what it's asked to do. Hub said the ships have a low-level version of its mind, so I'm guessing it will be like having command systems, but without all the omniscience and personality.

I hope.

Hub also told me that it didn't have any control over the ships, so that gives weight to the idea that the ships carry a separate program, one in which Hub isn't the boss.

Jack being gone is turning out to be good for me. Leaving him was something I dreaded. I'd been going over what I would do the last night I was here. At least a thousand different ways to say how I felt without giving away that I was leaving have been considered and discarded. Now, I won't have to do that. I'm relieved.

We chatted this morning while I ate breakfast, mind-chatted anyway. I tried to figure out if he wanted me to come there and see him again today without outright asking. Eventually, he seemed to get it and told me that he thought it would be best if I processed everything without pressure from him. It will only be for a few days, he'd said.

Yeah, a few days. Except I might not be here by the end of those few days.

I'd agreed with him, but it was hard to do. I can't hug him like he is now. There's no way to get a surreptitious kiss goodbye, though even thinking of kissing him in aquatic form is a little weird. For a few minutes, I consider asking Hub if I can change form and join him in the tank, but really, that's a step too far for me at this point. Plus, I don't want to go back to Earth with a trace and I'll get one if I change form. The last thing I want is my world thinking I'm an alien puppet about to take them for slaughter.

And really, they're going to freak as it is. I would freak. There will be epic levels of freaking out, without any doubt.

In keeping with my plan to make my movements seem normal for as long as possible, I take the transport toward the docks, but this time I bring my suit, so I can enter the work floor. I switch between this and going up onto the platform every other day or so. Jack usually came with me before, but I'm keeping up the habit even without him.

Hub should simply figure that I really like the docks. The other day, I delivered a painting of Drives Too Hard, but I couldn't tell who was who on the work floor until I contacted him via implant and he hopped in excitement. I'm not entirely sure what he thought of my painting—particularly considering that I did it on their shiny paper with their pigments, which are not subtly colored at all—but he conveyed excitement through the implant and seemed pleased to receive the gift.

And yes, I've figured out that Drives Too Hard is a "he." Or rather, as close a corollary to a male as can be assigned. They're actually very different in terms of gender, but for right now, in this life stage, the friendly Kassa is a he. In a few years...well...that will change. I wish I could stay and see that, but I can't. He's going to need the support of his friends when that time comes. I had hoped I would be one of those friends.

He introduced me to some of his work mates and while we were close, the subtle differences between them became apparent even to me. Drives Too Hard's eyes have a slightly more pronounced folded ridge beneath them. It makes them seem to tilt up at the ends, like a smile in the eyes. To them, they probably look as individual as all humans look to me.

And they were all very friendly, very funny in their own way, and absolutely lacking in social subtlety. I've been asked twice if Jack and I are going to "squish." Yes, I've been asked that. Drives Too Hard must have done some poking around about humans, just as I did to learn about the Kassa, because he hopped right in and told the asker that humans are secret about their squishing.

I can't be sure, because Kassa expressions are posture related, but I think that notion intrigued the other Kassa. I have zero doubt that someone in that group looked up human mating. None whatsoever.

Today when I arrive at the docks, open my implant, and ask for Drives Too Hard, he answers that he's in the dock where the new ships are and is working. I'm sort of bummed, but then I get a ping from a different Kassa.

You want to come in? Engine test today! I get an extremely excited translation, so I'm guessing that's an equally exciting activity.

Yes, who is this?

One of the many Kassa on the work floor is scurrying toward the glass in that way they do. I swear it looks like they're going to fall forward at any moment when they hurry. It stops and unfurls those fuzzy looking antennae, so that it has the most amusing crown around its head. *I'm Noisy Sleeper, brother-cousin of Drives Too Hard.*

I wave at the Kassa and hurry over to the little tunnel, which is an airlock. Luckily, I'm already suited. By the time the inner door opens, the Kassa is waiting, rather impatiently if the twitches are any indicator. It sticks out one of its upper arms toward me, the big manipulators that are their version of hands spread wide.

Good to meet you, Lysa! Shake, yes? Shake like human?

So, at least a few of the Kassa have indeed been digging into the human databanks. I extend my gloved hand and feel the rasp of the armored appendange as it slips into mine. One of the manipulators taps the back of my hand and I smile at the Kassa.

It's very good to meet you, Noisy Sleeper.

It lets me go without ceremony, then shuffles a bit and hops. There is certainly something exciting going on. It radiates from him like a physical thing, a corona of anticipation that should have a color, like a sun or the blue of a bright sky on a perfect day.

What's the engine test?

That was the right question, because I get a series of clicks coming through with the vague translation, *noises of excitement*. So, Noisy Sleeper is actually beyond words? Wow.

Come over, come over. We're going up to watch, he sends, backing up and ready to go.

I hurry after him as fast as the suit will let me. I'm getting more comfortable in the suits, which helps me to run, but the Kassa are extremely quick. If it came down to a chase, I would lose, which is a sobering thought when I think of what I'm going to do. At the tunnel entrance, a crowd of Kassa are mingling. I'm out of breath from running, so I'm glad to stop.

While I bend over and gasp, Noisy Sleeper taps my helmet and asks, *Are you ill? You are not normal now.*

Shaking my head with a grin, I marvel at how succinct they are about some things. *I'm fine. Running in this suit is difficult for me.*

Noisy Sleeper furls his antennae and another Kassa pushes him with a pair of manipulators. *Apologizing! I did not want to harm you!*

Looking between Noisy Sleeper and the Kassa that pushed him, I wave my hands downward and say, *I'm fine. Truly fine. Humans should be able to run better. I eat too much and don't practice running.*

I have no idea what the look the two Kassa exchange means, but I get hints of a head shake in there via the implant.

We go now. Can you go? Need to carry you?

The horrifying thought of being carried pushes back my fatigue. *Oh no, I'm fine. Quite fine. We're going up on the elevator?*

I can already see the open elevator door from here, so I answered my own question. Different groups of Kassa keep moving down the long quasi-hallway to other open elevator doors. I guess we're using all the elevators in this tunnel. Noisy Sleeper clicks and hisses at two Kassa and they take off for the next elevator, leaving he and I to take the first one in the tunnel. That's so nice of him.

I've got my breath by the time we get to the mid-level that puts us even with the ship. I capture the images of me standing in an elevator with a dozen Kassa, because the sight is just so funny and awesome. I'm taller than them by almost a head, so there I am, sticking up in my suit helmet from a crowd of excited bug-looking people. It's hilarious, so I capture the view from the front as well. If I get the chance, I really want to show this to my mom. She'll get a kick out of it.

There are a hundred or more Kassa all along the tunnel, all facing the glass and the ship beyond. Noisy Sleeper stands next to me and hops when it says, *Starting engines now.*

For a long time, nothing happens. After about five minutes, I tap Noisy Sleeper's manipulator where its pressed to the glass next to my hand. *Why are they testing engines?*

Leaving soon on mission. That ship. He points to the ship attached to the ladder and gantry that represent my only shot at getting up to a ship. This is the ship I've created all my plans around.

My stomach drops into my boots and my heart seems to skip a beat. Swallowing down an immediate sensation of panic, I try to remain calm and send, *When are they leaving? Today? Tomorrow?*

I know what the Kassa version of a shrug looks like from looking up their species, and Noisy Sleeper does that now. *Not sure. Soon. When's your tomorrow?*

My timeline just shrunk, I think. Then again, the Kassa definition of a day is very different from mine. Their day is about two weeks long in Earth time. I suck in a deep breath, reaching for calm and peace. I'm doing the right thing, the needed thing, so things have to work out. That's just the way the universe operates, I think. Asking the implant for time definitions, I find one that will suit the situation.

Will it be this work cycle? Next work cycle?

Noisy Sleeper rotates its head a little, which is their way of expressing approval. *Start of next work cycle!*

That means I have two days. Just two days. Their next work cycle starts in three days, right about mid-morning for me. At that time, Drives Too Hard and his brother-cousins will all go off shift and the next group will come on shift. I can't wait until that last day either, because I have no idea what process they use when they change shifts. For all I know it's an all day affair.

As I try to figure out if I've got the stones to really do this, a vibration starts in the glass and all the Kassa along the tunnel hop, unfurl antennae, and generally fidget. All faces are glued to the ship beyond the glass. They are enraptured. I watch the ship, thinking I'll see blue light come out of the propulsion like in the movies. Alas, nothing like that happens. There's no visible hint that the engines are running, only that vibration.

I know the Kassa can see using parts of the light spectrum I can't, so I wonder what they're seeing. After a minute or so of vibration, it stops and all the Kassa seem to deflate as one. Not really deflating, but more like a sigh, like they're relieved or something.

Did it go well?

Noisy Sleeper's eyes are shiny and his neck has a little extra curve in it. To me he looks relaxed and happy, like I might feel after a good meal. *Excellent. Very finely calibrated. Beautiful work!*

That's good news, I send. And I really mean that. After all, I'm going to need those engines.

And I'm going to need them in two days.

Thirty-Six

The cabinet bot delivers my quasi-luggage, pushing it along like the cabinet is getting ready to check its bags. It's sort of funny. I'm glad no one asked me why I wanted a rolling crate. This is the last piece to my puzzle. While I probably need to sleep, I can't sit still. I test the safety lines on the hook I specified for my crate and it attaches perfectly. I'll be able to hoist up the bag currently nestled inside the crate once I reach the top of the ladder. Assuming I reach it. Well, assuming a whole lot.

Once I'm done packing, I have a thirty-pound crate. The small items, the most important ones, will be tucked inside my suit. The camera, the portable control surface, as well as a few other things too important to risk will be stowed safely next to my body in the suit.

I'm ready.

The painting on my easel is covered by a cloth. I don't want anyone to see it until tomorrow. The painting is almost done, and I think I'm going to leave it this way.

Not quite finished. That sends a message too, and it's one I hope Hub will understand.

I'm fidgety now that I'm done. I think about unpacking my crate and packing it again for the third time. If I keep doing that, I'll eventually get sloppy and that would be bad. I need to focus my thoughts on something else altogether. It takes a few turns around my room and some self-talk, but I manage to convince myself that everything is packed perfectly and should be left alone. I've got to distract myself before my nerves get the better of me.

Looking up at the ceiling, I ask, "Hub, how is Heather doing?"

"Her visit with you was immensely helpful, Lysa. She is doing quite well and fully engaged in her orientation. She is, as you're fond of a saying, a real trooper."

I'm relieved to hear it. The way she looked when she came here was awful and I'm happy to hear she's joined into our little fray. "Did she get her lymphoma fixed?" I ask, not forgetting why it was so urgent she get help quickly.

"I'm not sure I should share medical information, Lysa."

"That's not fair! I mean, you brought her here because she had it bad. It's only right to let me know if I did the job correctly." Will that work? It would work on my mom.

It does, because Hub says, "In that case, I'm pleased to report that Heather is entirely well in that regard. She has been healed."

Clapping my hands, I say, "Bravo, Hub! Fantastic job."

"To you as well, Lysa."

We fall silent a moment, and I consider asking to talk to her again, but I don't think that's a good idea. The temptation to share something—anything—with another person might be too much. Best to avoid that.

"Is there anything else, Lysa?"

"No, goodnight Hub. And thank you for all that you do. I really mean that." I shouldn't say that stuff, but I have to. I have to say thank you before I go.

"You're welcome, Lysa. Goodnight to you too."

My fidgets have vanished. I'm glad I asked about her. If she's so much better for knowing the truth, then I'm doing the right thing, a good thing. Even if it means I never see Jack again or travel beyond my planet or live the eternal life of a Ranger out in space, I have to do what needs to be done.

Rather than sit here and dwell for my remaining hours, I climb into bed. For a little while, my brain won't slow down, but eventually, my tiredness overcomes my anxiety and at last, I can sleep.

*****

Since I cleared my calendar and marked my day as a non-working day, nothing wakes me. So of course, I sleep later than I wanted. Springing up out of my bed the moment I realize the time really does say eight o'clock gives me an immediate headache and a bad mood.

That won't do.

I'm not using my implant unless absolutely necessary, but I need it now, so I turn it on to order coffee, extra orange juice, and a full English breakfast. No one should judge me for that one, because I've got a rough day ahead. Then I run for the shower. The bot pings me before I've even rinsed off the soap suds, so I do my best not to lose my towel while retrieving the delicious smelling tray.

Getting dressed faster than I thought humanly possible, I try to savor my meal. It reminds me of my mom and a place we used to go on those rare occasions when we actually got our act together in time to see a Sunday matinee. That was when I was still little. She'd take me to this pub that served the best breakfasts. It was the only place I went where I didn't have to order a kid's meal. She and I would have this breakfast and get excited over whatever princess movie I was about to see.

I have a great mom. I didn't appreciate her enough and I hope to make some amends for that. *I'm going to see my mom.* The thought hits me like a punch, but a good punch. I've missed her so much my heart feels like someone is squeezing it for the juice. Now, I'm going to finally…at last…see her again.

I'm getting weepy-eyed all the sudden and that is almost the last thing I need today, so I drain my juice and bring my coffee into the bathroom to finish getting ready. I'll need a clear field of view, so I braid back two sections of hair and clip them together at the back of my head. I give it a shake and it stays put, so I'm good there.

Basic clothes are the rule of the day. No funny tee shirts about aliens, especially considering what I'm about to do. I put on a plain black tee, then realize I look like a scared goth. My nervousness has made me pale. Switching it for a nice sky-blue one works better.

"Yeah, a nice calm color. Calm is good," I say to myself in the mirror.

A pair of jeans and some slip-on skater shoes are the only other things I'm going to wear. I need to keep the weight down and my body free to move.

Calling the cabinet bot for my dishes, I gather them up and put them outside the door, then wipe off the table so that the surface is free of debris. Putting the environment suit I intend to wear on top of my rolling crate, I survey the room that's been mine for almost two months.

My room is clean, with everything put away. It barely seems anyone lived here. I've packed up the art supplies and left the box behind the easel. All that's left is my easel and the pictures I've made while here. I ordered some frames—which stick to the walls anywhere you put them in some mysterious way—and arranged many of them around the walls. The order they're in tells a story, and I hope Hub and Jack will understand the tale.

I can't know if it will translate, but it's the best I can do. The rest of the pictures, the ones that simply punctuate the story, are spread out on the table. There's just the one on the easel left. I lift off the cloth and fold it while I look for a moment. Will Hub understand? Will Jack?

I don't know. I hope so. That painting is the only of them that isn't signed, isn't complete.

With one last look around my room, I try to say goodbye, but what keeps nudging that aside is the hope that I'll come back. I'm returning to Earth, but I still feel like my future is here. I always wanted to work by digging up the past. I didn't realize that what I really wanted was to bring it back to life. Here, I can almost do that.

And I don't even need to finish high school to do it.

The bot passes my door as I step out and sends me a smiley face, so I say, "Thank you."

With that, I walk out, rolling my cabinet behind me.

Thirty-Seven

I'm not at all worried about this first part. I feel even better after seeing Esme on my way out of the wing. She greets me with a big smile and points at my cart. "Going somewhere special?"

With a wink and a smile so easy it almost surprises me, I say, "The Kassa like my art. I thought I'd do more for them."

The expression on her face makes me feel like garbage. She looks proud of me. "I'm so glad you're settling in."

"Give me another week and I'll be changing bodies and asking for a job." With that, I push through the door and exit the wing to the sound of her delighted laughter.

The subway ride goes well, but I start to get nervous when the little car comes. The butterflies in my stomach turn to bats the size of housecats as I put on my environment suit. With all the busy machines on the transport level zipping past with their mysterious crates and bubbles of water, I'm in a crowd, but also very alone.

The darkness when my car shoots down the shaft for the entrance level matches my sadness. As always, that darkness lifts, and so must my feelings, because I have work to do.

The suit slips up my torso, then one arm, then the other. This isn't the time to get sloppy, so I pay attention and do it right. Inside the suit are big pockets that Jack told me are for longer term support equipment. Given their locations near my hips, I'm guessing those are for various machines to take care of bladder needs and so on. For now, they function perfectly to hold my portable control surface and my camera.

Basically, anything that I can't leave behind goes inside. I bounce around experimentally before sealing myself up. I'm a little heavier with the gear, but the flaps on the pockets keep everything secure. I seal my shoes in after a moment of consideration. I have no idea if I can get more on the ship and the idea of being without shoes for however long bothers me for some reason.

I can't explain it, but there it is. I need shoes. Being barefoot while saving the planet is just out of the question.

Now comes the hard part. I ordered a utility belt suitable for the environment suits and I put that on, then clip each of my safety lines to it. If I was feeling heavy before, I'm really weighty now. The lines themselves are made of some super-light material, but the metal clips are heavy considering how many I have attached to my suit.

A final clip goes from me to the crate. The line for that will pay out as I climb. Inside the crate, my belongings are tied up in a bag that can resist the Kassa atmosphere. My cards with the Kassa glyphs are on a big ring, with the English on the back of each card. I've practiced, and I'm fairly quick with them, but we'll see how well I do when I'm nervous. That big ring goes on another clip at my chest. I flip it up and yes, I still have room to hold it. The position is a little awkward, but it won't get in my way as I climb.

I'm not taking the cart onto the ship, but it will ease my burden until I get to the ladder. Once I reach the top, I'll have to heave the bag up all that distance. I'm not sure I can do that, or that I'll have time, but I have no idea if there's food for humans on the ship. Then again, I can survive a good while without food, so if I have to drop it, I will. I've got enough proof inside my suit.

Yeah, and the spaceship. That's proof too.

When I seal the helmet, I wait for the pink light and feel the whispering stream of human-safe atmosphere against my neck. The tiny module that serves up the atmosphere from the gases outside weighs so little that I thought it was part of the helmet. My power readout tells me I'm at max, so I'm good.

I'm ready. I can do this.

The distance to the airlock is just enough that the sound of my too-rapid breathing starts to ratchet up my nerves. Without someone to talk to through the speakers in my helmet, my sounds are louder. The tightness in my chest makes my breaths almost raspy sounding. Before I dare turn on my implant to cycle the doors, I have to calm down. There's too much risk that some of my emotions will bleed through, and my mind is screaming about everything that might go wrong.

Taking a few deep breaths, I try to focus on something—anything—that will calm me down. Jack's face comes to mind, and then him as he is now. Grabbing that like a life raft, I imagine floating in the water, free of worry or fear. The warmth, the lift and fall of motion in water, the light making it all beautiful. It works, at least enough so that the heartbeat pounding in my ears dials down a notch.

Before I lose that fleeting and hard-won sense of peace, I open my implant to cycle the door and step inside. The wind inside buffets me about and I focus on warm water, floating with my face to the sun and nothing but endless, salty sea below me. When I step through, I shut off the implant for the last time.

Goodbye.

Glancing around the work floor, I don't see anything amiss. The space is huge, possibly a half-mile long in total and a quarter-mile wide. Size is so much different in space without any gravity outside to press down on construction. Looking around, I realize how beautiful it all is. I hadn't really noticed that before, but it is. The curve of the ceiling sloping up to a point so high I can no longer make out details, the way the ship beyond the glass reflects gray and blue into the room. It's a marvel.

The Kassa are at the far end, working around their beloved machines, as usual. No one is in my immediate area, but it won't take long for them to notice me. Pulling my cart as casually as possible, I start in the opposite direction, toward the ship.

While I'm in this area, no one should think anything is the matter. Once I cross into the area near the ladder and gangway to the ship, I'll have no excuses. Then it will be a matter of speed. Without my implant on, I can't hear if anyone pings me, but I hope that won't be considered out of character.

I've been careful to cultivate an impression that I feel uneasy with my implant, so even the Kassa know I leave it off at times. Waving two arms above them is the way they draw attention with each other, and they've learned that it works to get my attention too. So long as I face away, no one should think much of my not answering.

Plus, I let Hub and the Kassa know I wanted to come and paint this area in real life rather than from memory. I've conveyed images of what it looks like to paint to the Kassa, complete with easel and stool, so my cart shouldn't be cause for alarm.

At least, I hope so. That's the plan anyway.

My heart is back to pounding so hard that it hurts my ears by the time I get even with the end of the workspaces. The space is defined by a stripe of some kind on the floor. It looks like a non-color to me, noticeable only by the slight shimmer, but Jack told me it's very visible to the Kassa. It's their version of the bright yellow line striped by black we use to denote such areas on Earth.

Earth. I'm coming.

Looking back before I cross the line, I see three Kassa hurrying my way. One of them raises two arms. Unlike before, this posture doesn't look relaxed like a simple wave. The movement has purpose. I know they want me to stop.

I know I can't outrun them, but I run anyway. The ladder is at least two hundred yards away. That doesn't sound like much, but in a suit stuffed with gear and dragging a cart, it's a very long way indeed. My breath is bellowing when the first of the Kassa catches up with me.

I'm no good at recognizing them as individuals, particularly not when in a blind panic, but I stop and flip through my cards. I hold up the ones I need in order.

Please don't tell Hub. Let me go. I must go. I must do like Krissa food machine for my people.

The Kassa looks from my cards to me and I see something new. The way the antennae furl and unfurl is the same when they show confusion. I flip another card and hope that this one will break through. *Free will.*

The Kassa almost starts when he sees it, then surprises me by rotating quickly to face all the other Kassa, making a rapid clicking and hissing. The noise is so loud and sharp I can hear it through my suit. It resonates through the space like it does through my body. It's urgent. I can tell that much. All the Kassa except the one talking immediately drop face down on the deck and almost retreat into their armored bodies. I choke back a near cry because I know what this is from looking at the Kassa cultural databanks. This is the posture of silence, of hiding, of not making a noise. They will keep my secret.

They understand.

He turns back to me, his neck and head lowering, two manipulators reaching for my little stack of cards and flipping them till he holds the card he wants. He taps the glyph that means *Go*.

I run like my life depends on it. Not because of the Kassa, but because it's entirely possible that one of them might have accidentally communicated the irregularity on the work floor before getting the signal to be quiet. And if the Hub knows, then the Hub could stop me.

There are Kassa on the ladder above me, but I don't have time to worry about them. Unlike me, they can go up and down the ladder from both sides. Right now, they appear to be hurrying down the ladder from the back, probably so that they can get into the quiet position. I don't delay, parking my cart and unlatching the lid so that my bag with its many coils of line are visible. Making sure the end of that line is attached to me, I start climbing.

The ladder is far more frightening in real life than from a distance. It's not even really a ladder. It's more like a shallow stairway with treads only wide enough for a baby's foot. Each tread is heavily textured. The treads are so rough they would tear apart a human's soft, bare foot, but the boots on my environment suit are tough. Let's hope they're tough enough. This entire ladder is perfect for Kassa, but absolutely awful for humans. The only thing that makes this possible are the rungs on the side, which are wide enough for my hands and small enough for the clips.

The measurements on the drawing gave me enough data to work with, but if I don't place that first clip correctly, I'll run out of safety line. I wait as long as I can before that first clip goes on. Looking down, I find that the Kassa who followed me is no more than ten feet below, its neck extended and its antennae tightly furled around its head. The two that were on the ladder are now crouched at the foot of it, their heads tucked in and entirely still. Meeting the gaze of the one below me, I read uneasiness, even a bit of fear. I don't need an implant to know that.

The other two that initially ran after me are still on the work floor, but both are looking up at me. I have no doubt they're wondering what I'm doing, but it wouldn't be like them to think I was up to something bad. That's not their way. I think they might be lookouts. The way they survey me, then the giant glass windows separating the hangar bay from the station screams lookout. No, they don't think I'm up to any nefarious.

Are they confused about my purpose? Yes, probably. Suspicious about my purpose? No, definitely not.

Once the clip is on I feel less like I'm in mortal danger from the fall. I'm probably no more than forty feet up, but forty feet looks like a long distance from my perspective. The trembling in my arms and legs feels huge and obvious, but my gloved hands look steady to me. The shaking is making my fear worse. What if I lose my grip?

By the time the first safety line tugs at my middle and I reach for the second clip, I'm already breathing too hard and my thigh muscles are screaming for me to stop. Unclipping the spent line relieves me of a tiny bit of weight. Carefully, I clip that free end to a rung so it won't fall down and hit the Kassa below me. So far, so good. Then I make the mistake of looking up. There so much more to go. I've barely started on this long ladder.

Head down, I focus on each hand hold, each toe hold. Then I do it again. Over and over, and during each step, I think to myself, *You can do this. You can do this.*

I almost lose my grip somewhere along the course of my fifth safety line when the Kassa that was below me scrambles up the back of the ladder. It stops and turns around, following me up while waving downward at me. I know it can see how fatigued I'm getting, and probably doesn't want me to fall. I shake my head and look upward to let it know I won't stop. At last, it disappears to get below me again. I pause long enough to catch a little of my breath back.

Hooking my arm around the side rung is awkward, but it gives my cramping hands a tiny break and lets me stand on the narrow stair tread enough to relieve the burning agony in my thigh muscles. The pain is so great that my eyes tear up, but the last thing I need is blurry vision. I blink them away, whispering harsh things to myself about being tough, not being a baby…about not giving up.

The safety lines decrease in number, the weight of them falling away and giving that little extra I need right when I need it. As I near the top, my trembling limbs are so fatigued that I'm no longer entirely certain my hands are gripping the rungs until I see it with my eyes. I reach for another clip to find none.

All that's left is the second end to the one now tugging at my waist. Looking up, I see at least forty feet of ladder left. I don't want to look down, but I do. I almost fall at the sight of so much distance. The two Kassa at the bottom of the ladder appear tiny now, nothing more than brown dots.

What do I do? I can try to go down and unhook my clip, taking the time to hook and unhook with each step. Or I can go on without it. My arms are shaking visibly now. I know I'm hanging on with nothing but grit. I've got almost nothing left inside me. The temptation to let go and let the safety line catch me so I can rest is incredibly intense. It takes an almost physical effort to push it away.

I reverse course and take one shaky step back down. I'm not sure I can do it. My leg won't straighten again, no matter how hard I push. The squeal that escapes me echoes in the helmet, reverberating back to me in tones of pain and frustration. The Kassa below me pauses, looks from me to my line and then scrambles quickly downward. I can hardly believe my eyes, but it unhooks my line and darts back up to me with such ease that I almost hate it for its endurance. Scrambling past me on the back of the ladder, I meet its eyes for one brief second.

It's Drives Too Hard. I know it. I know it wasn't him when I started on this ladder, but I know it's him now. During these long minutes of intense concentration, I somehow missed the swap. I don't know whether it's the way he wears his tool belt or that strange little V of space in the brushy, moth-like antennae around his head, but I know this is him. If I could spend time looking at his face, I might recognize that extra fold below his eyes, but I don't need it.

There's a momentary tug, then the pull eases as he clips my safety line well above me. The line is enough to get me to the top. Just barely, but enough. I shake my head to try and push back the tears, but I want more than anything to be able to tell him how much this means to me. He looks down at me and slips fully around to the back of the ladder, leaving me room to climb.

The break has helped. My fingers feel more secure and my legs lighter, the song of pain in my thigh muscles lowering in volume. Maybe it's just that I can see the top and know how close I am. Rather than hurry, I place each foot with care, gripping each rung with cautious fingers.

And then I'm at the top.

Drives Too Hard follows me up and scurries a little away from me. He has to know what I'm doing, but either he doesn't fully understand that I mean to steal the ship or he's okay with it. Either way, I'm grateful, but time is pressing on me. The fact that the Kassa exercised their free will and solved the Krissa problem is probably my greatest ally.

After bending over and gasping like an oxygen-starved fish out of water, I look over the edge toward my almost invisible bag at the bottom of the long ladder. There's no way I can haul my bag up. What was I thinking to believe

I could? I unclip the line and, rather than let it fall where it might hurt someone far below, I hook it to the last rung of the ladder and turn away. If I starve, I starve.

Maybe I'll just take the ship through a drive through. A very big drive through. Fish sandwiches for all my friends. Perhaps I'm getting delirious, or the stress is taking a toll, but I laugh. It sounds more like a choke, but it was a laugh.

My legs feel like jelly and that first step on the gangway puts me on my knees. My leg muscles just won't work. Screaming in frustration, I hit at my legs with my fists until I start to feel the blows, then rise awkwardly, holding onto my knees to brace myself. The little tunnel that leads to the hatch is a few hundred feet away at least. I'll never make it.

Drives Too Hard doesn't approach me, but he follows me through each lurching step, his two top arms reaching out and pulling back every time I stumble. It's like he wants to help me, but can't bring himself to because he understands the rules. Free will, but no interference. I wonder if he'll help me if I simply can't do it. Would he break Hub's rule? Does that rule even apply to them?

Dizziness hits me so suddenly and intensely that I have no time to prepare for it, no time to sit or crouch. When my head clears, I find myself back on my knees with my arm hooked over the railing to the gangway. The floor far below me is a mere step away. Standing up is harder—much harder—this time. The scream of frustration in my helmet makes my ears ring, but it gives me strength.

Reaching the tunnel—or airlock since that's what it is—is like reaching an oasis after a long trip through the desert. My helmet bangs against the glass and I put my glove to the control surface. One last hurdle and I'm there. I've done it.

Nothing happens. Moving my hand, I press my palm to the surface again more firmly. Again, nothing.

With an angry cry, I realize why. Why hadn't I thought of that? Jack told me that our IDs don't go through the gloves for these suits. Humans are too fragile for a stronger implant. This door is still a part of the Hub, which means using my implant to open it will alert Hub in a way that physical opening will not. Anything relayed through the implant is relayed through Hub. I can't open the door. Well, I can, but this is going to hurt.

I know what's going to happen, but for some reason, the consequences don't give me pause. Fumbling for the seal that will unseat my glove, I feel something press against my back and jump in alarm. A Kassa arm reaches past me, the manipulator pressing against the plate. The door to the airlock hisses open and I step through, looking back at Drives Too Hard for just a second.

What he does next is almost too much. He presses two pairs of his manipulators together, the tips touching each other just so, the armored pads ever so slightly apart. Then he bows just a little.

Namaskar.

I know Hub explained to the Kassa what that meant. The words of translation are simple, but the meanings are many. Depending on how one holds their hands or bows, how one uses the word, or what form of the word they use, the meaning changes. Hub explained that to them after our first encounter. And what Drives Too Hard has done is how I would do it for someone that holds my greatest respect and love.

A sob tears at me, and it hurts my already raw throat. I hope with all my heart that I will see him again. He is my friend. I hold my arms up over my head and shake my hands, which is the best I can do to mimic the way they would greet a brother-cousin. I hope he understands.

Turning away, I have to hurry. The Kassa can go into this area, so I'm not overly worried that I've raised an alarm, but that doesn't mean anything at this point. The whole episode is an alarm waiting to happen.

The only purpose of this airlock is to reach the hatch and it contains an atmosphere safe for Kassa. There was no delay or warning, and there would have been if this wasn't a Kassa-safe atmosphere. That means the air in here is definitely not safe for me. I'm in the same position as I was before I got into this airlock.

My legs feel the tiniest bit better now, but with each step I feel a pulling, stinging sensation that will, no doubt, make me want to die tomorrow. Hurrying across the airlock, I see the gleaming deep blue of the ship's exterior around the hatch, the silver surface of the control panel bright against all that blue.

This hatch belongs to the ship, not the Hub, but even so, the ship is docked and I can't risk opening the implant. Not while I'm still on the station. I have to step over that barrier before I dare turn on my implant.

I have no idea what will happen when I take off my glove, but I can guess, and Drives Too Hard isn't here to help me this time. Gritting my teeth, I unseat the glove.

For a brief second, I think everything is going to be okay. Then it's not.

A searing pain envelopes my hand. It feels as if someone stuck my arm inside a vat of boiling oil. I scream as bubbles appear on my skin, the flesh opening under the power of the corrosive atmosphere. Slapping my burning hand to the control surface, the door opens and a warning flashes that the atmosphere is in standby. I leave a bloody smear on the plate and bits of my skin with it. Cradling my hand and screaming, I step over the threshold. Blood starts dripping from my hand and wrist, but immediately turns into a stream, painting the front of my suit in brilliant red.

I may have just killed myself after all.

Thirty-Eight

I open my implant, but my head is going fuzzy all the sudden. I have no idea if the ship works like Hub. Shouting in my helmet is loud, but it also helps me stay awake and aware. "Ship, can you hear me?"

Inside my head, I feel the answer, but it's soft-edged and strange. *I can hear you, Lysa.*

I have to assume that the ship knows who I am because I'm registered at the station. The voice is different than Hub's inside my head, so I'm hoping this really is an independent machine. "Talk to me out loud. Do you know what I am? Human? I need human atmosphere now!"

The ship answers me in my head and via the helmet simultaneously, "Human atmosphere in eighty-three seconds."

"Which way to the bridge? Show me!"

I'm in that same chamber I saw on the images Hub gave me. Beyond should be the room with the mysterious indentations, then the three hallways. I look down and see the front of my suit is now liberally splashed with red, long runners of it reaching all the way to my knees. I feel it pattering against the tops of my white boots. Letting go of my hand, there is a renewed flow. Despite the pain, I rotate my wrist and see the huge craters there. That's where most of the blood is coming from…and it's spurting.

With my gloved fingers, I push the melted looking flesh together and press hard. The big spurts diminish into steady pattering drops, but that's an improvement. The pain also clears some of the fog in my brain. I look up to find pink dashes lighting up the control surfaces. Running feels strange, almost like I'm floating a few inches above the deck. I can barely feel it through the boots of my suit. Even my lungs feel bubbly and broken, breathing now taking more effort than I remember.

Everything flies past me in a haze. All I see are wavering pink dashes of light and hallways that seem to narrow and widen even as I run. I lose it in one of the wavering hallways, slamming into the side so hard that my ears ring from the helmet's impact. It does help though, shaking me up enough that I can see again.

The end of the hallway is ahead and as I approach, a wide door slides open into a dim space. "I need human light!"

Lights come up and I suck in a bubbly breath at what I see. This is definitely the bridge. The excitement is enough to push back the darkness edging into my vision, like the creeping tendrils of unwanted vines. Clearly this isn't set up for humans, but I wouldn't expect it to be.

There are wide benches at different spots around the walls, giant silvery areas depicting the locations of control panels and screens. The screens are blank now, but the starkness makes the room even brighter as the lights come up.

In the center, there's another wide bench, the edges curved upward. In front of that bench is a pedestal.

"I need a view outside. Where's the helm or whatever else I can use to move the ship?"

My voice sounds weaker than I've ever heard it before, breathy, the words not as loud as they should be considering how hard I'm trying to talk. There's a wet hint to the words and when I cough, a fine mist of red paints the inside of my helmet. I feel like my body is ebbing away, becoming less substantial somehow.

The entire upper half of the room opposite me becomes a viewscreen, and I'm a little revived by what I see. The stars.

The pedestal in front of the bigger bench glows to life. It's beautiful. Silver and blue and radiant. A blue-ish dome of light springs to life above it. I've not seen this before and I have zero idea how to interact with it.

"I need Earth, the human home-world. Do you know where that is?"

"I do, Lysa. Observe and confirm."

I have no clue what that means, but then the blue dome of light changes. Shapes coalesce inside, and I stagger toward it. There's a little rail around the pedestal and I lean on it for support. Otherwise, I would fall. I want to sleep, but then, inside the light I see the unmistakable form of Earth. The Australian landmass, a shape every schoolchild knows, spins past me, then I see the other continents and smile. I'm almost surprised that I can smile, given the situation, but I can. *Home.*

"Yes, that's it! Take me there!"

"I cannot, Lysa."

My heart plummets. Was all this for nothing? Am I bleeding to death for no reason? "What do you mean, you can't? Why can't you?"

"We are currently docked."

Gritting my teeth, I shuffle around the pedestal until I half-fall onto the bench. Keeping my fingers pinched on my wrist is harder than it should be. "Undock."

"I require authorization, Lysa."

My head drops until my helmet bangs on the pedestal's railing and wakes me back up. I know what the ship just said, but the words aren't sinking in. I can't bring up the resources inside myself to deal with it. I can't.

But I have to.

"How do I get authorization, ship?" My voice is nothing more than a whisper. I hope my thoughts are louder.

A hum sends the faintest vibration through my helmet. Opening my eyes, I look up. I can't even really lift my head anymore, only my eyes want to obey me. A control surface rises from a little spot on the pedestal only a foot from my helmet. A choked noise that I meant to be a laugh escapes me.

It needs my hand.

My hand that is nothing more than cratered meat, bone, and blood. Using my gloved hand to lift my useless one to the surface, I find that I can't move the fingers enough to open them and lay my hand flat. This hand no longer obeys me. It's way past that. Letting go of my wrist, I press my fingers down with my other hand, the stream of blood picking up speed as soon as I let go. I can hear the patters of it hitting my boots again. *Tap, tap, plop.* This time I can also feel the tiny impacts of it. Fissures open along the joints as I press, but it doesn't matter.

I have the ridiculous thought that I'll never paint with that hand again. Of course, I already know I won't do anything with that hand again. Or any other part of me. But this is okay. It's good. It's the right thing.

As long as I can get to Earth and bring the ship, I'll have given them proof. My portable control surface has enough imagery. I just need to live long enough to give the instructions to the ship to relay my data. There must be bots on board that can get it out of my suit. I don't have to be alive for that.

Finally, contact is made between my ID and the control surface. It glows with that silvery light. There is an eternal moment of nothing before the hum of the ship coming to life around me begins. I'm not sure if my face is smiling, but my mind is. I know that much.

"Go to Earth. Over North America. Get close enough to be seen, but not so close that you'll hurt anything. Take me home. Can you do that?"

"Yes, Lysa."

"Then go. Home, take me home."

I don't feel the ship moving, but I know it is from the way the girders of the station retreat on the viewscreen. The progress is very slow, but none of that matters now.

"Opening a portal," the ships says, the voice competent and sure.

The sensation that I'm falling asleep fades a little when the bridge floods with light. Pink and purple light washes out the blue controls and fills every crevice with that extraordinary light. I pick my head up and my entire body tingles with the sight of it. Again, I bathe in the feeling of eternity, of endlessness. The portal is immense, so big and bright. The blue swirls seem alive, twisting along the seams of color. And like before, I feel it like a force, urging me on, urging me forward.

It seems close, but I know the portal is still some distance from us. I have a little time, a moment or two. While I have this moment of awareness, I focus my comms on the Hub and send, *Can you hear me, Hub?*

Yes, Lysa. I can hear you.

The soft kindness of Hub's voice undoes me, and tears fall on my cheeks. They feel hot against my skin. The sob makes more tiny red spots join the others on the inside of my helmet. Soon, I won't be able to see through all the red.

I'm sorry I stole your ship. So sorry.

I know, Lysa.

I had to. Free will, you know. You remember?

I do. The hub's voice pauses in my head, then it sends, *Lysa, you are gravely injured. I cannot help you on the ship.*

That's okay, Hub. I just have to get the ship to Earth. It's all okay.

There's so much more in my head that I can't say, so much that I feel. I want to tell Hub how much being here has meant to me, how much I care for it and all that it keeps safe inside the station. For Jack. I want to somehow let Hub know that my only regret is that I will miss spending my life with them. I want it to know my heart, but I can't anymore. The pain is bad, but the feeling of slipping away is even worse.

Hub...I...

I know, Lysa. I hear you. All will be as it will. I'm here with you. I will always be with you.

And then I feel it, emotions so strong they have weight. A love so powerful that it erases my fear and eases my pain. This is the love of a planet's worth of life joined into one being, projected onto me like a blanket on a cold day. It's Hub's goodbye gift to me, to make my death less horrible. To let me know that I'm loved.

The smell of jasmine fills my nose. The faint murmur of cotton against cotton, of skirts in motion. It tickles my ears and my memories. Those are the smells and sounds of comfort. Grandmother? Is she here?

In my mind, it all comes together. My grandmother's smile as we sat in the museum that day. Her dark eyes tilting up at the edges as she explained life, the warm urging I felt in front of the portal when others felt only fear, the way Hub opened its history to me, even meeting Heather and hearing her tale. All of it comes together in a cluster of coincidences that can't be what they seem. Or can they?

Hub, did you know? Did you know I would do this?

No, Lysa. I only hoped.

The portal is growing, no longer entirely visible in the viewscreen. The center is brighter, closer. Suddenly, I'm afraid of it. Afraid of what will happen. Afraid it won't be enough.

My vision blurs against the light and I'm transported into something that feels like memory, but can't possibly be one. It has to be a dream, a dying dream.

The room with the wall indentations I just went through is there, but this time there are environment suits in each depression. They fit perfectly. Spread on the floor around me is another suit, and I see my hands playing with the control surface on a sleeve. Except, those aren't my hands. These are child hands, almost those of a baby, chubby and small, the fingers blunted and soft.

And there is a birthmark on one hand, a discolored spot I know well. The tiny birthmark, shaped almost like a heart, is sharply defined and new on this child's hand, just below the knuckle. I don't have that birthmark, but my mother does. This hand isn't mine. It's my mother's.

A noise makes me look up just as a woman rounds the corner into the space. She is young, and her beauty is heart-breaking. He sari gleams and sways with her long, confident strides. Her hair tumbles down her back in a deep brown, almost black wave. Behind her, a blond-haired man with a smile softening his features pauses to lean against the wall.

Grandmother? Grandfather? It can't be.

As the woman reaches me, her skirts swish. Kneeling, she says, "Barbara, you know these aren't toys. Come and see. We're almost there." Looking to the side, she says to a cabinet bot near me. "You're supposed to watch her, not help her make mischief."

She tousles my hair, then stands and takes the man's hand. I get up to follow, listening as they murmur and laugh. The bright color of her sari and one slender foot are the last I see as they disappear around the corner ahead of me.

What is this? What does this mean? Why is she calling me by my mother's name?

I'm brought out of the vision and back into my hurting body by another hum. I look to see a sort of cabinet bot entering the bridge. The bot is different, but clearly of the same general format. It rolls up near me and the top unfolds like a table. I think it wants me to get on it. It flashes a sad face on the panel, then a red cross.

I can't move. I simply can't. I've gone past that.

The center of the portal is so close it feels alive. Warm and alive. The momentary panic of before vanishes under the spell of it. A stretchy feeling begins within me, a tug of atoms that wish to go their own way, to fly free as they will.

Hub, I'm afraid.
I know, Lysa.
What's going to happen?
What must happen.

There's a crackling feeling as the portal envelops the ship. Some part of me wants to survive, even now when it's far too late for such desires. The urge is there though, and that deep animal part of me opens my eyes wide, ready for fight or flight. The light is everywhere. *So beautiful.* All I can do is let my head fall back against the bench and watch it come. When the bridge enters the portal, I feel as if I'm stretched like taffy, as long as a galaxy and as thin as a spider's thread. The last thing I hear is my own halting, bubbling breaths in the otherwise perfect silence. The pink and purple light takes my stolen ship home.

Home.

Then, the silence is complete. The light, gone.

Epilogue

Jack shoots around his tank in frustration. This is the first time he's ever felt constrained by the tank, by the mere fact that he is immersed in liquid. As the image of Lysa fades and she disappears into the portal, his mental voice grows sharp, but also filled with pain.

Why did it have to be like that? Why did she do that? Why didn't you tell me she would do this? Why did she leave?

Jack, this was her choice. I did not choose this for her. It's her will, her right. She wanted it and she had to do it alone. I cannot interfere. Her life is hers to give.

Making no effort to hide his anguish, Jack sends, *Will she survive?*

I don't know, Jack.

What will happen to them now? To Earth? Did she save them?

I don't know, Jack. All things will change now. I will collect data and recalculate, but it will take time. I'll send a ship with drones to begin gathering the data. We'll know then and there will be much work to do.

Jack mental voice is silent, his mind filled with too many things to articulate. The human girl who looks so different from him—but grew to mean so much—is gone. He would have gone with her. He would have left it all behind for her.

I love her, Hub. She is my light.

I know, Jack.

The thought flits though his mind that she left no message for him. He didn't mean to send it, but Hub must have heard it anyway, because it answers the thought. *She did leave a message for you.*

She did? Show me?

Jack can't see the same way a human can in his current form, but his trace takes over and his mind fills with images of her room. The pictures along the wall weren't hung there the last time he was inside. He looks, realizes there is order to it, and finds the beginning.

The view of the station and the Bluriani ship, her room, him at the door, him lying on the table being replicated…a dozen more. The final one is his message. Lysa standing at her tank, her hand against the glass where he floats. She drew him as she saw him. It is painted with love.

There is one more, Jack.

The mental tug toward the easel pulls him away from his message, and he looks at the unfinished painting there. Two figures, with a smaller one tucked into a pouch, face a bright light in the distance. They are leaning together, a posture that speaks of comfort. There is an air of destruction, but behind the figures are flowers—Earth flowers—as if the figures were standing at the edge of a field in bloom. Before them is destruction, but a single step back would return them to the field full of colorful life. The edges of the painting are hazy and incomplete, as if the image were not yet set in stone...as if it could change.

Who are they, Hub?
They are the Bluriani, and I understand the message.
What is the message?
Hope.

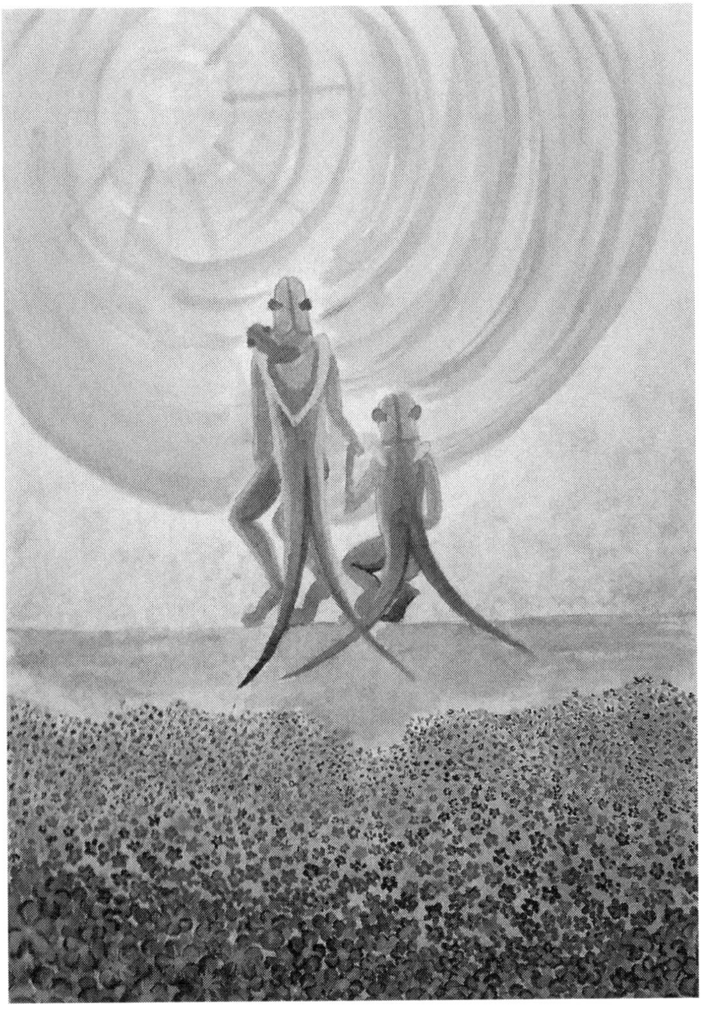

From the Author

Thank you for taking the time to read *Portals*, book one of *Into The Galaxy*. This isn't a long series, but instead, a mere two-book duology. *Portals: Saving Earth* continues (and completes) the tale of the invasion that isn't. There are many layers to the puzzle of Hub, many secrets to be revealed in those pages, and an enemy to be reckoned with. I hope you enjoy it and that you enjoyed this volume.

Believe it or not, this book took almost three years to write. Three years. Begun as the seeds to a short story, I realized very quickly that Lysa, Hub, and Jack would need time and effort if I were to do justice to their lives and worlds. Rather than publish quickly, I decided to take that time and write both books before publishing. It was hard labor, but one filled with love...a true passion project.

Lysa is a painter, though not yet very skilled. I decided to create her paintings. It helped me to know her, so she could better tell you her story. (Also, I'm an extremely bad painter, but I do love slapping paint around onto any handy surface.) The Bluriani painting is included in this book, but you can find a few of her paintings on a secret web page just for you: http://www.annchristy.com/Portals

Now is when I hit you up for a review. I don't like to ask, but reviews are very hard to come by and they are vital. Without sufficient reviews, my book won't be offered to readers who might like it. It will create no buzz, no warm tickling of the machine algorithms that decide which books are good and which should be relegated to the deeps. So, I ask you humbly, but sincerely: Will you write a review? It needn't be long or complex. A few words will do the job, and you'll be significantly contributing to the work that I do! Thank you.

If you'd like to read the story of how Hub came to exist, you can get it free when you sign up my VIP Newsletter list. I don't spam, or send out constant updates, but I do try to communicate once a month or so, and I usually have a drawing for some exclusive (and very cool) swag. You can sign up here: http://www.annchristy.com/portalsviplist

Again, thank you for reading. From my home by the tempestuous sea to your home, wherever you are in this beautiful world, I send you greetings. Until next time.

—Ann Christy

About the Author

Ann Christy is a retired naval officer and secret science fiction author. She lives by the sea under the benevolent rule of her canine overlord and an extremely foul-mouthed cat. She's been known to call writing fiction a form of mental zombie-ism in reverse. She gets to put a little piece of her brain into yours and stay there with you—safely tucked away inside your gray matter—for as long as you remember the story. She hopes you enjoyed the meal.

Acknowledgements

I'd like to take a moment to thank Daniel O'Brien. Dan was helping me to understand a culture I've never lived, as well as the Hindu religion. While only touched on in the novel, I wanted to be respectful, without limiting all my characters to people who are exactly like me. While I've got a global roll-call of cultures and ethnic variations swimming around in my DNA (surprise!), I want to include everyone in the worlds I create. The world is full of interesting, brave, and wonderful people. I want to write them.

Dan was patient, kind, and laughed at me only when necessary. He recommended books for me to read and put up with my endless questions. Sadly, as I was writing this book, Dan lost his battle with cancer. His smiles and good heart have been, and will continue to be, deeply missed.

All errors made must be laid at my door. Most certainly, Dan would have caught them and in his gentle way, explained to me how I was wrong. After he left the world, I simply couldn't bear to ask another to do what he was doing. I will miss him.

Made in United States
Troutdale, OR
09/13/2023